THE RELUCTANT COURIER

A MARRIAGE OF CONVENIENCE HISTORICAL ROMANCE SET DURING THE AMERICAN REVOLUTION

THE COURIERS
BOOK ONE

ELSA STANLEY

GLOSSARY

redcoats: British soldiers
regulars: also British soldiers
lobsterbacks: also British soldiers. I didn't use this in the book
because I couldn't do so with a straight face.
Continentals: American soldiers; soldiers in the Continental Army
Partisan Corps: an elite, mobile fighting force within the Continental
army.
Whig: someone who is on the Continental/
American side of the war
Tory: someone who is on the British side of
the war

CHAPTER 1

Rachel Staples had never been brave before. She was considering being brave today, if her sister would let her.

"You don't have to do this," Hannah said. "In fact, I'd rather you not. You've never made a delivery before." Hannah barely finished her sentence before a wracking cough shook her body.

Rachel reached for her sister, but Hannah waved her off, still coughing. It was the same sickness that had suffocated their mother only months before, and Rachel couldn't bear to see Hannah like this. Anything she could do to help Hannah recover, she would. Even if it seemed impossible.

"Must this be done today?" she asked. Perhaps they could allow Hannah time to recover.

Then she could make the delivery when she felt better.

"The British soldiers have been setting up camp for nearly a week. Redcoats have already taken supplies from Ezekiel's store. We've waited long enough."

The presence of British soldiers anywhere on the continent was cause for concern, but a whole camp of them not two miles outside of town – that was cause for alarm. Everyone in town was talking about the scores of redcoats infesting the countryside, and Rachel had barely slept in the last few days thinking of it. *They'll take all of our food and starve us out,* Abigail had said. Not to mention how the redcoats were rumored to treat women.

"Perhaps Lieutenant Feldman's troops can wait a few more days for their winter clothes. If we put this off…" It was a desperate grab at *any* reason to delay the inevitable, and Rachel knew that. They were due to make another delivery to a Continental regiment the following day.

Hannah shook her head. "We need to keep delivering supplies. The Continental Army depends on us. You know that."

Rachel studied her sister, who had grown thinner in the last week, standing huddled in her cloak. Her breath fogged the cold air in front of her. The cellar was lit by a single candle, and Hannah's face was pale and grave in the dim light. Rachel did have to do this. For their work to continue – the work their mother had started – she had to deliver these supplies.

"What do you need me to do?"

Her voice was steady enough, wasn't it?

"Rachel." Hannah pinned her with a look, as if expecting her to burst into tears at any moment.

Rachel did feel like crying, but she was trying to appear composed. Their mother was always composed, even when her husband had abandoned her on her deathbed.

"Tell me what to do, and I'll see that it's done."

Her sister's blonde eyebrows drew together. "If you're certain."

Rachel wasn't certain at all, but she had to at least try to be brave.

"We've loaded the wagon with any supplies that can be spared. Be friendly. Tell them you're there to deliver supplies. Appear dimwitted." Hannah's eyes moved over Rachel's wool cloak and green homespun dress. "Good. You look pretty but not too pretty."

"I'm not sure if that's a compliment or not."

"Speak to one of their officers if you can," Hannah continued, brushing past Rachel's attempt at levity. "Mention –" she coughed again. "Mention the fact that you might be making similar deliveries as far west as Trenton, and that you'd appreciate their discretion. If they are suspicious of us, then our future deliveries will be all the more dangerous."

"So." Rachel crossed her arms. "Deliver the supplies, smile prettily, and gain their trust and cooperation?"

"If it's possible. This is also a test. How they treat a woman coming into their camp alone will tell us a great deal about them."

"So I'm to be bait?" Rachel shifted her weight from foot to foot. The walls in the cellar, lined with jars of food and boxes of supplies, seemed to be closing in.

Hannah put a steadying hand on her shoulder. "Someone has to be. You know I would go myself. Perhaps I should."

"No. You must get well."

"Mother would have gone, even if she was ill."

"She would have," Rachel said. "But we are not her." Much as they both tried to be, each in their own ways.

"Are you certain you can do this?"

Rachel could still say no. Hannah wouldn't be surprised. None of their friends would be surprised. But that was what made Rachel want to say yes.

"I'll do it."

Hannah carried her candle to the trunk that rested in the corner of the cellar. She was only twenty-seven, but she moved like she was sixty since she'd taken ill. "Let's get you ready, then."

She pulled a heavy bag out of the trunk. "Are you armed?"

"I've a dagger and a pistol." Rachel never went anywhere without at least a dagger these days. One couldn't be too careful.

"Extra powder and shot?"

Rachel patted her skirts, feeling the comforting weight of the pistol and ammunition tucked in hidden pockets. She may not be brave, but her mother had made sure she could protect herself if she needed to.

"Extra food and a canteen?"

"I'll only be gone an hour, two at the most," Rachel said.

Hannah pinned her with a look so much like their mother it made Rachel's heart ache. She pulled an apple and a wedge of cheese out of her own pocket. "Take these, just in case. And you've supplies to light a fire?"

Rachel shook her head. She was woefully unprepared for this.

"You've never delivered supplies before." Hannah pulled a rucksack out of the trunk and dusted it off. "How would you know what to pack?"

"I suppose I wouldn't."

Hannah gave Rachel the rucksack and directed her to fill it with supplies from the trunk: extra flint and kindling, a blanket, and an extra dagger for good measure.

"I think you're as ready as you can be." Hannah wrapped her arms around Rachel's shoulders, surprising her.

Rachel hesitated for a moment, then let herself be comforted. She took a deep breath, and let it out slowly. Her heart still beat far too fast. They climbed out of the cellar and walked out of the shack that stood above it. Hannah and her husband lived on the outskirts of Freehold, on a hill overlooking the road, which made her house a perfect place to begin endeavors like this. The horse and wagon stood ready, the horse moving his hooves through the snow as if he was nervous too. Rachel pulled on her hat and gloves and climbed up onto the wagon seat.

"Rachel," Hannah said. "If things go poorly and you are captured, do you know what you must do?"

"I won't be captured." She wouldn't, would she?

"But if you are, I need to know –" Hannah looked toward the horizon, where the sun was beginning to paint the snow in oranges and pinks. "I need to know that you'll do what you must."

"I will." Hopefully it wouldn't come to that.

Rachel could do this. She would ride to the British camp, let the soldiers unload the wagon, talk to them if she could, then turn around and leave. Everything would be fine. She told herself that, but her hands were shaking.

Rachel slowed the wagon as she approached the British camp. Their outpost stood out like a stain on the snowy landscape, interrupting the rocks and trees outside of Rachel's town. Rough-hewn logs formed a wall around the side of the camp that faced the road, where it wasn't naturally protected by the forest or a rocky hillside.

Two guards stood at the entrance. The red coats with white straps they wore had inspired a healthy fear in Rachel since she was a child. *Turn the wagon around. Turn the wagon around and go back the way you came.*

Rachel didn't listen to that inner voice; instead, she stretched her lips into a smile.

"State your business," one of the guards said.

Rachel tilted her chin up, meeting the man's eyes. *Confidence.* "I'm here with supplies: musket balls and powder. And some provisions as well."

Both guards looked at her wagon with interest written across their faces. "Come in."

Rachel flicked her reins. Curious eyes followed her from all directions as the wagon rumbled into the camp. She kept the smile on her face and tried to breathe deeply. The sooner she delivered the supplies, the sooner she could leave.

"Gentlemen," she called to the soldiers who milled about. "I've some supplies to unload. Who can help me?"

Soldiers formed a line to what must be their supply tent, and passed each crate from the wagon to the tent. It appeared to be like any army camp Rachel had seen; canvas tents interspersed with cookfires and a makeshift paddock built for horses.

"No ale?" someone called to her.

"Not this time. Perhaps on my next trip."

Her horse shifted his weight, and Rachel loosened her grip on the reins. No need to make him nervous as well. She stood up, pretending to stretch her arms while she got a good look around. How had this many soldiers encamped here so quickly? It had only been a week since the first redcoats were spotted in this area. A tall white man approached the wagon. He wore a powdered wig, and his uniform was spotless.

"My thanks for the supplies," he said. "I am the Sergeant here. And you live in Freehold, do you not?"

Rachel's smile fell, but she forced it back into place. "Have we met, Sergeant?"

Hannah hadn't told her they would know who she was.

The man ran a hand down her horse's flank. "I have my sources."

"Well, I wanted to make sure you all felt welcome here," Rachel said. "We do our best to help with the war effort. I frequently deliver supplies to His Majesty's troops."

"How patriotic of you."

"I take this road east to Long Branch, and as far west as Trenton sometimes. I hope you won't mind."

His eyebrows rose. "I'm sure we can be accommodating. What is your name?"

"Miss Staples. And I'd thank you for your discretion."

"Thank *you*, Miss Staples. Do you need an escort home?"

"No, thank you."

A scream cut through the air. Rachel jumped, and it rattled the wagon seat. The scream was silenced just as quickly. The soldiers moved all around her, not seeming to care about the awful sound that raised goosebumps on Rachel's arms.

The Sergeant picked up a barrel off the bed of the wagon. "I am Sergeant Neumann. Come see me if you have any trouble with the men."

"Of course. Thank you."

He carried the barrel into the supply tent. That was enough. Rachel turned her wagon around and rode toward the entrance of the camp. She kept her head held high and didn't look behind her, not even when more screams rent the air. They sounded like a different person this time. Perspiration dripped down Rachel's back, and she looked ahead at the snowy horizon. She gripped her dagger with one hand and the reins with the other. The guards waved at her as she left. She gave them what she hoped was a convincing smile.

"Miss Staples!"

She stopped the wagon, her heart pounding. Had they discovered what she had done? So quickly?

Sergeant Neumann approached her, carrying the tarp that had covered the supplies in the wagon. "You must have dropped this."

He laid it in the back of the wagon.

"Be careful," he said. "It's dangerous for a woman to be out alone."

"Thank –" Rachel swallowed hard. "Thank you, Sergeant. Good day."

Captain Mark Johnson wished desperately for a cup of coffee. As he and his men had spent the night in a cave, though, there was no coffee to be had. He shifted his weight, keeping his head down below the edge of a boulder.

"Complete this assignment," he told himself, "and you get a furlough."

"Talking to yourself, Captain?" Will said from beside him.

"It's nothing to concern yourself with."

"This is going to be the easiest assignment we've done all year," he said to his men.

There was no movement in the army camp below them – the British soldiers were still sleeping, apparently, so they could still converse.

Will snorted. "Saying that is bad fortune."

"Except this time it's true." He raised his head high enough to see over the rocks they hid behind, then ducked back down again. "This encampment of redcoats has been a real nuisance to the nearby towns, and they've only been here a week."

"Gathering information?" Jim said from beside him. "That would be imperative before further action."

Mark nodded. "We're not going to engage. Just observe."

"Why do we not watch from the trees?" Will said, looking up at the forest that surrounded the other side of the camp.

"Not this time." Mark shuddered at the thought of climbing a tree with his knee the way it was. "Too risky."

Jim's breath fogged in front of him as he exhaled. "I agree."

"No shooting anyone?" Will crossed his arms, huddling into his cloak. "Where's the fun in that?"

"Another day," Mark said. His rifle quivered in his hands – just slightly. He set the rifle aside and gripped the rock instead. He didn't want to have to kill anyone today.

The sooner this war was over, the better. And yet Mark doubted he'd live to see the end of it.

"When will we go?" Jim said. He adjusted his cloak and ran his hands over his pockets, double-checking his supplies. Jim noticed *everything* and was invaluable on assignments like this one.

"As soon as it's light enough to see."

They watched in silence as the sky turned from black to gray. Will shifted his weight. "As soon as we get back to camp, I'm getting some coffee."

"Me too," Mark said.

"Will you leave right away?" Jim said.

"Yes. I can be home by tomorrow night if all goes well. You two will do fine in my stead."

Jim clapped Mark on the shoulder, and he startled. "I'm sure you'll be better and back with us before you know it."

"I hope so."

Once they saw movement in the camp below them, Will and Jim moved away from Mark on either side, taking their own places. Mark wrapped his fur cloak more tightly around himself and tugged his tricorne hat lower on his brow.

"Deep breaths," he told himself. He was usually calm in the midst of even the worst battles, but lately he'd been more agitated before every assignment. He'd have to solve that problem if he wanted to retain his captaincy.

He pulled his rifle back across his lap and kept his left leg straight. He didn't want to irritate his knee even more. British soldiers in the camp below them were waking up and beginning their day, much the same as any Continental soldier would. Mark's stomach growled at the smell of bacon wafting up from their cook fires, but he was much too nervous to eat. There were more soldiers in this camp than their reports had suggested. What were they all doing here, outside a little town called Freehold, fifteen miles from the coast?

Mark maintained his position until it was fully light, shifting from time to time so his muscles didn't cramp up. His men did the same. They'd done this type of assignment many times in the year they'd been together. *Information saves lives,* Colonel Staples told his officers at least once a week. The more they learned today, the more successful their future assignments would be, and the fewer men would have to die.

The soft plodding of hooves in the snow and the creaking of wagon wheels drew Mark's eyes back to the road. A wagon approached the camp, stopping in front of the two guards. The driver removed their – her – hood. Mark squinted, and yes, that was a woman. Her blonde hair was braided to one side and gleamed against her brown cloak. Mark gripped his rifle harder. She was approaching an entire camp of redcoats alone?

Jim met Mark's eyes and shook his head.

Chastened, Mark sat back. Whoever this woman was, she wasn't his responsibility. Her wagon lurched into the camp, and soldiers surrounded her. Mark risked moving closer so he could see better. Wooden crates and barrels sat in orderly rows in the bed of the wagon. A line of soldiers formed from the wagon to one of the tents, and they passed the supplies along the line.

Mark shook his head. "They even unload supplies with ruthless precision."

Some days he wondered if the Continental Army stood a chance.

The woman sat still on the seat of the wagon. So far, none of the soldiers had come near her. If she was delivering supplies, which was how it appeared, then perhaps she was known to these redcoats. Perhaps they would treat her well. A scream echoed through the snowy landscape, and Mark startled at the sound, pulling his dagger out of its sheath.

"Captain!" Will hissed in his direction, and Mark ducked back down just as quickly. There was another scream. Mark put his head between his knees, trying to breathe.

"Captain?" Jim's voice was soft beside him. He had risked his own position to help Mark calm himself.

Mark took a shuddering breath and raised his head. The screaming – a different person this time – didn't stop. It was coming from the camp, and none of the soldiers appeared to care. Jim nudged his shoulder. Mark waved his hand, gesturing that he was fine. The woman – was she all right? He forced his eyes back to the camp, where the woman visibly startled when another scream cut through the air. She looked around quickly. Was that a dagger in her hand? After that, she turned her wagon around. One of the regulars paused to talk to her for a moment, but she flicked the reins and rode out of the camp. He tugged on his hat. *Concentrate.* Was that another set of hooves approaching? Down the road to the west, two redcoats on horseback approached the camp, passing the woman driving her wagon.

"Prisoners."

Mark saw them at the same time that Will uttered the word. Tied behind the horses were two lines of men, six in total. Their heads were bent low, and they limped along toward their deaths. Blood stained the snow beneath their bare feet, smears of reddish brown making a gruesome trail. Mark's body went hot, then cold. Those four lines of blood behind the prisoners were all that Mark could see. He – he couldn't look away.

Will gripped one of his shoulders – now Will was next to him too? Were the prisoners in pain, or were their feet numb by now? Perhaps the cold was a mercy. They were still a ways down the road from the camp. There was time.

Mark tied his handkerchief around his face, just below his eyes. He was halfway down the hill, picking his way over the icy rocks and trying not to fall, before he heard Jim and Will following him. His knee protested, but he ignored the pain. He hid behind another outcropping of rock at the base of the hill, near the road. The two officers and their prisoners were far enough ahead that they hadn't seen him yet. He raised his rifle, then lowered it with a sigh. A gunshot would bring the other soldiers running. He reached for a rock instead, and threw it, hitting one of the officers in the head. Mark used the man's momentary disorientation to run over and club him with the butt of his rifle. The man went down with a dull thud onto the snowy road.

Will knocked the other officer to the ground, but the man didn't surrender without a fight. While Jim tied up the man that Mark had knocked out, Mark untied the prisoners and led them into the forest. Once they were all concealed from view, including the bound and gagged redcoats and their horses, Mark caught his breath. What next?

Mark's knee throbbed from his scramble down the hill, but the further damage to his knee would be worth it if they could get these prisoners to safety.

"Captain?" Will tied a strip of fabric around a bleeding gash on one of his legs.

Jim came over to join them, holding his hand over his rapidly-swelling eye. Mark had managed to complicate a simple assignment, but his men were with him.

"We have to get as far away from here as we can."

Mark hobbled back through the trees until he could see down the road again. The woman's wagon was just disappearing around a bend.

"That was impulsive." Will came up beside him. "Not that I didn't enjoy it."

"You're never impulsive," Jim added.

Guilt weighed on Mark – especially as both of his men had been injured – but he didn't regret his actions.

"I'll apologize later," Mark said. "If we move fast, we can use that wagon."

Mark's men looked where he was pointing, and nodded their agreement. They made their way through the forest, leaving the redcoats tied up in the snow. Thankfully the woman wasn't driving very fast. Mark's limp made him lag behind, but the prisoners were well enough to keep up with Will and Jim.

The men moved to the bed of the wagon, climbing in and lying flat. Mark scrambled up beside the woman on the wagon seat. Will and Jim tied the redcoat's horses to the back of the wagon and set about covering the prisoners with the tarp.

The woman turned to face him, her face pale. A knife pressed against his throat before Mark could blink. He leaned away. He had never had a woman hold a knife to his throat before, and he liked it more than he thought he would. Blonde eyebrows met each other over brown eyes as she glared at him. Mark held his palms up.

"Good day," he said, keeping his voice casual. "We'll be borrowing your wagon."

Her dark eyes went wide. "All of you?"

"I'm afraid so," Will piped up from the back of the wagon.

The woman turned back to frown at Mark. "I see."

Her voice was barely a thread, but she was remarkably calm,

given the situation. She handed him the reins, then sat stiffly in her seat, her knife gripped in her lap.

"We mean you no harm," Mark said. "We need a ride, and you have excellent timing."

He flicked the reins. With a wagon for transport (and as long as they met no trouble on the road), they could be back at their own camp in a few hours.

"Where are you going?" the woman asked.

"That's not for you to know."

"You *were* delivering supplies to the British army," Will put in from behind them.

"You understand why we won't tell you where we're going."

The woman's thin lips twisted. "Fair enough." She scooted farther from Mark on the wagon bench, her face straight ahead. He wanted to pull her against his side. She had to be cold. They rode like this for a few minutes, and Mark gradually relaxed - not completely - but enough for him to enjoy the beauty of the day. There was a particular kind of relief that came with getting out of a dangerous situation, and he let himself enjoy it. His men stayed quiet, and the woman beside him looked at the horizon, her back straight. The top of her head barely came to his shoulder. What role did she play in all of this? She'd put herself in danger by being out on the road anywhere near a British camp; why did he need to protect her?

The wood of the wagon seat creaked, and by the time Mark looked over, the tail of the young woman's cloak disappeared into the dense forest on the side of the road.

Mark sighed.

"I was wondering when she would do that," Jim said.

"Can you blame her? She's had to sit next to the Captain for the last twenty minutes," Will added.

Mark pulled the wagon to a stop. It'd be best to go on horseback, with his knee being the way it was. He climbed down and untied one of the horses.

"I'll go after her," Mark said. It had begun to snow, and he didn't want to be out on the road for a moment longer than he needed to. "You get back to camp. We'll be right behind you. And Will, bandage that leg, for heaven's sake."

His men took him at his word and got the wagon moving again. Meanwhile, Mark mounted the horse and nudged him toward the forest. Hopefully the woman hadn't gone far.

Rachel tucked herself into the gap of a tree, trying to catch her breath, panic racing through her. She'd ridden away from the British camp safely. That was supposed to be the hard part. Now a very large man dressed all in leather was pursuing her into the forest.

"Um, Miss?"a deep voice called. "I know you're around here somewhere. Although it was clever to drag your feet so I can't see where your footprints lead."

His voice was perfectly congenial, as if they were having a conversation about the weather.

"I mean you no harm, Miss. If you'll come with me, we can get back to our journey and you'll soon have the use of your wagon back."

The cold handle of Rachel's pistol comforted her, and she pulled it from the pocket of her skirt. It was at times like this that Rachel wished that Mother were still here. Or that Rachel was more like her mother in any discernible way. As it was, Rachel's hand only shook a little bit when she stepped out from behind the tree and pointed the pistol at the man's head. He was a Captain – his men had called him that. Her knife hadn't seemed to bother the Captain; perhaps a pistol would.

"Woah there." He raised his hands and the horse backed up a step. "No need for that."

His palms were scraped and bloody. Of all of the things to notice at the moment. Rachel brought her eyes back to his face. She kept eye contact with him, willing him to see her as a credible threat and not just a woman with a gun. He seemed to be sizing her up as well. She couldn't tell his age, for his dark hair was pulled back and his tricorne hat kept most of his face in shadow. His fur cloak made him look enormous, and Rachel took an involuntary step back.

"I have no reason to trust you."

"The men that were with us were prisoners of the redcoats. We needed your wagon to conceal them."

"I don't know what you'll do with those prisoners."

He lowered his hands, blood dripping off of them onto the snow. Wasn't he concerned about his hands? Perhaps Rachel was losing her faculties; she had bigger concerns than a stranger's injured hands.

"It's the middle of winter and you're alone, on foot." The man was still talking. "You're not safe out here."

"You're right, I'm not. Anyone could steal my wagon, leaving me defenseless. Imagine that."

"I wouldn't say ' defenseless.'" The Captain was grinning now, his teeth white against his tanned skin. "From the way you're holding that pistol, you know what you're doing."

"Of course I do," Rachel said. She was tempted to fire the pistol and show him how well she knew what she was doing, but that would be too loud. And she wouldn't risk hurting the horse. "Now, please leave me alone."

"I'm sorry, Miss. I can't do that. You'll find I'm very stubborn."

Rachel's mind frantically searched for other options. She needed to get away from him so she could get back to Hannah's. The last thing she needed was him following her.

"I'm sure the —" Rachel wasn't sure where this sentence was going, but she grasped for ideas. "I'm sure the regulars will be patrolling this area. You've no desire to be found by them, do you?"

The man set his jaw. In a roundabout way, it was comforting to know that the British were his enemy as well. If he was a Captain, was he a Continental? Did he know her father? Did he know her brother?

"If you truly mean me no harm, then let me ride that horse, since you've taken my wagon."

"Of course." He climbed down, stumbling a bit as his feet hit the ground.

Rachel mounted the horse, patting its neck, and some of her fear eased. If this man intended to harm her, he wouldn't have given her that advantage. He probably wouldn't have come after her at all.

He stood beside the horse, glancing around.

"How will I get my horse and wagon back?" Rachel said.

"You live in Freehold?" he asked.

Rachel nodded.

"I will return them to you in a few days' time."

"Very well." It wasn't as if he'd given her a choice. "Excuse me, then."

Rachel turned the horse toward the road, and as she studied the terrain in front of her, she noticed the crimson blanket beneath the horse's saddle.

"Oh no." She stopped the horse.

The Captain looked up at her. "What is it?"

"You stole this horse from the redcoats, didn't you?" The red and white crown insignia on the saddle blanket wasn't subtle.

Rachel climbed down from the horse and started unbuckling the saddle, muttering to herself.

"We'd just taken their prisoners. We weren't exactly going to leave them with their horses. They'd probably stolen these horses from a local town anyway."

Rachel laughed, and the Captain smiled at her. He was really quite handsome when he wasn't making her life more difficult. She finished unsaddling the horse and handed the saddle and blanket to the Captain.

"Hide those somewhere, will you?"

He limped over to a fallen log and concealed the saddle and blanket inside. He came back toward her and helped her climb onto the horse bareback. They reached the road and Rachel studied the landscape for a full minute before urging the horse back toward Freehold. The Captain kept up with her, but barely, limping along.

"What's wrong with your leg?" she said.

"I wrenched my knee last week."

"Ah. Well, best of luck, Captain. I look forward to the return of my wagon and horse."

The man stopped walking, looking up at her. "Will you at least let me escort you back to Freehold?"

"Why?"

"I want to make sure you're safe." The sincerity in those words brought Rachel up short. The man had done nothing but make her life difficult, but he did appear to care for her safety.

"Fine. You may escort me to Freehold." She slowed the horse to a walk so he could keep up.

After a few minutes, the distant sound of hoofbeats grew closer, and Rachel looked over her shoulder. Eight redcoats on horseback appeared on the horizon, and she froze.

The Captain must've seen the panic on her face. "You delivered them supplies this morning. Be friendly and innocent. I'll be watching."

And with that, he was gone, into the trees. How had he moved so quickly with an injured knee? Rachel felt like a deer in the sights of a hunter as the regulars approached. She tried to take the Captain's words to heart, but she couldn't move. She had her pistol and knife, but they were no match for eight trained soldiers.

The soldiers approached her, looking at her carefully. "Didn't you have a wagon, Miss?"

"Yes, uh – I did." Her throat closed up, forcing her to swallow. "Thieves took it."

One of the officers frowned. "We've had some thievery ourselves. The Continentals made off with some of our prisoners about an hour ago. We're searching the countryside for them. You haven't seen them, have you?"

Rachel shook her head, looking the man in the eye. "I must hurry toward my home, then, with such dangerous men about."

The man pulled his horse around in front of Rachel. "They stole two of our horses, too. You're sure you haven't seen them?"

"I'm sure." Rachel saw in the man's face that he didn't believe her as she uttered the words. "It was probably the same men who took my wagon."

The redcoats were surrounding her now.

"I'm afraid you'll need to come back with us, Miss Staples."

CHAPTER 2

Mark didn't care if this Miss Staples had delivered supplies to the redcoats that very morning. These officers bore her no goodwill. In fact, they looked ready to tie her up and drag her back to their camp. He stepped onto the road with his hands raised. He couldn't allow this woman to be captured because of him. Cold poured through his body at the thought of going back with them. But he didn't have a choice, did he?

"Good day, gentlemen." Mark stepped toward the man who had been intimidating Miss Staples. "Your quarrel is with me, I'm afraid."

The powdered wigs on the heads of eight officers turned toward him. For a moment, everyone was too stunned to move. Mark was counting on them taking him and letting Miss Staples go. If they took her anyway, then he was ten kinds of a fool. But he had to try.

"Miss Staples was not involved. I used her as a decoy, but she's done nothing wrong."

"I see," the nearest officer said.

Mark saw the blow coming and accepted it, with one last glance at Miss Staples before everything went dark.

"Now, Miss Staples, I'm afraid you'll need to come with us," one of the officers said.

Rachel tore her eyes from where the Captain was bleeding in the snow. "Of course."

They threw the Captain over the back of one of their horses like a sack of potatoes, and he groaned but didn't regain consciousness. He need not have revealed himself to the regulars. That thought echoed through Rachel's frantic mind on the ride back to the redcoats' camp. He could have disappeared into the trees and made his way to safety. But when he saw that she was threatened, he stepped forward. That almost made up for him stealing her wagon.

Rachel rode into camp behind the procession of officers that took the Captain with them. Sergeant Neumann stood at the entrance to his tent, squinting up at her with his mouth in a firm line. Rachel climbed down off the horse she rode and dusted off her skirts.

"Ah, Miss Staples," he said. "I'd hoped to see you again, but not this soon. I'm told you were found in the company of a man. We suspect he has stolen some of our prisoners."

Rachel looked the man in the eye. "Entirely inconvenient for myself as well, I assure you."

"So you have no association with him?"

"I don't even know his name." At least she didn't have to lie. "Meeting him on the road was bad luck."

"I see." He gave her a long look, and an awkward silence fell between them.

Rachel knew from dealing with her father that the Sergeant was using this silence to make her nervous. It was working.

"You wouldn't mind if we questioned him then?" he said.

"Of course not."

"Good. Well then, Miss Staples, you are free to go." He gestured to some of his officers and two of them approached. "Two of my men will escort you back to your home in Freehold. We would not want you getting lost again."

"Thank you," Rachel said, her mind spinning. "Good day, Sergeant."

The men who were assigned to escort her back home rode a few paces behind her, talking between themselves. The day was wearing on her, and the twenty-minute ride felt like it took an hour. She should be paying more attention to their conversation, but her mind was too frantic. The Captain was even now in the British camp, unconscious. What were they doing to him? She didn't trust the man, and didn't entirely like him, but she certainly didn't want him in the hands of the enemy.

As they rode back into Freehold, Rachel took the most direct route home. A few people they passed by gave her strange looks, and she tried to reassure them without words that she was all right. Her home appeared at the end of the lane, yellow with white trim, and Rachel rode around the house to her barn.

The officers didn't dismount, which was a good sign. "This is your home, Miss Staples?" one of them said.

"Yes. Thank you, gentlemen, for the escort. Good day."

They went on their way back to their camp, their figures fading as they went down the road.

Rachel shook off the lingering unease and took the horse to her barn. "I suppose you're stuck with me now," she said to the gelding.

He took an apple from her hand and munched on it happily. "I hope you like your new life."

Once she got the new horse – she'd have to name him – acquainted with her other animals, she went inside her house. The remains of her breakfast early that morning were scattered all over the kitchen, and she tidied up absently. That morning felt like an eternity ago.

The regulars hadn't been gone for twenty minutes when her first curious visitor appeared.

"Well?" Abigail, who used to be her closest friend, appeared in her kitchen doorway.

Rachel turned, and Abigail kept right on talking.

"How did it go? I saw you, riding into town like a queen with two redcoats behind you."

Rachel put a hand to her pounding heart. "I —" she swallowed hard. "Abigail, I'm not supposed to discuss this with you. Ezekiel doesn't want you to be involved with our work any more. You must honor his wishes."

This sobered her friend. "That doesn't mean I can't discuss it with you."

"It was fine," Rachel said. No need to tell her friend all of the details. She respected Ezekiel, Abigail's husband. Though she didn't agree with his decision, he had the right to say what his wife could and could not do.

"Are you sure you're well? You were gone much longer than expected; the camp's only a mile away, yet you've been gone for hours."

Abigail sat down at the kitchen table, making herself at home. She was the ideal American woman in her blue homespun that matched her eyes, her blonde hair in a neat knot at the back of her neck. Rachel felt like she'd been through a battle, and it wasn't even noon.

"Yes, I'm fine. It was a lot of excitement."

"That's the second time you've said 'fine' in as many sentences. But I'll let that one pass. Why did they escort you back home?"

Pouring herself a cup of cold coffee, Rachel sat down across from Abigail. She recounted the morning's events in broad strokes, not telling Abigail about the men who'd stolen the wagon. That would only inspire her friend's curiosity.

"You must be exhausted," Abigail said. "You were gone by the time I rose at half-past six this morning." She placed her hand over Rachel's. "I was surprised you agreed to deliver those supplies."

Rachel pulled her hand back. "You're not supposed to know about that."

"I saw you loading the wagon last night," Abigail said. "It doesn't take a genius to think of what you were doing. Not that I don't think you are perfectly capable of delivering supplies to a camp full of enemy soldiers. You've always just been content to stay at home."

Those words pressed against Rachel's chest like a suffocating weight.

"You know Hannah's been ill. I didn't want her to tax herself further."

Abigail's eyes grew serious. "How is she?"

"Not well," Rachel said. "I'm going to feed the animals and ride over there this afternoon to see her."

She wished she could stay with Hannah until she was better, but she had her own household to manage.

"Why don't I do your chores for you tomorrow, so you can stay with your sister?"

"Truly?" Rachel set her mug down.

"Of course. I'm happy to help."

The weight of her worry eased – just slightly. "Thank you."

"Are you sure you're all right?" Abigail looked at her intently. "You're pale."

"I'm –" Rachel stopped herself before she could say 'fine' again. "I'm only tired."

Abigail stood. "It was good of you to go. I hope whatever you did today made some progress for us."

"There is no more 'us,'" Rachel said, as gently as she could. "It would be easier if you accepted that."

Walking back to Rachel's door, Abigail gave her a weary smile. "I don't know if I can."

Once Abigail had gone, Rachel allowed herself to lean her head on her forearms, crossed on the table before her. Abigail had been her closest friend, and perhaps she could be again if Abigail would make peace with her husband's commands. This was one of the many reasons that Rachel would never marry. Sighing, Rachel stood from the table and forced her tired body to move.

She wiped down half of her kitchen table before tossing the rag down and giving up. The Captain kept intruding on her thoughts. He had foolishly given himself up to the redcoats in an effort to protect her. He may have inconvenienced her by taking her wagon, but he had acted honorably. And Rachel had heard that morning what the redcoats did to their prisoners.

Rachel walked through her empty sitting room and went upstairs to her brother's bedroom. Luke was away, fighting for the Cause, so his furniture was covered in cloth to keep the dust away. Rachel rummaged through his highboy dresser until she found an old pair of his breeches and a shirt, then took the clothes to her bedroom. Her own clothes – damp from her romp through the snow – were tossed onto Rachel's bed in a heap, and Rachel put on her brother's clothes instead. They hung off of her smaller frame, but it would be easier for her to move without being seen if she wasn't wearing a gown.

"What am I doing?" she asked her reflection in the looking glass.

She braided her tangled hair and tucked a cap over it. Once darkness fell, Rachel would make her way back to the camp. The Captain had risked his life for her; it was only fair that she do the same.

Mark awoke to a splitting headache and blood dripping into his eyes. He went to wipe his eyes but discovered that he couldn't lift his hands. Rope pinned his arms to his sides, and tree bark scraped at the back of his head. Once he opened his eyes, he squinted against the brightness of the snow. The smell of death, a smell he had become well-acquainted with, hit his nostrils as soon as he took a breath. He was sitting on the cold ground, in a clearing. He was inside the British camp, judging by the tents. Immediately near him, though, were other prisoners. Nausea battled with the fear in his stomach, and he was glad he hadn't had that cup of coffee this morning.

None of the other prisoners looked like they were in any condition to speak to him. Mark hadn't been captured before, but he'd trained other soldiers on what to do if they were captured. If only he could take his own advice. He took a deep breath, trying to calm himself, but that only brought the smell further into his body. The sun was beginning to set, and it was even colder than it had been earlier. Footsteps made Mark turn his head to face the sound. He blinked the blood out of his eyes, trying to make the clearing stop spinning.

"Ah, you're awake." A British officer strode toward him, his impeccable uniform out of place with the men that were rotting, tied to trees, around him.

Mark met the man's eyes as best he could. This was a Sergeant, judging by his uniform. He wore a powdered wig, but he looked to be about Mark's age.

He was grim, expressionless.

The Sergeant came to stand in front of Mark. "I have a problem, and perhaps you can solve it for me."

Mark cleared his throat. "I shall certainly try."

"Two of my officers were injured earlier today. Six of my prisoners were taken, along with two horses."

So they hadn't found the prisoners yet – perhaps Will and Jim had made it safely back to their camp. At least there was that.

"My officers said that they were attacked by three men who had their faces covered. They couldn't tell me much more about them, only that they were wearing furs. Like you. You wouldn't happen to be one of those men, would you?"

"No. I'm sorry – I wish I could be more helpful." Mark met the man's blank eyes and closed his mouth, refusing to prattle on and incriminate himself.

"You told my men you were using Miss Staples as a decoy. Which one was the lie?" He shifted his weight. "I certainly hope you didn't lie to me."

He *had* told them that, hadn't he? But he'd been trying to keep Miss Staples – that was her name – safe, so he couldn't regret his moment of bravado. Had they harmed her? Where was she? The last thing Mark had seen before they knocked him out was the panicked look on her face.

"I was lying to your officers," Mark said. "I worried for Miss Staples' safety."

"I see," the Sergeant said. "Well, we don't take kindly to liars here, I'm afraid."

Mark's stomach lurched, and he swallowed back the bile in his throat. He'd heard of what the redcoats did to their prisoners – in fact, he'd heard it that very morning.

"The sun will set soon," Sergeant Neumann said. "And it will grow colder. I'm not a barbarian, despite what you may think. During the winter, there's no need for torture –" He gave a slight smile. "We do punish our own men. And those special prisoners. Must keep order and all."

"As you can see –" the Sergeant gestured around the clearing to the other prisoners. "-- I prefer to let the winter do the work for me."

Mark could see that clearly enough. He was already cold; how much worse would it get when he was left here overnight? Nobody knew he was here except Miss Staples; his men would still assume he was on his way back to them.

Sergeant Neumann gestured to two of his men who came into the clearing. One of them untied the rope that bound Mark to the tree. The other held him down while they removed his fur cloak, boots, and stockings. They tied him up again – Mark's head was still spinning too much to fight them – and left him in his leather shirt and breeches.

"We'll leave you here for now," Sergeant Neumann said. "I'll come back in a few hours to see if you'd like to be more forthcoming. In the meantime, my men thank you for these fine boots."

They were out of the clearing without another word. Desperation clawed up Mark's throat as he realized how defenseless he was. They'd taken his weapons while he was unconscious, and now he had nothing.

"Best to just accept it, lad," one of the other prisoners slurred. He looked to be barely holding onto consciousness. "More peaceful that way."

As soon as darkness fell, Rachel made her way back to the camp on foot, carrying her rucksack. Her heart pounded and she felt light-headed, making it difficult for her to walk steadily, but she needed to do this. She took a wide path around the camp, sticking to the forest, and moved toward the back of the enclosure, where the log walls met the forest. That was where the screams had come from that morning.

All was quiet now, with only a low hum of voices and the crackling of cook fires. What on earth was she doing, skulking around a British camp, alone, after dark? Hannah would have her head if she found out about this. This was pure foolishness. But the Captain had risked his life for her. She had to at least see what she could do to help. She would find out where he was located, and then – perhaps – in the morning, she could ride to her father's camp and get help. Rachel shook her head as she waded through the snow. She would solve that problem later. Her only aim right now was to find out where the man was.

Near the rear of the camp, the smell changed from supper to – well, to death. Rachel's stomach clenched at the idea of anyone being imprisoned there, but she'd have to face it. Solid walls of thick logs prevented Rachel from climbing over them. But there were trees. And Rachel was wearing breeches.

She tightened the straps of her rucksack so its contents wouldn't rattle, then started to climb. The tree was too cold for her hands to find purchase, though.

"God bless you Hannah for making sure I was prepared," she said softly, pulling the length of rope out of her rucksack.

With the help of the rope, she climbed the tree and found a perch that was close enough to see. She tucked the hood of her cloak over her head and crouched as close to the tree trunk as she could.

There were about ten men in a clearing in the camp, most of them tied to trees. Some were struggling against their bonds now that the redcoats had left them alone. Some were in various stages of decay. The Captain was easy to spot across the clearing – tied to a tree, his dark head hung low. Blood covered his face and he looked to be asleep. Rachel shivered. It was below freezing outside, and the night would only get colder.

The prisoners were left in the cold? Exposed? Some didn't have shoes on. Rachel sat back against the tree trunk and looked up at the stars and the full moon. If she was to get help for the Captain, it wouldn't be until the morning. There was no way he would make it through the night if she didn't do something.

Still, she sat frozen in that tree until she was shaking with cold. If she did this, she was throwing her lot in with a strange man. She didn't even know his name. If she did this...

Rachel shook her head. No. She would act, then consider the consequences later. This was the right thing to do – she knew it as certainly as she knew that delivering the bullets this morning had been the right thing to do.

She tied the end of the rope securely around the branch of the tree, then slid down the rope into the camp. Knees bent, she dropped to the ground and crouched behind another tree. She'd need to make it across the clearing to get to him, and the light of the full moon meant that she could be seen *so* easily.

"Don't make me regret this," she whispered before she took her first step across the clearing.

The Captain didn't move when Rachel crouched behind the tree he was tied to.

Her dagger made quick work of his bonds, and she knelt in front of him.

"Can you move?"

He squinted at her through the blood covering his face, but they didn't have time for him to consider her question. Rachel pulled the Captain to his feet and he stumbled toward her. What had they done to him?

"I'll be fine." His voice was barely audible "Go."

She tugged him along, trying not to look behind her and failing miserably. There was a man tied to the tree next to the Captain's – maybe they could...

"He's gone," the Captain said. "Nothing we can do for him."

She led the Captain to the rope. Her hands ached just looking at it, but there was nothing for it. She grasped the ice-cold rope and used the tree trunk as a brace, climbing clumsily toward its branches. Rachel didn't look to see if the Captain was beneath her still, but she felt his weight moving the rope around, so hopefully he was keeping up. Shouts from below them meant that the redcoats had noticed the Captain's absence.

Rachel tried to climb faster, but her hand slipped and she slid down the rope, nearly landing on the Captain's head. He gripped her leg with one arm, holding her in place. She grabbed the rope again and climbed, reaching the branch and hauling herself up onto it. Torches glowed in the darkness, and the pop of rifles urged her on. She reached the branch of the tree and scrambled toward the trunk. The tree was cold and her hands were growing numb, though, so she slipped out of the tree and landed in an ungraceful heap in the snow, thankfully on the outside of the camp.

Mark's sluggish mind struggled to keep up with what was happening. This was the same Miss Staples he had encountered earlier. What was she doing here? He was too grateful to question it, though. He gritted his teeth through the pain in his hands and feet and climbed after her. She landed in the snow outside the camp. After a moment, she was up again and running.

A bullet shattered the tree limb right next to Mark's arm. Saying his prayers, Mark jumped from the tree into the snow after her. The voices and gunfire were all around them now. The hairs on his arms stood up, and he glanced around frantically. There was no outrunning or outfighting this many soldiers, especially since he had no boots; they had to hide.

Miss Staples came back and grabbed his hand, pulling him along. He flinched as her hand made contact with his palm, raw from climbing the rope. She dropped his hand, looking apologetic, and he moved past her.

"I know a place," he said.

She blinked at him for a moment, then thankfully followed his lead. He ducked closer to the wall of the outpost and followed it to the north. They scrambled up the rocky hill above the British camp, slipping and sliding and moving far too slowly. The redcoats were gaining on them.

He rounded the top of the hill and looked down. A frosty stream flowed lazily at the bottom, a darker shadow in the moonlight. If they could make it across that stream, they could find the cave where he and his men had camped out the night before.

"Down the hill," he said to Miss Staples, who scrambled up beside him.

His knee and hands were in agony, but he could acknowledge that pain later. If they lived.

"You must be daft," Rachel said to the Captain. They stood at the bottom of a steep hill that Rachel had no desire to ever encounter again. And he was crossing the stream.

It was only about a foot deep, but that water had to be frigid, and she had no desire to lose a toe to frostbite. The redcoats had crested the top of the hill above them, their torches glowing ominously.

The Captain was already halfway across the stream, and he glanced back at her. "If you don't walk, I'll carry you."

"Fine." Heavy-handed man. Although she was grateful for his taking charge of the situation. She'd gotten him untied and out of the British camp; she hadn't had a plan beyond that. And apparently he had a place where they could hide.

Gritting her teeth, she stepped into the frigid stream. It was worse than she imagined it would be. Rachel thought she had been cold before, but the icy water made the whole bottom half of her body ache. She slipped on a rock, and for a terrifying moment she thought she'd fall into the stream. Providentially she caught herself with one hand. The Captain hurried his pace once he'd made it across the stream, and Rachel scrambled to catch up.

"It's just through here," he said.

A rock outcropping was mostly covered in snow, but the Captain had slowed his pace and was squinting at one side of it. He dug through a spot in the snow until he revealed a gap in the rock. Surely not. That gap was barely large enough to hold one person, let alone a normal-sized woman and an abnormally large soldier.

He didn't give her a choice, though. He took her by the shoulders and tucked her into the gap, then crowded in beside her. They ducked down behind the wall of snow, and the Captain scooped more snow in front of them.

Rachel leaned her head back against the cold rock, trying to catch her breath. The redcoats had been friendly enough to her, but now she'd helped their prisoner escape. Had any of them seen her? Had they recognized her? A warm arm closed around her shoulders.

"Easy." She barely heard the Captain's voice, but the deep rumble of it was enough to take the edge off of her panic.

They waited for what felt like an eternity. Eventually the voices died down and all was quiet again.

"We'll wait another minute."

The Captain stuck his head out of their hiding place and pushed the wall of snow aside.

"Let's go."

He led her along the side of the hill until they came upon a cave. She wouldn't have known it was there if he didn't lead her to it. As it was, she could barely make out the entrance to the cave in the moonlight. Once inside, they stood side-by-side against the wall, trying not to move. There were still sounds of movement in the distance and the occasional flash of a torch.

If this man wasn't with her, Rachel would've been caught. Would they have recognized her? Surely they would have, even though her clothes were different and her hair was tucked away. Had she ruined everything for herself and her friends? She should have waited for Hannah to be well enough to make the delivery. Rachel's place was at home; she had no business trying to be brave.

As they stood there in the dark, the pain of the cold spread through Rachel's body from her dip in the stream. The Captain must have noticed her shaking.

"Take off your wet clothes," he ordered quietly.

"But -"

"Do as I say," he said. "Unless you'd rather contend with frostbite?"

Rachel found herself following his orders and removing her sodden cloak and outer jacket. She lay them next to her on the floor of the cave. That finished, Rachel stood in her breeches and loose shirt, even colder than she had been before. She crossed her arms and hunched her shoulders, trying to keep in as much warmth as she could.

"Come here." His voice was gravelly and barely audible. What did he intend?

But she was too cold to argue, so she stepped toward him.

"I'm going to help you warm up. I'm half-frozen myself. No need for alarm."

Then he wrapped his arms around her back, and pulled her flush against his body. His leather shirt smelled like woodsmoke and he was so *warm* she wanted to curl up against him like a cat. She rested her palms against his chest and leaned her head against him, waiting for his warmth to seep into her. His heartbeat was steady; how was he so calm?

"Are your feet wet as well?" he said softly.

She nodded against his chest.

"We'll get your shoes off as soon as it's safe to light a fire."

"All right," she said.

She wasn't sure how long they stood there, but even with the Captain helping her keep warm, the night was brutally cold, and a light snow fell. After a few minutes, he let go of her and went to the entrance of the cave. They'd been standing in the dark long enough that Rachel could make out his profile as he squinted into the night.

"They must have given up for now," he said. "I believe we can light a fire."

"I've a flint." Rachel pulled the flint from where it hung around her neck, grateful for Hannah's insistence that she bring it along.

"My men and I have stayed in this cave before," he said, then disappeared into the back of the cave.

He reappeared with an armful of wood and arranged it on the floor. Rachel struck her flint, and they worked together to coax a fire into lighting their cave.

Rachel squinted against the firelight at first, but once her eyes grew accustomed to it, she studied the cave around her. They were near the back of the cave, about ten feet from the entrance, where the blowing snow glittered in the firelight. It was dusty, but it was out of the snow.

"Do you think we'll be safe here?" she said to the Captain, who was still tending to the fire.

He shrugged. "Safe enough."

"Won't they see us?"

His face was half-shadowed. "I think they've given up for the night. It's worth the risk of a fire; the cold will get to us more quickly than any British soldiers. You fell into the stream?"

"I caught myself. Mostly."

"I'm sure you did." A dimple appeared in one of his cheeks. Rachel found herself smiling back.

The Captain rested his bare feet in front of the fire. Without his hat on, his face looked younger, less severe.

Rachel cleared her throat. "They took your cloak and boots?"

"Yes," he said.

That was a grim thought. His bare feet had cuts and scrapes from their scramble up the hill, but the cold had to be painful as they warmed up. "I can help," she said. "I brought supplies."

"You did?"

Rachel nodded.

"Did the regulars allow you to go back to your home?"

"They escorted me back. I borrowed some clothes from my brother, as you can see."

"So you were safe at home." He frowned, then looked at her across the fire. "Why did you come back for me?"

He was leaning forward, elbows on his knees, his dark eyes reflecting the firelight.

"I didn't intend to. I was only going to see where you were, so I could get help for you."

"And why didn't you get help?"

"I didn't think you'd live out the night, tied to that tree in the cold."

He glanced at the fire, then his eyes fixed on hers again. "I wouldn't have. But you should have stayed home."

"I beg your pardon?"

"It was reckless and foolish to come after me alone like that."

Now he was scolding her for saving his life? "What would you have had me do? Leave you to die?"

He leaned back on his hands, winced, and leaned forward again. "Do you know what British soldiers are known to do to women?"

"You don't think I do?"

"You did ride into a camp of them alone."

A tear escaped her eyes, then another. She buried her face in her hands. Her father hated it when she cried, and this man would be no different.

"Are you crying?" His voice held astonishment.

"Of course I'm crying. I just saved your life and you're scolding me for it."

For a few minutes, there was nothing but the crackling of the fire between them. Rachel tried to calm herself. They weren't through this danger yet; she couldn't afford to break down now.

"I only meant –" he said.

"I don't wish to speak of it any more," Rachel said. She was hanging onto her composure by a thread.

"Fine."

He went to the entrance of the cave, where he cleaned his palms and the wound on his head with some snow from outside. Rachel pulled her rucksack toward her to get out some bandages for him. While she was at it, she got out the food that Hannah had insisted she pack. Her stomach growled at the sight of the salted meat, hard biscuits, and apples. It would make a lovely supper, and perhaps it would calm her down. She wiped her eyes with the back of her hand and set out two modest portions of food, saving the rest. The Captain had come to sit next to the fire again and was studying the flames.

"Here." She handed him the bandages. He deftly wrapped them around his palms, tying each one off with his teeth. Then he wrapped his poor feet with bandages.

"Can I look at your head wound?"

"No." His tone brooked no argument. "It's fine."

Fine then. She changed the subject. "Would you like some supper?"

He looked at her, surprised. "You came far more prepared than I did."

She handed him his share of the food.

"Thank you." He met her eyes, and seemed to be trying to apologize with his gaze.

Rachel didn't want to talk about it anymore, though. "You're welcome."

Perhaps they could go their separate ways, once they were warm and dry enough to leave. Rachel started in on her supper, and the food calmed her nerves.

"I suppose I should introduce myself." The Captain bit into his apple and chewed with gusto. "I'm Mark Johnson."

"Rachel Staples." She chewed on a piece of salted meat. Mark. The name fit him.

"Are you related to Colonel Clive Staples?"

Rachel froze with a piece of meat halfway to her mouth. "You know him?"

"He's my commanding officer."

"He – he's my father." Rachel set down her food. "You're in the Partisan Corps?"

"I am. Your father recruited me last year out of the cavalry."

"Do you know my brother Luke as well?" She might as well find out now.

"No. I've heard of him from your father, but we haven't crossed paths. You have a sister too, don't you?"

"Yes, Hannah. She lives near here." Rachel took a sip of water from her canteen, trying to steady her nerves.

"Does your father know you deliver supplies to the British?"

"No."

Rachel busied herself re-packing her rucksack, making sure the food would stay fresh and dry. She also pulled out the small blanket that Hannah had insisted she pack, and wrapped it around herself. Anything to give her the hope of feeling warm again.

"I see," he said.

He was judging her again, though he had no idea what he was speaking of. And if he told her father – "You must not tell him."

"Why ever not?" He set his food aside and glared at her. "You're aiding the enemy."

Rachel opened her mouth to respond, then closed it again. She couldn't tell him – not without risking everything she and her friends had worked for in the last year.

"Things are not always what they appear," she told him.

"How could they not be? I watched you deliver a wagon full of supplies to the camp. You spoke to Sergeant Neumann like you were the best of friends."

"You were watching me?"

Was he blushing? "Not just you. I was watching the entire camp. My men and I were –" He snapped his jaw shut. "I'm not going to tell you what we were doing. You can't be trusted."

That suited Rachel just fine. "We need not know much about each other. I will want my wagon and horse back, though. Since you took them from me."

A muscle ticked in his jaw. "Of course. We'll see that they're brought back to your home."

"And how do I know that you're telling the truth?"

"It's frustrating not being able to trust a person, isn't it?"

Rachel sighed. She couldn't have a conversation with this man without wanting to wring his neck. Her back was growing cold, so she turned to face the back of the cave, warming her other side. Without conversation, though, the quiet outside the cave unsettled her. Call her a fool, but she needed to talk to keep herself calm.

"What will you do tonight?" she said. It was very cold and very dark outside. Would he consider staying here for the night? Would she?

CHAPTER 3

Mark met Rachel's eyes across the fire. He had no idea what to tell her. He *always* had a plan. But today had turned out differently than he'd expected in so many ways.

"I'm not sure," he confessed. "What was your plan?"

"To rescue you, and then return to my home."

He felt like a cad for making her cry over that. It had been foolish of her to rescue him, but she'd saved his life. She was beautiful and compelling, and he'd already hurt her feelings.

"Is it possible to travel tonight?"

She looked doubtfully toward the entrance of the cave. The wind had picked up and snow was blowing, howling in the night. "Probably not."

"Then we'll stay here."

"Together?"

"It's not safe to travel. Even the redcoats know that, which is why they've left us alone."

She looked so vulnerable, swathed in her blanket with only her face peeking out. "You'll be a gentleman?"

"Haven't I been so far?"

"You have, but we haven't had to spend the night together yet."

"Yes, I'll be a gentleman. We can keep to our sides of the fire." It would be cold, but they wouldn't freeze to death.

"Very well." She stared back into the fire, the flames casting shadows across her face. Rachel had to be a few years younger than him, with light hair and dark eyes. She'd been afraid when she'd rescued him. But she'd done it.

A few minutes passed in silence where Mark wasn't sure what to say. He'd never been alone in a room with a woman before, apart from his mother. Add that to the fact that Rachel was compelling to him, and he was an awkward mess.

"We'll leave at dawn," Mark said. "As soon as it's light outside. Then you can be on your way, and nobody needs to know that we spent the night together."

"Good. And you'll bring my wagon back to me?"

"Yes. I'm due to take a furlough, so I'll be able to bring your wagon and horse back myself." It would take him out of his way, but he owed her that courtesy at least.

"Is your enlistment over?" She frowned, studying him.

"My enlistment's been over for months. I've stayed on because I've wanted to finish the work that we are doing."

"Will you return for the spring campaign?"

"Probably. I haven't another career; being a soldier is all I'm good for, so I might as well continue."

"Surely that's not true."

Mark sighed. If only she knew. "It is. Now we should get some sleep, if we can."

He lay as close to the fire as he could and settled in to sleep. He'd hear if there was any disturbance outside, and he was exhausted from little sleep the night before. Across the fire, Rachel seemed to be trying to settle in as well. How could even the way she sighed be so attractive? It was good that after tomorrow he wouldn't see very much of her. He was just starting to drift off when he heard her soft footsteps coming toward him.

"Mark?"

"What is it?"

She was moving her things closer to him. "I'm going to sleep next to you. It might be warmer for both of us."

"That's fine." It was more than fine, but Mark reined in his wayward thoughts.

He scooted further from the fire so she could set up a warmer spot between himself and the fire, and she settled in beside him, laying on her back. Even having her next to him made him warmer. But of course, having her next to him made it difficult for him to sleep. She settled the blanket over both of them, and Mark was immediately grateful for the warmth.

"I can't sleep," she muttered.

"Close your eyes and count to a hundred."

"That won't work. Can we talk instead?"

He sighed. "What would you like to talk about?"

"Tell me how you came to be a soldier. You claim that being a soldier is the only thing you are good at. Why is that?"

"That question is a bit personal, isn't it?"

"Captain," she said, and heaven help him that he loved hearing his title from her lips. "We're sleeping next to each other. It can't get more personal than that."

It very much could, but now was not the time to bring that up. "Fine."

Mark rested his injured hands across his chest. The fatigue brought on by the day made him more open than he'd even been with his men. "My father owned a shipping company. He – I had no talent for numbers. He was also a Tory. Being on the side of the British, he hated it when I took an interest in the Cause."

"And you were good at being a soldier?" she guessed.

"I was," Mark said. "It had the added benefit of making my father angry. I've never looked back."

"I see. Have you any other family?"

"Only my mother."

She yawned. "My mother died this year. It was a fever." Her eyes drifted shut. "Hannah has that same fever now. That's why I made the delivery today..." She yawned again. "I've never been – never been brave enough."

Never been brave enough? Surely she couldn't be serious.

Rachel woke up... warm. It was strange. She lived alone in her family's home, and she was cold at night from October to April. But this morning she was warm. Her head was on a firm surface, and there was a heartbeat beneath her ear. She snuggled closer, enjoying the feeling of peace and safety. A warm arm wrapped around her shoulders. As Rachel's mind woke up, she realized that she was wrapped in an embrace with a practical stranger, and she sat up.

It was barely gray inside the cave, and the fire had gone out. Mark sat up too, rubbing a hand down his face. Stubble covered his jaw. Her breath fogged in front of her and she had the absurd idea to throw herself into his arms again.

"Good morning." His voice was rough, and of course Rachel found it appealing. He sat up and leaned forward, looking like he was trying valiantly to convince himself to get up.

"Good morning." Rachel busied herself getting dressed in her cold-but-dry outer clothes to hide the blush on her cheeks.

"We must go," Mark said, once he had shaken himself from his stupor.

They packed up their scant belongings and Rachel was almost sad to leave the cave. It had been a strange interlude, and now she must face the consequences for everything she had done the day before. Beginning with assuring her sister that she was alive.

"Will you return to your home?" he said quietly as they left the cave and made their way down the hillside. He walked gingerly on his bandaged bare feet.

It was barely light enough to see, but that made their path safer.

Rachel shook her head. "I need to go to my sister's. She lives two miles from here. Then I'll return home."

"I'll escort you."

"That's not necessary."

"Perhaps not, but I'll be escorting you anyway."

Rachel was tired and hungry, and the sips she took from her canteen were doing nothing to help. So she saved her argument for later. The bottom of the hill met the road that led back to Freehold. Mark crossed the road at a sprint and ducked into the trees. Rachel followed him. They stuck to the forest, darting from tree to tree. Gunshots tore through the air and the sound of hooves approached.

"You there!" a voice called. "Stop, in the name of the King!"

Yes, those were redcoats. Rachel took off in the direction of Hannah's house.

Rachel had hoped to avoid this. But with a British soldier pursuing them on horseback and more coming, she didn't have a choice. Hannah's home was only about a quarter mile through the forest by now. If they were on the road, they wouldn't have stood a chance against soldiers on horseback, but the density of the trees was slowing the horses down. A gunshot sounded particularly close, and Rachel ran faster, her lungs burning. What would it feel like to be shot?

The shack behind Hannah's house appeared in the distance. Hopefully they weren't putting Hannah in danger, but Rachel didn't see another way.

Rachel threw open the door to the shack, shoved Mark inside, and barred the door behind her, breathing hard. The soft thud of footsteps outside told her the redcoats had dismounted and were approaching the building. The trap door in the middle of the floor came open easily, and Rachel tugged Mark toward it.

"Down there?" he said, sounding dazed.

"Yes, go!"

He scrambled down the ladder, and she went after him, pulling the trapdoor closed when she was down in the cellar with him.

"You there!" one of the soldiers called. "If you and your companion want to live, you will come out at once."

The hair on the back of Rachel's neck stood up. Mark was beside her, but she couldn't see him in the darkness of the cellar. The shack above their heads looked flimsy, but Rachel and her friends had reinforced it from the inside for an occasion like this.

"We may have to do something you don't like," the soldier continued.

Rachel counted twenty full seconds of silence, her heart pounding in her ears. The door to the shack above them rattled, but held firm.

"Very well." The man said.

At first, she thought nothing had happened. But soon she heard the crackling of wood and smelled the smoke.

Mark fought back his panic. They had no choice but to leave the cellar...but could they, if the redcoats had lit the shack on fire? He managed to stay calm in combat situations (mostly), but being trapped in a cellar beneath a burning building was an entirely different matter. He'd always thought he'd die on a battlefield, not trapped like this. As the building above them caught fire in earnest, the crackling grew louder and the smell of smoke drifted down to them.

How long would it take them to suffocate? Mark didn't want to take a deep breath and inhale more smoke, and that lack of air only made his panic spiral higher.

A small, calloused hand gripped his bandaged one.

"Come," Rachel said, raising her voice against the sound of the flames.

He followed blindly behind her, shuffling his feet across the small room.

"You'll have to duck your head." She took his hand and placed it on a low ceiling, much lower than the ceiling in the cellar.

Mark bent over and followed her lead. He had no idea how far they went, or where they were going, but they were passing through a tunnel made of freezing-cold earth.

"We can sit here," she said.

It was cold and dark, but they were safe, and they had somehow moved away from the fire. Her hand was still in his, and he clung to her like a lifeline. Feeling behind him, he sat down on the dirt and leaned against a wall. He could still smell and taste the smoke, but it wasn't quite so thick here.

"I take it this tunnel is ventilated?"

"It is," she said. "We can escape if need be, but hiding is best right now."

Her voice was barely above a whisper, and Mark wished his heart wasn't beating so loudly so he could hear more sounds around them. Rachel's shoulder brushed his, and acting on impulse, he wrapped an arm around her. It was to help them both stay warm. It wasn't at all because Mark couldn't believe that this miraculous woman had saved his life again.

He wasn't sure if he should recruit her to join his regiment or marry her. Or both. Probably neither, though, since she was supplying the enemy. A pity. How did she know about this place? And how had a shack managed to keep British soldiers out?

The burning shack made a creaking groan, then the ground shook. It was far too loud for any conversation, so they sat there, huddled in the darkness. Once all was quiet again and the fire had presumably burned itself out, Rachel tugged on his hand.

"Not yet," he said.

They waited several more minutes before crawling back through the tunnel. Mark felt his way along the ceiling before he could stand up again. A flame of light flared in the darkness, and Rachel held a candle aloft in front of her.

Once she lit a candle, Rachel could see enough to know that this cellar would need to be repaired before she and her friends could use it again. Part of the ceiling had caved in, and soot coated the small, cramped room. But they were alive, and they could hide here for the time being.

"How did you know this was here?" Mark asked. He sat down on the cot in the corner of the room.

"This cellar?"

He nodded. "This cellar has a convenient tunnel for escaping British soldiers. Did you dig it yourself? I wouldn't be surprised."

Rachel warmed at his praise. It was a strange compliment, but a compliment nonetheless. "It was used to smuggle Madeira, years ago."

"Madeira? But we're fifteen miles from the coast."

"Exactly."

"You're not going to tell me how you knew of this place?"

She shook her head.

"Why did the shack above us keep the redcoats out? It looked from the outside like it was barely standing. And yet they weren't able to break in."

This, she could tell him without compromising anyone else's secrets. "It was reinforced from the inside."

"I see."

Rachel held the candle up toward the ceiling, studying the damage the fire did. "Do you think the rest of the ceiling will cave in?" she asked Mark, to change the subject.

"We should assume it will."

Well, *that* would be unpleasant.

Mark looked around. "We can sit next to that trunk."

"How will that help us?"

"If the ceiling caves in, it will land on the trunk and we'll be in the gap." He crossed the room and huddled against the trunk, showing her what he meant.

"I suppose that makes sense."

"Unless you're in a hurry to leave?"

Rachel sat down next to him on the cold ground. "I'm not."

"Perhaps we can both be on our way soon."

"I'm in no hurry." In reality, she was. She had things to do and her sister to check on. Had the redcoats questioned Hannah? Had they harmed her?

"You don't have anyone expecting you back?"

Hannah might be concerned that she hadn't stopped by, but she wasn't expecting Rachel per se. Abigail would be worried about her, but she would assume she was at Hannah's.

"Not particularly."

"You're not married?"

Now why would he ask that? She squinted at him in the dim light. Was he blushing?

"I'm not. Are you?"

If he could ask personal questions, she certainly could as well.

"I am not married. But my men will worry if I don't turn up in camp today."

Rachel leaned back against the trunk. How, even after everything they'd been through, did Mark smell so good? It was irritating. He shouldn't be this appealing.

"You could have stayed with your men, you know."

"I couldn't have."

"I was doing fine without you." Rachel's own words pulled her up short. For someone who wasn't brave, she'd accomplished a great deal: she'd entered the enemy camp, conversed with their Sergeant, gotten away successfully, and then gone back and rescued one of their prisoners. It hadn't been easy, and she was tired, hungry, and sore, but she had done it. Perhaps she could be brave.

"You were," Mark agreed. "I thank you for saving my life."

"You're welcome."

They both stilled at the sound of approaching hoofbeats on the ground above them.

Mark extinguished the candle that Rachel had lit, and pulled her against him. He held his breath as the ceiling shook faintly. The hoofbeats stopped, and two riders dismounted. All of this to be caught now? Frustration burned in Mark's gut. These redcoats were tenacious. Perhaps they were bored as well; it was a dangerous combination for the residents of nearby towns. And for Mark and Rachel at that moment. They dare not crawl back into the tunnel, lest they make any noise. Rachel was cold as well, tucked into his side. He'd counted to two hundred before he heard the horses moving away again. Rachel let out a long breath beside him, but didn't speak. After another few minutes, Mark dared to sit up straight – he was uncomfortable enough without being hunched over.

"We'll stay here for now," he said in a low voice.

Rachel nodded, then pulled her rucksack into her lap. She pulled out the rest of the food she'd saved from the night before, and handed him half. He murmured his thanks and tried to eat slowly, but the single biscuit and piece of dried venison were gone before he could even taste them. Rachel dozed after a time, her head against his shoulder, but Mark was too afraid to sleep.

It was supposed to be over. He was supposed to be on a furlough right now, finding his way through the ways his mind had changed in the last few years. Now he was trapped with a strange woman who he didn't quite trust, and he wasn't sure what would happen next.

"You can't have slept well last night," she murmured against his shoulder. "You should take some rest while you can."

Strangely, he *had* slept well last night. It had been cold, but bearable with the fire nearby, a borrowed blanket, and someone to share warmth with. Rachel pulled her blanket out of her rucksack and tucked it over both of their laps, making sure his bandaged feet were covered.

How long had it been since someone had cared for him, even in the smallest way? Mark was moved by that small gesture, and he looked away from Rachel, confused. She hardly knew him, and in their short acquaintance he'd certainly done little to merit such care. Strange.

Mark couldn't get comfortable, though. His hands and feet ached from their cuts and scrapes, his head ached from the blow he took the day before, and he was still hungry.

After a time, Rachel sat up. "I can see you're not going to be able to relax. How long do you think we should wait out here?"

"Is there somewhere else nearby where we can take shelter?"

"We're on my sister's land." Rachel tucked a strand of blonde hair behind her ear. "We can hide at her house if we need to."

Mark had never met Hannah, but the Colonel had nothing but praise for his eldest daughter, so he supposed she was trustworthy. Colonel Staples had spoken little of Rachel beyond a passing mention, but apparently Hannah was a paragon of womanhood, having married a Continental herself.

"I think it would be wise, in case they are still looking for us," Mark said. "We'll wait out here for another hour or so, then hide at Hannah's until nightfall, if she's agreeable to that."

"And then you'll be on your way?"

She didn't need to sound so eager to see him gone. "Yes."

"Hannah will have some extra clothing and boots you can borrow, I'm sure."

"I'd be grateful," Mark said.

Rachel leaned her head against his shoulder again, rubbing her cheek against the leather.

"Your shirt is so soft," she said. "It's lovely. Where did you get it?"

Mark wouldn't normally be this open with someone he barely knew, but what was the harm? After today, he might never see her again.

"I traded for the leather with some of the Iroquois that lived near my home in New York. I'm not sure what they do to make it so soft and supple, but it's far superior to anything else I've seen."

She ran a finger down his sleeve, ever so slowly, and the faint touch made goosebumps rise on his arms. This woman was only admiring the workmanship of his clothing, but his body took interest nonetheless.

"I suppose leather is preferable for the work you do. What *do* you do in the Partisan Corps? My father isn't very forthcoming about your work."

She didn't sound like she was fishing for information that she could give to the redcoats; she was probably bored and trying to make conversation. Still, Mark wasn't sure how much to reveal.

"We, ah – we spend most of our time in the forest. Colonel Staples says that our primary role is to gather information. We like to think of our work as shortening the war and preventing as many deaths as we can."

Mark couldn't help laughing at his own words. He believed they *were* preventing deaths, but he'd still seen far too much death to ever be at peace again.

"My sister told me that the Corps inadvertently saved her husband's life," Rachel said.

"Oh?"

Rachel nodded. "His name is Isaac Wellington, and his division was encamped at Fort Washington a few months ago. You – well, I don't know if it was you specifically – but Isaac wrote to Hannah that one of the Partisan Corps units warned them that the regulars were coming. If they hadn't had that warning, then many more of them would have died. Isaac was manning a cannon on the walls of the fort; he could have been one of the first to be killed if they didn't have any warning."

"Well," Mark said. He and his men had helped with that particular assignment, but he didn't remember very much of it. "I'm glad."

This conversation was making him feel far too many confusing emotions, so he shifted it to her.

"What about you?"

"What about me?" Her blonde eyebrows, smudged with ash, drew together in a frown. "There's not much to tell."

"I'm certain you're wrong about that," he said. "I know nothing about you besides your name. And that you're brave to the point of foolishness." He said the words lightly so she wouldn't take offense.

"What do you do?"

Rachel looked away from him and at the opposite wall. "Spend time with my friends. Take care of my family's home."

"Do you grow crops?"

Do you grow crops? Mark chastised himself. What kind of question was that to ask a woman?

"I do," Rachel said. She didn't seem to be put off by his question. "Only enough to get by. Some wheat, some hemp, some herbs in the spring."

"That must be a great deal of work."

"It is."

What else could he ask her about? Mark cast about in his mind for anything to talk about besides crops. "You, uh – do you wear breeches often?"

Mark groaned and covered his face with his sooty, bandaged hands. "I'm sorry. Forget I asked that question. I don't spend time with many women."

To his utter surprise, Rachel laughed. Really laughed, from the depths of her soul, until she covered her mouth to suppress the noise.

At least he had made her laugh. That was good, right?

When she recovered her composure, she smiled at him. "You're doing fine. And I only wear breeches when rescuing men from enemy encampments."

"So not very often, I hope?"

"Not very often," she said. She was still smiling at him, and two of her bottom teeth were slightly crooked. Why did he find that endearing? "I wouldn't have been able to climb that tree in a gown, or move easily through the snow."

She answered his awkward question so frankly, and met his eyes so steadily, that Mark felt emboldened to ask more.

"How did you learn to climb a tree like that?"

"Didn't you climb trees as a child? My brother and sister and I ran wild in these hills as children."

Mark shook his head. "I was never allowed. My parents were strict."

"Ah," she said. "Well, I'm sorry for that. You climbed that rope just fine. I suppose all of that – strength –" she gestured to his shoulders and arms – "comes in handy. I'm sure you'd be a natural at climbing a tree."

Her last few words were spoken so quickly that Mark almost missed the part where Rachel Staples had given him an outright compliment.

"You think I'm strong?"

She curled the blanket between her fingers. "You must be, looking like that," she said to her lap.

Despite the desperateness (and strangeness) of their circumstances, Mark found himself smiling.

CHAPTER 4

After waiting another hour or so, Mark thought it was safe to cross the yard to Hannah's home. Rachel led the way out of the ruined shack, and they wiped their feet on the snow so they wouldn't track soot across the yard to Hannah's home. Rachel pulled a key out of her pocket and unlocked the kitchen door, ushering Mark inside. Her stomach sank. The kitchen was cold and the fire had gone out. There was so much to do, and all she wanted to do was sleep in a warm bed for ten hours or so. After a hot meal. And a bath. But none of that would happen until she made sure her sister was all right.

"If you can get the fire going," she said to Mark. "I'll check on Hannah."

She lit a candle and carried it with her through the sitting room and up the stairs. Hannah's bedroom was dark, and her sister was asleep in the bed. Rachel set the candle down and felt Hannah's forehead. It was still overly warm, but she seemed to be sleeping peacefully. There was nothing Rachel could do for Hannah at the moment then, so she could attend to herself and Mark. Rachel eased open a drawer in Hannah's dresser, and pulled out some clean clothes for herself. In the wardrobe she found an extra pair of boots that might fit Mark, and some stockings. Perhaps she could lend him a cloak as well, and he could return them when he returned her wagon.

She changed her clothes and set Luke's clothes in a pile to launder later. Her hair was hopelessly tangled now, but she didn't have the energy to attend to it at the moment.

Downstairs, Mark had gotten the fire going and put a pot of coffee on for them. Rachel poured herself a cup and let it warm her from the inside out.

"The doors are all locked," Mark said. "I checked."

"Good. I don't know if the redcoats already looked for us here, but we can hide you here until dark."

Mark sat down at the kitchen table with his coffee. "How is Hannah?"

"Improving, I think. We'll let her sleep and make sure her house is taken care of."

Rachel stood, though she wanted to lay her head down on the table. "I'll get you some supplies to clean yourself up."

Hannah kept her medical supplies in a cabinet off the kitchen, and Rachel retrieved bandages and a bottle of liquor.

She also set the boots and stockings she'd brought downstairs on the table.

"You can borrow these."

Mark's jaw dropped. "Truly?"

"Of course. I'm not going to let you walk back to your camp with only bandages on your feet."

He set the bandages on the table next to him. "Thank you."

"If you can look around for some food for us, I'll heat some water."

Rachel took the pot outside and retrieved some snow to melt. When she came back in the door, Mark was leaning against the kitchen table, pain written across his face.

"What's wrong?"

"My knee," he said. "It was easy to ignore the pain when we were running for our lives, but now…"

Poor man. She placed a gentle hand on his shoulder and set the pot down on the floor.

"Sit down," she said. Rachel may not be very brave (yet), but she certainly knew how to take care of a person.

She set the snow to melt over the fire and opened Hannah's cabinet. Some bread, butter, and cheese would do nicely. And Hannah had some apples in her cellar.

They were both still covered in soot, dirt, and blood, so Rachel poured the melted snow into two basins and set Mark's on the kitchen table. He washed gratefully, the soot running off of his forearms in rivulets. That done, they ate the food remarkably fast, barely saying a word between them.

Once her stomach was full for the first time in a full day, Rachel sat back. The fatigue weighed heavier on her now. Mark had to be tired as well. It was late afternoon, and the sun was beginning to slant golden rays into the kitchen.

"How far away is your camp?" she asked Mark.

He yawned. "Ten miles or so."

Ten miles? He couldn't expect to walk that tonight, could he? Especially given the condition of his feet and knee. The regulars might be looking for him as well – in fact, it was safe to assume they hadn't given up their search.

Mark rested his cheek against his palm. He still had blood running down the side of his face from where the redcoats had struck him. Surely he couldn't travel in this condition.

"Do you live here too?"

Rachel was so lost in her own thoughts that she didn't hear his question for a moment.

"No. I keep my family's home in Freehold. My sister lives with her husband, when he's not fighting for the Continentals."

"Will your home be safe if you stay here tonight?"

"It will have to be. I have a friend who knew I might be at

Hannah's today – she said she'd take care of my animals." Abigail would keep her word; Rachel was sure of that.

Rachel blew out a breath. "You're not going back to your camp tonight."

"I can –"

"No. I'd only worry about you and come after you again."

That got a smile out of him. "Are you suggesting I stay here?"

"It might be best."

Though they'd already spent a full day together, this was differ-ent. There was more intention in this. And there was Hannah to consider.

"Your sister won't mind?"

"I'll tell her when she wakes. I'm sure she'll understand."

"I'll be gone first thing in the morning, then."

"You can borrow one of my horses if you'd like," Rachel said.

"I'd be grateful."

Rachel took their basins of dirty water and dumped them outside, then refilled the water from the pot hanging over the fire.

"Let's get you cleaned up."

Mark watched, bemused, as Rachel filled one of the basins with warm water again and cleaned his head wound with a clean cloth. Since they'd arrived at Hannah's home, he'd seen a change come over her. She was more confident, and nurturing at the expense of her own comfort. How often had Mark had someone in his life to take care of him as she already had?

Rarely. It was – it was moving.

His head ached like the devil and her poking and prodding at it only made it worse, but he knew it needed to be done.

He suppressed a curse when Rachel poured liquor over the wound.

"Sorry," she said softly.

"It's all right."

She moved his hair out of the way to bandage the wound, untying and re-tying the scrap of leather that held it at the base of his neck. Mark closed his eyes, enjoying being touched. Did she spend more time sifting her fingers through his hair, or was he imagining things?

Next, she examined his hands, running a fingertip over his scraped and bruised palms. Mark shivered, fighting the urge to pull his rough hands back from her thorough perusal. She cleaned the scrapes and bandaged the heels of his palms.

"I'm going to have a look at your feet as well."

The soles of his feet stung as she unwrapped the wet, bloody bandages. She clucked her tongue.

"I've seen Continental soldiers go without shoes before," she said softly. "But I've never looked too closely."

Warm water engulfed one of his feet, stinging even worse, but Rachel didn't seem to mind that he was gritting his teeth as she washed his foot. Seeing her kneeling before him, performing such a humble task without complaint – Mark wasn't sure how to feel about it.

She dried his foot with a soft towel and wrapped it in bandages again. Her fingers grasped the stocking on the table before Mark covered her hand in his.

"I can put my own stockings on." His voice was gruff, and he cleared his throat.

"Fine, then."

She turned to his other foot, repeating the process. Once both of his feet were bandaged, Rachel stood, drying her hands on the towel.

"I don't suppose there's anything I can do for your knee."

"There isn't," Mark said.

"Hannah has some laudanum. That might help with your head as well."

"No thank you." Mark hated the taste of the stuff, and how much it addled his mind. Though he felt safer than he had two hours ago, they were still in danger. He must be alert.

"Why don't you sit in front of the fire on the sofa?" Rachel gestured through to the sitting room. "You must still be cold."

Would he ever feel warm? He stood carefully and accepted her help walking to the sitting room. She wrapped an arm around his waist and he leaned on her. His knee ached more now than when he first injured it. She proved surprisingly sturdy for having such a slight frame, and he leaned on her more heavily with every halting step. By the time they reached the sitting room, Mark was sweating as he lowered himself onto the blue plush sofa. Rachel brought him a blanket and wrapped it around his shoulders as if he was a child, then sat on the chair opposite the sofa.

"Do you need anything else?"

Would it be strange if he asked her to sit next to him? Probably.

"No, thank you. You've been very kind."

"Good. I'm going to check on Hannah again."

She rose to her feet, and Mark could see the fatigue settling on her shoulders. Rachel had to be just as exhausted as he, and yet she was taking care of him.

"Thank you again," he called after her, wishing there was more he could do for her.

Before she went upstairs to see Hannah, Rachel wrapped another blanket around her shoulders. Mark looked miserable, huddled on the couch, and she wished there was more she could do for him.

It was full dark now, so she carried a candle upstairs and made sure Hannah was asleep in her bed still – she was – before turning down the spare bedroom for herself. She'd have to check on Mark once more, but then she could fall into bed and sleep for hours.

Mark didn't look at her when she went back into the sitting

room. He'd begun to shake, so hard his teeth were chattering. Alarm raised the hairs on the back of Rachel's neck.

"What's wrong?" she asked.

He looked at her with bleakness in his dark eyes. "I don't know. I can't – I can't stop shaking."

Rachel had seen this before. She felt as helpless now as she did when it had been her father shaking uncontrollably, so she did the only thing she could. She sat next to him on the sofa and took his hand. It was an overly familiar gesture, but Rachel didn't know of another way to help. He gripped her hand like his life depended on it. When his shaking didn't subside, Rachel wrapped her arms around his shoulders and pulled his head against her chest. This is what she would do to comfort a child, but sometimes adults weren't very different in what they needed.

"Listen to my heartbeat," she said. "Count, if you must."

He nodded against her chest, and her body felt warm all over. Now was not the time to get distracted by how she was reacting to his nearness.

"Thank you," he said.

"You're welcome."

"Are you cold?" she asked after a few minutes.

"Yes."

"Are you sure I can't do anything?"

"Your – your voice helps," he said. "It's soothing."

"What would you like me to talk about?"

It wasn't lost on Rachel that she had asked him to talk to her the night before when she couldn't sleep. Now he was asking the same comfort of her.

"Tell me what your family does for Christmas."

"Christmas?"

"It is in a few weeks, is it not?"

"Ah –" Rachel swallowed hard. "My sister and I have celebrated with my mother the last few years, but she won't be here. So I expect

Hannah and I will have a modest meal. Decorate the house with boughs of greenery."

"What was she like?"

"My mother?"

"Yes."

"She was..." Rachel sighed. Two months ago, she couldn't even bring up her mother's name without tears. But she was healing. Slowly. Now it felt good to talk about her. "She was brave."

"Then you take after her."

Rachel laughed. "One can only hope."

"That's fair." Mark yawned. "I wish things could have been different for your mother. That she could have lived."

"So do I," Rachel said. His yawn must be contagious, for she found herself yawning too.

Mark's shaking had eased, but he made no move to leave her side. She didn't want him to, strangely. It was nice, sitting on the sofa with him like this. Rachel felt safe. Relaxed, for the first time in over a day.

After a time, he sat up, turning to face her. "Thank you."

Rachel frowned. "For what?"

"For sitting with me. Nobody else has ever done that for me."

Did he think she would've left him alone? "You're welcome."

His brown eyes were so warm in the firelight, and he leaned closer, pressing his lips to the corner of her mouth. Just a featherlight touch, then they were gone. Heat radiated outward from the spot, and Rachel wanted to feel *good* after all they'd been through, so she took the back of his neck and pulled him against her, kissing him in earnest. Mark seemed shocked for a moment, but he quickly took charge of the kiss, cupping her cheek with his palm. It was fire and warmth and everything good after nothing but cold. Rachel pulled back, her heart pounding. Mark appeared to be similarly affected, but he sat back, putting space between them. She held still, waiting to see what he would do.

His shoulders drooped as he sighed. "I'm sorry. I shouldn't have done that."

"You shouldn't have kissed me?"

"Yes."

"Why not?" That stung.

"I took advantage of you."

Rachel tilted her head. "You didn't, Mark. If anything, I took advantage of *you*. Perhaps I should be the one apologizing."

Mark's lips thinned, lips that had been soft in contrast to the roughness of his stubble. His cheeks were still red, and he didn't meet her eyes. *Should* she apologize? Rachel had been the one to turn the exchange into a true kiss, but Mark had kissed her back. Quite forcefully. Rachel's body was still humming with the energy of it.

"I suppose we're both to blame." Rachel leaned back against the sofa and put her feet up on a stool nearby, putting space between them again. "It's nice and warm here, so we could sit together for a few more minutes, couldn't we?"

But after kissing Rachel Staples – the first person Mark had ever kissed in his life – he felt like he was home. Rachel had settled next to him with her feet up, and she hadn't seemed inclined to talk more, which was a blessing, because Mark could scarcely string two words together. It was an entirely different feeling from his episode earlier in the evening. Yes, his heart was pounding, and yes, he felt too warm, but it was pleasant in a way that could become an addiction if he allowed it. Eventually he relaxed. By the time he did, Rachel had fallen asleep against his shoulder, her blonde eyelashes fanned out over her cheeks. He was exhausted from all they had been through, and a yawn overtook his body. It wouldn't hurt to rest here for a few more minutes.

Rachel awoke to a knocking at the door and footsteps on the stairs.

"Hannah?" a voice called. "It's Abigail. We're coming in."

Mark startled awake beside her, sitting up and dislodging her from where she was wrapped around him. Of course, the blanket she'd pulled over them was wrapped around them both, so there was no untangling herself. Hannah was staring at them from the bottom of the stairs, mouth agape. Abigail and her husband Ezekiel came in the door.

"Forgive me," Abigail said. "We wanted to make sure you were all —" she looked at Rachel and Mark. "All right."

Rachel opened her mouth to speak, but no sound came out. Fear and dread churned in her stomach at the three people staring at her with varying degrees of shock and horror. Mark, bless him, unwrapped himself from the blanket and stood up, leaning heavily on the sofa.

"Good morning," he said calmly. "I am Captain Mark Johnson. Miss Staples and I have had a bit of an adventure, and she was caring for me."

Rachel groaned and hung her head, covering her eyes with a hand.

"I can see that," Ezekiel said. "Hannah, you would permit such sin under your own roof?"

Hannah rolled her eyes. "I'm sure nothing untoward happened. Did it?"

"No!" Rachel said. "This is all a misunderstanding."

Ezekiel took Abigail's arm. "Come, Abigail. I wanted to rid you of their influence for a reason."

They were out the door before Rachel could blink. Mark sat back down on the sofa next to her, stretching his leg out in front of him. Rachel uncovered her eyes and looked at her sister.

"Captain Mark Johnson," she said. "I recognize that name."

"He's in the Partisan Corps," Rachel supplied.

"Ah, yes. Father mentioned him in one of his letters."

"Father writes you letters?"

Hannah ignored Rachel's question and sank down into the chair opposite them. She looked between Rachel and Mark. "Why don't you tell me the whole story?"

CHAPTER 5

"I can see you're feeling better." Rachel rubbed her hands down her face. "I need some coffee. We all need some coffee. Mark, you can speak to my sister while I go make us some."

She stood and made her way into the kitchen. Panic rose in Mark's stomach as he turned to face Hannah. Rachel's elder sister looked just like her, with fair hair and dark eyes, but Hannah's demeanor was much more serious, while Rachel's was soft, gentle.

"I, uh –" Mark had no idea what to say. Where did he start?

Sounds from the kitchen indicated that Rachel was indeed making coffee, and breakfast, from the smell of it.

"How did you meet my sister?" Hannah asked. "Did you rescue her?"

Mark laughed. "On the contrary. She rescued me."

"Are we speaking of the same Rachel Staples? My sister rescued *you*, a member of the Partisan Corps?"

"She did." Something stirred in Mark's stomach. Why did Hannah find that so hard to believe? "She saved me from a camp full of British soldiers."

"By herself?"

"Yes, by herself."

"This was yesterday?" Hannah said.

He shook his head. "The day before. I – uh, my men and I were –" A pounding on the door interrupted Mark's thoughts. "Are you expecting someone?"

"No. Are you?" Hannah may be ill, but she thought as quickly as her sister. She leaned forward and whispered. "Are the redcoats still looking for you?"

"Maybe."

"You'd better hide, just in case. That wardrobe has a false back to it."

She pointed to a harmless-looking wardrobe in the corner of the room. Mark ignored his aching knee and climbed into the cramped space.

Rachel's mind was just beginning to function again when there was a knock at the front door. She set down her coffee and went to the sitting room. She had to look frightful, but there was no time for vanity. Did everyone in Freehold want to stop by this morning and witness her disgrace?

Hannah was opening the door when Rachel came into the sitting room. Two redcoats stood on the doorstep.

"Good day, Miss," one of the soldiers said. "Well, we came to see if you had seen a man we were hunting."

"A man?"

"Yes," he said. "An escaped prisoner of ours. We knocked on your door yesterday but you didn't answer. He had dark hair and was dressed all in leather, and he wouldn't have any shoes unless he managed to steal some."

"I've been ill," Hannah said. "I was in bed all day yesterday."

Rachel froze where she was, not wanting to draw attention to herself. The soldiers stepped back.

"We tracked him to a shack on this property. We had to burn the shack down, unfortunately."

Rachel fought to keep an impassive expression.

"Wouldn't the man have died in the fire?" Hannah said.

"We think so," the redcoat said. "But we wanted to be certain you hadn't seen a man skulking around the property. We wouldn't want anything to happen to you."

"Thank you for your concern," Hannah said. "And I'm sorry I can't help you more."

"Well." The men tipped their hats. "We hope you recover quickly. Good day."

Hannah pushed the door shut, and leaned against it, facing Rachel. They waited until they heard the footsteps recede, and Rachel looked out the front window, just to make sure they were truly gone.

"Now tell me the story of how a very handsome soldier came to stay in this house with you last night." Hannah sat down on the chair and looked at Rachel expectantly.

"I can hear you, you know." Mark's muffled voice came from inside the wardrobe in the corner of the room.

"This doesn't concern you," Hannah said with a raised voice. "You can stay there until my sister and I have finished our conversation."

That gentle imperiousness reminded Rachel so much of their mother that it made her heart ache.

"May I have a cup of coffee at least?" Mark said.

"When we have finished," Hannah replied.

She turned back to Rachel. "Now, tell me the whole story. Captain Johnson said you rescued him from the redcoats' camp, but surely he was exaggerating. How did the two of you meet?"

Rachel swallowed down her irritation and related the main points of the story to her sister, ending with her rescue of Mark.

"I see," Hannah said. "And then what happened?"

"We uh – the Captain hid us in a cave nearby. We avoided being found by the redcoats."

"And how long did you stay in this cave?"

Rachel paused. "Until yesterday morning. We were pursued when we left the cave, and we hid in the cellar. The redcoats burned the shack down, I'm afraid. We'll have to rebuild it."

"Rachel," Hannah said evenly. "You stayed overnight in a cave. With a man."

Rachel stood, knowing where this was going. "Hannah, don't you dare –"

"Captain Johnson, you may come out now!" she called, a grin spreading over her face.

Mark climbed out of the wardrobe, far too gracefully for such a large man, and picked up the remaining cup of coffee on the side table. His hands shook as he brought the cup to his lips. Rachel tried not to notice, but notice she did. Was he all right?

"My sister tells me that you spent a night in a cave with her," Hannah said. "And I saw with my own eyes that you slept together here last night."

"I heard the entire conversation, you know," Mark said.

"Is it true?"

"You don't believe her?" Mark raised his eyebrows, pinning Hannah with an intimidating look.

"Of course I believe her. I merely wanted to give you a chance to defend yourself."

"It was necessary," he said. "Nothing untoward happened."

"I know that. We all know that," Hannah said. "But there is my sister's reputation to consider. Abigail and Ezekiel saw you, and they've probably already spread the word all over town."

Rachel set her coffee down and clasped her hands. This couldn't be happening. "Surely there's a way out of this."

"I believe there's only one way to salvage your reputation, and I think you know what that is."

"I am prepared to do what is necessary," Mark said.

Why was he so quick to agree? "Hannah – "

"Now, I'm going to have some breakfast, because, for the first time in days, I have an appetite." She stood. "I'll leave you two to work this out."

Hannah took her cup of coffee into the kitchen, where she put on her cloak and went outside.

"Let's get this settled," Mark said. "Will your minister marry us today? That seems best."

Rachel's eyes went wide. "Marry us? Today?"

"Of course. Why would we wait?"

He'd actually stunned the woman into silence. Mark sat back on the sofa and closed his eyes.

"I – I don't want to marry you."

"I don't want to marry you either, but we haven't much choice in the matter, have we?"

"I suppose we don't," Rachel said. She stopped pacing and faced the window, looking out onto the snowy landscape. "I swore I would never marry a soldier."

"Why?" Mark said.

"Does it matter?"

"It matters to me."

She frowned. "Are you going to stop being a soldier?"

"Of course not. But I'd still like to know." Hopefully the sincerity in his voice would help Rachel let down her guard around him.

"It would be like not having a husband. I'd have to do all the work of keeping a house by myself."

"Is that different from the way you are living already? Don't you keep your family's house alone?"

"I wasn't finished," she said.

"I'm sorry," Mark said. "Please, continue."

"But to answer your question, yes I do keep my family's house alone. But that is my choice. If we married and had our own home, it would belong to *you*, and I would be your property."

Mark had more questions, but he didn't want to interrupt her again.

"I would hardly see you. I'd constantly be worried whether you were alive or dead."

"All of this is true," Mark said. "Everything you've said. But we still must marry for the sake of your reputation. My position as a Captain would be at stake as well, especially as my commanding officer is your father."

Mark's position might be at stake even if he and Rachel married today. He didn't think the Colonel would take kindly to him "ruining" his daughter.

"I hadn't thought of that," Rachel confessed.

"Is there anything I could do that would assuage your fears?"

"I'm not sure."

"These friends of yours that saw us – are they likely to be discreet? Is there a chance they could keep what they saw a secret?"

Rachel shook her head. "I love Abigail, but she's a horrible gossip. And Ezekiel, her husband, will likely make it his personal responsibility to reform our sinful ways."

Mark sighed. "I see."

Surely she could see that they had no choice, couldn't she? "Why don't we speak to your minister?"

"I think that's wise," Hannah said, coming in from the kitchen. "Reverend Alder will understand, Rachel."

Mark hoped the minister did understand. He didn't want everyone in Freehold thinking the worst of him, and he didn't want to ruin Rachel's good standing in town. Guilt and shame weighed on him, but he was also frustrated. He didn't deserve this. Rachel didn't deserve this. He could only hope that they could make the most of a bad situation.

✳

Rachel had sworn never to marry a soldier, and now she might be forced to. She thought of her mother and the resignation on her face when Father had kept them all up with one of his nightmares but refused to discuss it the next day. She thought of Hannah, and how it had been six months since she'd seen her Isaac. Marriage to a soldier wasn't something Rachel could bear, especially not one as strong-willed as Mark Johnson. Rachel was meek enough as it was; she would fade away into a very small version of herself if she married Mark.

After Rachel took a few minutes to freshen up and make herself more presentable, Hannah wished them good luck. They rode in silence from Hannah's home just outside of Freehold to the minister's house. Mark looked around him as they rode. What did he think of Freehold? How did it compare to where he had grown up? Mrs. Elliott, Ezekiel's mother, was walking to the church with some of the older women in town. She frowned at Rachel, her lips set in a thin line, and Rachel gave her a friendly smile, her heart sinking. Why did she feel shame? She had done nothing wrong. As much as Rachel didn't claim to care about her reputation, she found with the thinning of Mrs. Elliott's wrinkled, colorless lips that she did care. Far too much.

Reverend Alder answered his door quickly, as if he was expecting them. "Ah, Miss Rachel. Good day."

"May we come in?" Rachel said. She felt as if she was being watched after days of being pursued by redcoats.

"Of course."

The minister waited until they were gathered in front of his fireplace with coffee and fresh biscuits to bring up what he had to know they were there for.

"So, I talked to Ezekiel Elliott an hour or so ago," Reverend Alder said. "He told me quite the tale of sin and debauchery, but I'd rather hear your side of the story Miss Rachel, before assuming the worst."

"Thank you for that." Rachel sipped her coffee, her appetite gone. "This is Mark Johnson."

"Pleased to meet you," Mark said.

"And you're a Continental?" Reverend Alder said.

"Yes. Did Mr. Elliott tell you that?" Mark asked.

The older man waved his hand. "You have a look about you."

It was true. If any man looked like a soldier, it was Mark Johnson.

"Could we keep my profession a secret, Reverend?" Mark said. "I'd rather be known as 'Mr. Johnson' here. I don't know who can be trusted."

Rachel hadn't thought of that.

"Of course," Reverend Alder said. "Continue with your story, Miss Rachel."

"Well, I met Captain Johnson on the road two days ago. He was freeing some prisoners that had been on their way to the redcoats' camp just outside of town."

"I see," the minister said.

"Captain Johnson ended up being captured by the redcoats, so I rescued him." Rachel didn't give Reverend Alder the chance to be shocked at how Rachel could possibly do something like that; she plowed right on with her story.

"We had to stay in a cave together overnight in order to survive," Rachel said.

"Ezekiel didn't tell me that part."

"He didn't know that part," Rachel continued. "And I'm telling this to you because we have done nothing wrong. We've nothing to hide."

"Very well. Continue."

"The regulars continued to pursue us yesterday, and we took shelter at Hannah's house. Captain Johnson had numerous injuries and was unable to return to his camp, so he stayed at Hannah's house."

Reverend Alder looked between the two of them for a moment, his eyes magnified behind his spectacles. "That doesn't explain how Ezekiel found you 'intertwined in a passionate embrace' on Hannah's sofa."

Rachel looked to Mark, heat creeping up her cheeks. She hated how ashamed she felt, though they had done nothing wrong.

"Miss Staples and I were talking on the sofa last night," Mark said. "We did nothing more sinful than falling asleep after an exhausting few days."

He pinned the minister with a look that was downright intimidating, and Reverend Alder squirmed in his seat.

"I see," he said. "Well, Miss Rachel, I've known you your whole life. I didn't believe Ezekiel's story when he told it to me, and I'm glad you've cleared things up for me. It was a very brave thing you did, rescuing the Captain here from the redcoats."

Rachel swallowed around the sudden lump in her throat. "Thank you."

"That doesn't change what happened this morning, though," he said. "And what Ezekiel has already told half the town."

"We came to you to see how to best resolve this situation," Mark said.

Reverend Alder took a sip of his coffee. "I'm afraid in cases like this, marriage is the only path back to respectability."

"There's no other way?" Rachel said.

"What other way would you suggest, Miss Staples?"

"I —" He was right. In cases like this, she'd never heard of a couple solving the problem in any other way. "There probably isn't one."

"And Captain, are you willing to marry Miss Staples?"

"I am," Mark said.

The minister looked at her expectantly.

"Fine," she said.

"Good." Reverend Alder clapped his hands together, causing Mark to jump. "Sorry, Captain. Probably startle easily these days, don't you?"

Mark's cheeks darkened. "Not a problem."

"I can perform the ceremony at your home tomorrow, Miss Staples. I'm available in the morning. If Captain Johnson is to stay at your home tonight, I'd advise having a chaperone stay with you tonight. And perhaps...don't share a bed. Or a sofa."

He looked back and forth between Rachel and Mark. "That was a joke."

"'Tis too soon to joke about this, Reverend," Rachel said.

"Ah," he said. "My apologies. Good day to you."

With that, they were dismissed from the minister's warm, comfortable home that smelled like books and candle wax. Rachel helped Mark stand, and they walked together to where they had horses tied up outside.

Rachel looked around, but thankfully nobody was in view.

"Let's go home," Rachel said. She mounted her horse, and Mark did the same. "I suppose we're to be married tomorrow."

CHAPTER 6

The most direct path to Rachel's home was through town, so they rode as quickly as they could. Thankfully it was bitterly cold today, so not many people were out. When they reached Rachel's home, she led Mark around the back to the barn, where they put away the horses together. Rachel made sure her other animals were cared for, and Mark helped, despite his bandaged hands.

"I suppose I'll show you the house," she said, and led Mark through the snow to her back door. The fire had gone out, but otherwise everything in her kitchen looked to be in order.

Mark sat at her kitchen table and looked around. What did he see? Was her home as fine as his own? When Rachel sat in her kitchen, she saw the apples that Mother had hung up to dry last year in the rafters. The worn kitchen table that her grandfather had made. Luke's favorite baking pan hanging from the wall next to the fireplace. It wasn't the finest house in Freehold, but it was large and well-constructed, and it had sheltered her family for decades. She felt safe here, in a way that she didn't feel safe anywhere else.

Rachel cleared her throat. The man had to be exhausted, and she was nothing if not a good hostess.

"I'll show you to your room."

His uneven footsteps behind her on the stairs indicated that he followed her.

Rachel pointed out each bedroom at the top of the stairs before leading him to her own room. "You can rest here for now, while I get one of the other rooms ready for myself. If a friend of mine acts as our chaperone tonight, then she can share that room with me."

Mark looked pale and drawn as he brushed past her into the room. He sat on the edge of the bed, staring at his feet with a vacant look in his eyes.

"Do you need anything else?"

He finally looked up and met her eyes. "No, thank you."

"All right." Not sure what else to say, Rachel left him sitting on the bed. She wanted to help him – he was just as much a victim of their situation as she – but she wasn't sure what to do. *Do what needs to be done next.* That was what her mother had always said. With that burst of grief in her heart, Rachel set about preparing Hannah's old room for guests.

"Surely you can't intend for your marriage to this man to be chaste."

A soft female voice filtered through Mark's consciousness, and he opened his eyes. He was lying on his side, facing a wall. He was still wearing the boots and cloak he'd borrowed from Hannah's husband. And he was in Rachel's bedroom.

"I assure you, I do," Rachel said. She didn't mention the fact that she'd already kissed him. Why not? Perhaps their kiss hadn't been as noteworthy for Rachel as it had been for him. He would have to work to improve.

They must be standing in the doorway, but Mark didn't move to face them. What else would Rachel say if she didn't know he heard her?

The woman sighed. "A waste, if you ask me."

"Granny, aren't chaperones supposed to be dour and prudish?"

"You asked me at the last moment. I'm the best you've got for hanging onto a shred of respectability."

"Come," Rachel said. "Let's make some supper."

Their footsteps faded away. When he heard them moving around downstairs, Mark sat up. His head spun, and he put his hands to his head. He needed a furlough desperately, and now his plans for a few weeks of peace and quiet were gone. Once the room stopped spinning, Mark rinsed his face and hands in the wash basin on the nightstand, and re-wrapped the bandages on his hands.

The room was simply appointed, but like everything else he'd seen in the house, the furniture was finely made and well cared-for. A stack of books sat on the other nightstand, and green curtains shielded the room from the fading daylight. Mark shook off his lingering fatigue. His hands still ached and walking hurt, but he had much to be thankful for. He was relatively unscathed after being captured by the enemy. But he was to be married. Tomorrow. He couldn't avoid that thought forever, much as he tried.

If any man was unfit to be a husband, it was Mark. What kind of model had he had, given who his father was? Before yesterday, Mark had no intentions of marrying. But his only comfort was that he and his new wife would probably see little of each other until the end of the war. He would let his knee recover as much as it could, then go back to his work. Mark made his way down the stairs, regretting what he had put his knee through in the last few days. Clearing his throat in the doorway, he found Rachel and her friend with aprons tied over their dresses, cooking supper.

"You're alive!" Rachel said. She looked genuinely relieved to see him, and Mark found himself smiling back. "Mark, this is my friend Violet Greene."

"Granny, to my friends," the woman added.

"May he call you 'Granny'?" Rachel asked.

The woman tilted her head and looked at him shrewdly. She was Black, with a purple cloth tied around her graying hair. "Mrs. Greene will do for now."

Mark stood up straighter. "Pleased to meet you, Mrs. Greene."

He had the absurd urge to straighten his waistcoat. Instead of doing that, though, he sat down at the table again. The kitchen was lit by candles in the fading daylight, and smelled of meat and vegetables.

"How are you feeling?" Rachel chopped up a carrot and added it to a pot that simmered over the fire.

"Fine," Mark said. "As good as can be expected."

"I'm told you've had an exciting couple of days," Mrs. Greene said.

"We have."

"Now tell me something, Captain. Rachel says that she helped you escape from the redcoat camp. By herself." The woman's gray eyebrows rose toward the purple scarf at her brow. "I don't believe it."

Why was everyone in Rachel's life surprised by this? "She did."

Granny pulled some sort of dough out of a bowl and punched it. She was slightly taller than Rachel, and moved about Rachel's kitchen as if it was her own. Perhaps she spent a lot of time here.

"I never knew Rachel had it in her. Well done."

"Thank you." Rachel gave a wan smile, then turned back to the vegetables she was chopping.

"Of course," Granny said. "If I could deliver supplies without arousing suspicion, you know I would. As it is, it looks like you'll be making deliveries for the time being. Since you're so good at it."

Rachel gave Granny a quelling look, and Mark sat up straighter at the table.

How often were they delivering supplies to the redcoats? Mark had met Rachel's sister, the minister, and Granny now, and none of them *seemed* like Tories. And yet they were aiding the British side of the war?

"What are you delivering?" Mark asked, trying to keep his voice mild.

Granny looked sweet and innocent, but there was authority in her voice that Mark had to respect. "There's no need for you to know. I'm told you won't be here for long, anyway."

"That is my intent," Mark said. "I want to make sure Rachel's reputation hasn't been harmed, then I'll be on my way."

"It sounds like you'll be a perfect husband for her, then."

Mark was trying not to think about how poor of a husband he would be. "I hope so."

They ate a quiet dinner together, and Mark helped with the cleanup. This was – well, it was pleasant. Rachel didn't seem overly concerned about them getting married the next day, so Mark pretended not to be as well.

"Rachel and I will share a room," Granny said as they ascended the stairs for the night. "Pleasant dreams, Captain."

Mark gave the women a nod and retired to his – Rachel's – room. After he couldn't put it off any longer, he undressed and got into bed. A single candle still burned on the nightstand, and the moonlight shone in through the window.

Of course he was still exhausted despite his nap that afternoon, but his mind was too busy to sleep. What was he doing here? He was supposed to be reporting to the Colonel what they had found out about the British camp, and then he was supposed to be on a furlough, visiting his mother. Now, his plans had all gone out the window, so to speak.

"And now I'm hours away from marrying," he said to the ceiling. Did the room feel smaller?

Mark's thoughts swirled faster. Night time had not been his friend lately. He recognized the signs of an impending episode, and sat up, concentrating on the light of the single candle that still burned. Pacing usually helped, but he wouldn't put his knee through that. Instead, Mark rested his elbows on his knees and tried to breathe deeply. Would this get worse as the war went on? And what would Rachel think? This was one of the countless reasons that Mark was unfit to marry, and unfit to serve as a soldier. His heart felt as if it would leap out of his chest, and his vision blurred. Mark closed his eyes.

The bedroom door clicked shut, and Granny gave Rachel a look. Rachel was already in bed, attempting to read but not recalling a word, and she looked up from her book.

"I like him," she said in a low voice.

"You're not the one marrying him." She said the words lightly, but Granny's approval made Rachel feel better about the whole thing.

"I'm hopeful for you, Rachel."

Granny took off her headscarf and folded it, laying it on the dresser in the corner. Next came her apron, skirt, and bodice, all folded neatly in a pile. Rachel had known Granny for her whole life, and the older woman had become a surrogate grandmother to her, especially after her mother's death.

The bedframe creaked under Granny's slight weight as she climbed into bed next to Rachel. Her book would have to wait for another night. Rachel set her book on the nightstand and blew out the last candle.

"I've no idea how to be a wife," she spoke into the darkness. "All I know is that I *don't* want to be the wife my mother was."

"Your mother was a hero," Granny said.

"I know. But she became so – small – with my father. She loved him, but when her love wasn't enough to heal him, it broke her heart. I *felt* her heartbreak day by day. She had less and less energy, as if she was wasting away before my eyes. In the end, she barely put up a fight against the fever that took her."

"Your mother did love your father," Granny said. "I saw what it did to her as well. She confessed to me, after he'd had one of his nightmares...he refused to do anything about them. Even acknowledge them."

"What should I do?" Rachel said. If Granny didn't have some good advice for her, then Rachel wasn't sure what she'd do.

"I'm not sure, honey. My Mr. Greene is different from your father in that respect. He knows his limitations."

"Does it bother you?" Rachel searched for the words to put Mr. Greene's problems tactfully. "That your husband has a hard time –"

"Leaving our home? There's no need to mince words. Neither he nor I are ashamed of his difficulties. They came honestly. We both do our best. In fact, our struggles have brought us closer together."

That was Rachel's true concern in marrying a soldier, and a concern she hadn't shared with Mark. She'd already seen how the war had affected his body. Only time would tell how it had affected his mind and heart. He seemed kind enough now, but what if he came back from the war a different person?

"You're not alone, Rachel. Whatever comes, you have a family who loves you. We'll help you through it."

Granny's words brought tears to Rachel's eyes, and she brushed them away.

"You'd be an insult to all womankind if you didn't bed him, though."

Rachel gave a watery laugh. "I'll bear that in mind."

"He can't know about our work, though. Hannah would tell you the same," Granny said softly. "We don't want what happened to Abigail to happen to you. I don't want any more of my girls getting their wings clipped if I can help it."

"I'll be careful," Rachel said.

"I'm sure you'll find your way." Granny patted her arm. "Now get some rest. Tomorrow is your wedding day."

Of course Granny fell asleep quickly; she wasn't entering into matrimony the next day. Rachel lay awake, though, staring at the ceiling. How could she marry Mark and keep hold of who she was? And how could she keep her work a secret from him?

Mark's headache had come and gone since the redcoats had knocked him out two days before, but on the day of his wedding it was back in full force. He'd finally fallen asleep some time before dawn, but now it was time to get up and he was more exhausted than the day before. Granny opened his door with a bang, and Mark jumped.

"Good morning, young man. Today's your wedding day, and I'm here to help you prepare." Today she was wearing a blue scarf over her hair, but her brown dress and cream-colored apron were the same as the day before.

Mark cleared his throat. "Prepare?"

"I suppose you've nothing suitable to wear."

He shook his head. "Only the clothes I'm wearing." Which were dirty and stained with blood.

She tutted and pulled open the highboy dresser in the corner. "Luke has some things that will fit you until we can get you some new garments."

"I won't need new garments," he said. "I've plenty at my army camp."

"You'll wear these for today, though." Granny laid out a clean shirt, waistcoat, and pair of breeches on the nightstand. "I trust you know how to style your own hair?"

"Style it?" Mark blinked. "Make sure it's combed and tied back, you mean?"

"Good enough." She curtsied, then turned toward the door. "We'll see you downstairs when you are presentable."

She bustled through the door again, leaving Mark with a smile on his face. He liked her, and he was glad that Rachel had her in her life.

Downstairs, Granny had made a pot of coffee, and the kitchen smelled like warm spices, making his stomach growl. Mark tugged on his borrowed waistcoat, hoping his appearance met with her approval.

"Where's Rachel?"

"Collecting Hannah and the minister. They'll be back presently," Granny said. "Then we can have the wedding."

"Will Hannah be well enough?"

"I believe so," Granny said. "Besides, I can't act as a witness, so Hannah has to be there."

"You can't?" Why would that be? Mark cleared his throat when he realized what her legal standing was, because of her skin color. "Oh. I'm sorry."

She met his eyes steadily.

"Things will be different one day," she said. "Perhaps not in my lifetime. But one day."

"I hope so," Mark said.

He poured himself a cup of coffee and sat down at the kitchen table, watching her work. Luke's clothes were too small, but they were a nice change after wearing the same clothes for days. After Mark finished his cup of coffee and started on a second, Rachel came in the kitchen door, cheeks pink from the cold, laughing at something the minister said. Hannah came in after her, looking pale but better than the day before. Greetings were exchanged, and Mark felt like the outsider he always had been. These people had known each other their whole lives, and Mark was a stranger. Not only that, but he had made Rachel into a scandal in her own town.

Rachel hung up her cloak, and underneath she was wearing a green dress with cream-colored trim that suited her. Her hair was pulled back. This must be how she normally dressed; a woman of a new country, strong and independent. Her clothes were homespun.

She didn't put on airs. But there was a light and softness to Rachel Staples that drew Mark in, and made him want to be a part of her life. Even if it would be for a short time.

Once everyone had taken their cloaks and hats off, Reverend Alder smiled at them.

"Shall we have a wedding?"

They all filed into the sitting room, with Rachel and Mark standing with the minister in front of the fire, and the other women sitting on the sofa. Mark faced Rachel. She sobered when she looked at him, her dark eyes steady. He took her hands, hoping she couldn't tell how clammy his own were. Mark put all of his energy into repeating his vows and hiding the cold fear that coursed through him. His entire concentration was on his wedding vows, so he jumped when the front door creaked open.

CHAPTER 7

Rachel felt Mark's startle as Colonel Clive Staples walked into the sitting room as if he owned the place. Which, in fact, he did. He looked much as he always did, with his immaculate blue and red uniform, and white breeches. There were a few more lines on his austere face, but other than that, he seemed to be in good health.

Father paused, took in the room, and addressed Mark. "What's all this, Captain?"

"I – uh," Mark looked like he might faint. "I'm marrying your daughter, sir."

"This should be a good story." Mark's two men, the ones he had taken her wagon with, entered the room behind Father. They were both tall and muscular (of course they were), and both deeply tanned, one more so than the other.

Mark took a deep breath. "Rachel, these are two of my sergeants: Will Townsend and Jim Sturgeon."

"Pleased to meet you," Rachel said.

"Clive," Reverend Alder said, addressing her father. "Your

daughter and Captain Johnson were about to be married, as the Captain said. Would you like me to stop the ceremony?"

Rachel held her breath. Father looked between her and Mark, then sat down on the sofa next to Granny.

"By all means, continue."

"What?" Rachel said.

"You should have been married years ago, but I haven't had time to arrange it. Captain Johnson's a good man. Go ahead, Reverend."

"Colonel?" Mark turned to face her father, his throat bobbing with a harsh swallow. "Don't you wish to discuss this?"

Father shook his head. "After the ceremony."

Rachel turned back to Mark, her heart pounding. His hand was clammy even through the bandages; he looked as panicked as she felt. Mark licked his lips.

"Rachel, may I have a word before we continue?"

Rachel nodded.

"Excuse us," Mark said. He led her, limping, into the kitchen. "Is there somewhere more private we can talk?"

Rachel tugged him through a door off the kitchen, which was an old servants' quarters that they only used when someone was ill and couldn't go up the stairs. Inside was a small bed and nightstand, covered with dust cloths. Mark shut the door behind her and leaned against it, his eyes closed.

"Are you all right?" Rachel said.

He rubbed a bandaged hand down his face and opened his dark eyes. "I didn't expect your father to walk in."

"Nor did I." There was a room full of people waiting in the sitting room for them, and Rachel could practically feel their curiosity through the walls.

Mark dropped his hand. "I don't want you to feel trapped in this marriage. If you desire, we can walk out there and discuss the matter with everyone in that room. I'm sure we can find another way."

Rachel shook her head. "I've thought it through, as I'm sure you have too. There isn't another way. Not without disgracing both of us. I may be trapped, but you are too."

"I'm sorry," he said.

"I am too." Rachel had been worrying about this possible marriage since they'd first discussed it two days before, but now she found herself wanting to comfort Mark. "I think we can be friends at least, can we not?"

He nodded.

"That is a fine start to any marriage. As long as you are agreeable to it."

He managed a half-hearted smile. "I am."

Then he took her hand again and led her back out to the room full of very curious people.

Mark got through the wedding somehow. Afterwards, Granny escorted everyone into the kitchen for a late breakfast and set places for Jim and Will. Rachel kept a light grip on his injured hand, and didn't leave his side the whole time. Amidst the conversation and laughter (everyone seemed to enjoy this wedding more than the bride and groom), he felt his Colonel's eyes on him.Once the party dispersed, and Reverend Alder and Granny went home, they were left with Will, Jim, and Colonel Staples sitting at the kitchen table with cold mugs of cider. Hannah was dozing on the sofa in the sitting room, and nobody had the heart to wake her.

"Your Sergeants told me what happened the other day," Colonel Staples said without preamble. "When I sent you to that camp, you were to observe, nothing more. Clearly more happened than that. Perhaps you'd like to enlighten me."

Mark met the older man's pale blue eyes, hoping he saw the honesty in Mark's face. "Did my Sergeants tell you what we noted about the redcoat camp?"

"They did."

"We were nearly finished when I saw the regulars bringing prisoners into the camp. They were a fair distance away, so I – well, I couldn't let them enter that camp. I knew they wouldn't come out." Mark's cheeks heated. His decision had been reckless.

Colonel Staples crossed his arms but didn't give Mark any other indication of what he was thinking, so Mark continued.

"We freed the prisoners and bound the officers that escorted them. Fortunately, your daughter happened to be passing by with a horse and a wagon. She helped us get the prisoners to safety."

It was a creative retelling of events, but hopefully it was close enough to the truth to pass muster.

"We brought your wagon and horse back, by the way," Will put in.

"Thank you," Rachel replied softly.

"But your Sergeants made it back to camp with the prisoners in tow, and you did not. That is what confuses me." Colonel Staples said. "And what was my daughter doing near a redcoat camp with a horse and a wagon?"

"I didn't know who Mark and his men were," Rachel put in. "So when they took my wagon, I tried to run away. Mark pursued me. He wanted to make sure I was safe. Then, when some of the regulars found us, he allowed them to take him back to camp rather than risk harm to me."

"Is this true?" the Colonel asked.

Mark nodded. "The regulars took me back to camp, and Rachel rescued me."

"How?" Colonel Staples looked at Rachel expectantly. He didn't seem surprised.

Interesting that Colonel Staples believed Rachel capable of such a feat. Nobody else in her life seemed to.

"I climbed one of the trees and slid down a rope into the camp," Rachel said.

Colonel Staples raised his eyebrows at his daughter. "You were well-armed?"

"A pistol and my daggers."

"Good." He gave Rachel a look that made Mark's heart ache. How would his life be different if his own father had been proud of him? Rachel didn't seem to register the pride in her father's face, though. Did she know what a gift that was?

"So Rachel rescued you from the camp…I take it you were pursued?"

"We hid in the cave my men and I had stayed in the night before. We had to spend the night there. It was too dangerous to travel farther."

"Thus the marriage," Colonel Staples said.

Mark refused to feel shame. Rachel and he had committed no sin. Mark carried enough guilt for sins he *had* committed.

"Well, this all worked out then. And how is your knee?"

The knee in question ached as he shifted his weight. "Much the same."

"Would the redcoats recognize you on sight? Rumor has it that they have quite the presence around town."

"Sergeant Neumann, their leader, would." Mark took a sip of his cider. "He is the one who questioned me. Maybe a few others."

"Nobody I've spoken to has seen Sergeant Neumann in town yet," Rachel added.

"It's still a risk," Colonel Staples said. "I know you've expected a furlough, Captain, but these redcoats are more of a threat than we previously thought."

"I agree," Mark said, his heart sinking. "What would you like me to do?"

Colonel Staples looked at Will and Jim. "Your sergeants will continue to gather information about these redcoats with the rest of your unit until we can decide which action to take. You will stay here with Rachel, and if you gather any information from people in town, communicate it to your men." He stood. "I'm going to look around. Write to your mother and tell her you're not coming to see her yet."

Mark's heart sank as he saw all of his carefully laid plans falling apart before his eyes. But he didn't let any of that show. "Yes, sir."

"In fact, Captain, come with me out to the barn for a moment. I have some things to show you about the property."

Mark put on his borrowed cloak and followed Colonel Staples out into the yard, his knee paining him with every step. Colonel Staples moved briskly for a man of fifty, his cloak billowing out behind him as they walked across the packed snow.

"We won't go far," the Colonel said over his shoulder. "I know how your knee pains you."

"Thank you." Mark said.

Once they were inside the barn, Colonel Staples gestured to a wooden bench in the corner. "Sit down."

He didn't have to ask Mark twice. Mark eased himself onto the bench, taking note of the well-kept barn and curious animals. The smell of hay was comforting; he'd spent a great deal of time in the stables when he was growing up, and those were much more pleasant memories than the ones in his home.

As always, the Colonel got right to the point. "This turn of events is fortunate."

"How so?"

"I have an assignment for you. It will be easier to complete now that you're married to Rachel."

An assignment? Mark didn't say anything, merely let his commanding officer continue.

"I'm after some information, and you're in the perfect position to obtain it. Furthermore, you staying for a few weeks will add legitimacy to your marriage and protect Rachel from scandal. If you have to be here, you might as well be working for the Cause."

"What kind of information are you looking for?"

"Have you heard of Lieutenant Miles Feldman? He commands a unit of about fifty men. They're encamped five miles west of here."

Mark shook his head.

Colonel Staples paced, his hands clasped behind his back. "Well, Lieutenant Feldman's unit has been very successful. Much more successful than others in the area. When I spoke to him yesterday and asked him why, he said that they received regular supply deliveries from a group of women."

"Supply deliveries?"

"Clothing, boots, even ammunition. These deliveries have been coming every week or so. When I asked him who was delivering them, he named a Mrs. Wellington."

Mark wasn't sure who this Mrs. Wellington was.

"Hannah," the older man said, when Mark didn't respond. "Hannah has been delivering them supplies."

"I see," Mark said. But he didn't see. Was this a problem? And what about Rachel delivering supplies to the regulars?

"I want you to find out more about this," Colonel Staples said. "Hannah is cunning and knows how to take care of herself, but I want you to find out if she is in danger. Someone else may be leading this operation, and Hannah may be doing this against her will. I want you to watch Rachel as well. I don't think Rachel would be involved with something like this –"

"Why not?" Mark couldn't help interrupting.

"Rachel is as loyal to the Cause as anyone, but she prefers to stay at home. She's unlikely to risk her life by delivering supplies to Continental troops. Of course Rachel's just as capable, but I believe she's less likely to be involved. Keep an eye on her too, of course, but I'm fairly certain that Hannah is the one involved with this."

Mark was beginning to understand. In a strange way, having an assignment made him feel better about his marriage to a woman he barely knew and didn't trust. "So you'll need to know the patterns of their deliveries, what they are delivering, and who is involved?"

"Yes," the Colonel said. "And how they are accomplishing such a feat. Everyone is short on supplies, and I worry about the future of the Continental Army if our men don't have boots this winter."

"So these supply deliveries...you approve of Hannah being involved?"

"I'm not certain," Colonel Staples said. "That is for her husband to decide. Is this assignment something you can do for me?"

"Yes," Mark said.

"Oh, and Captain? Don't tell anyone about this. Not even your men."

"Yes, sir."

"Good." Colonel Staples helped Mark stand in a gesture that was too paternal for Mark's fragile emotions.

"Let me show you around the property now that you're part of the family."

Mark had gone outside with her father, and Rachel hadn't been invited to be a part of that conversation. She wasn't sure what they were talking about, and she told herself she didn't care. Instead of pacing in the kitchen, Rachel went to find Hannah. Her sister was still in the sitting room, propped on the couch with a book in hand.

Rachel sank down onto the soft cushions next to her sister. "How are you feeling?"

"Tired, but much better than a few days ago." Hannah smiled. "Isaac should be home any day now, and that will help."

Hannah had been saying that for weeks, and Rachel's heart ached for her sister. She could never come to care for Mark as much as Hannah loved Isaac. Rachel didn't think she'd survive it.

"How are *you* feeling?" Hannah asked Rachel.

"I don't know at the moment." And it was true; her emotions were a blur and she didn't want to stop to consider them. Not yet.

"Will you be able to deliver those clothes in the next few days?" Hannah said.

That was right. They were due to make a delivery to Lieutenant Feldman's troops – in fact, they should have done so a few days ago.

Rachel's stomach lurched. In truth, she was terrified to make another delivery after the way the last one had gone. But Hannah didn't think she was capable, and if Rachel didn't make the delivery, then she'd be proving her sister right.

"Yes, I can," Rachel said with more conviction than she felt.

"Are you certain?"

"Yes," Rachel repeated. "If you get the clothes to Granny's house, I can pick them up from there."

Hannah set her book aside and picked up her mug of cider. "And you won't tell your new husband what you are doing?"

"I don't see how I can, not without risking everything we've worked for. It's a miracle he hasn't told Father he saw me in the redcoat camp."

"True," Hannah said.

Rachel didn't like deceiving Mark any more than she had to, but there was no other way. Was there?

"I know that look on your face, Rachel," Hannah said. "There is no other way. I trust Isaac implicitly, but he has no idea what we do."

So far, Mark had given Rachel no reason not to trust him. And she knew that he didn't trust her. They'd have a hard enough time getting along without adding that further strain between them.

"Remember what happened to Abigail," Hannah said.

"You're right," she said. She pulled Hannah to her feet. "Let's get you back home so you can rest."

"You're concentrating awfully hard over there, Captain," Will said from the doorway of the study.

Mark's cheeks burned as he wrote his mother's address on the front of the letter, and he tucked it into his pocket. His injured hands ached from the writing, and he shook them out. It was strange to be sitting in his commanding officer's study and using the man's favorite pen, but Colonel Staples had insisted.

"Staples is still walking the property," Will said. "Making sure the fences are intact, things like that. Then we'll go with him back to camp and get the rest of the unit."

"Good," Mark said.

"In the meantime, though," Jim said, entering the room after Will. "We need to make sure that you're prepared for your marriage to Miss Staples."

"Ah, but she's Mrs. Johnson now," Will said.

A strange thought, but one that filled Mark's chest with pride. She bore his name.

"So," Will continued. "Shall we take ourselves off to the local pub and celebrate your marriage?"

Jim shook his head before Will could answer. "Colonel Staples said that Mark is to keep out of sight in Freehold as much as possible."

"You ruin all of our fun," Will said.

"But I keep us alive most of the time," Jim replied.

"That is true."

"We do have some advice to offer," Jim said. "I've seen you with women before."

"Neither of you are married," Mark pointed out, making sure the desk looked the same as he had found it. Colonel Staples' study was as neat as Mark would have predicted, and Mark wanted it to stay that way.

"Yes, but both of us have sisters," Jim replied.

They went out to the kitchen, and everyone else had left, thankfully. Mark wasn't sure where they had gone, but he was glad to have a few moments' peace with his friends. Jim pulled open the trap door to the cellar, and, after a moment, emerged with a jug of cider. They each poured themselves a healthy cup and Mark took a long drink.

"Before we begin," Mark said, savoring the flavor on his tongue. "What happened to the prisoners? Did they make the journey safely?"

"They did," Will said. "They had been captured in a skirmish near Howell, and they were grateful not to become prisoners of war."

That set Mark's heart at ease. At least some good had come out of his impulsiveness. "And how is your leg?"

Mark hadn't seen the severity of Will's injury, only that he had tied his cravat around it when they freed the prisoners.

Will waved his hand. "Only a scratch. Didn't even need to be stitched."

"And I see your eye is healing," Mark said to Jim.

The other man tilted his face from side to side. "I've been applying a cold

compress to reduce the swelling."

Good. "Now that I know all that, tell me whatever I need to know about marriage. And please do it before Rachel gets back."

Will took a sip of his cider and cleared his throat. "So, Captain, my esteemed colleague and I are here to educate you on the finer points of being a decent husband. Whether you are a *good* husband is entirely up to you."

"Let's begin with decency," Jim continued. "Lesson one: listening and observing. What does Rachel want more than anything in the world?"

Mark thought through his interactions with his new wife. "To take care of her sister?"

"*Why* does she want to take care of her sister?" Will said.

"Her mother is dead," Mark said. "Her father and brother spend most of their time at war. I think Hannah is the only family she has nearby."

"Good," Jim said. "So Hannah's welfare is important to Rachel? It must be important to you as well."

Movement in front of the house made them all pause their conversation.

"That will have to be good enough for now," Will said in a low voice. "We'll leave soon, and you'll have to muddle through on your own."

Rachel came in the front door and took off her hat and cloak. Mark stood, and in his haste to greet her, knocked over his cup of cider, spilling it all over the table and his shirt. Cheeks flaming, he tried to mop up the mess before anyone noticed, but Will and Jim were trying very hard not to laugh.

"Oh," Rachel said. "Let me help you with that."

She wet a towel and dabbed it against his shirt, which was now stained. "My father is taking Hannah home. I had planned to help her, but Father insisted. He wants to spend more time with her."

She was standing very close to him, dabbing at his shirt slowly. Mark held himself still, afraid to move.

"I was thinking about cooking supper. Do you have any preferences?"

"Not at all." Mark cleared his throat. "Anything you cook would be...would be good." Why was he nervous around her? Perhaps because he could feel Will and Jim's eyes on him.

"I'll get you a clean shirt from upstairs," she said. "This will have to be washed."

"He'll need some new pants too," Will said, helpfully. Jim smacked his friend in the back of the head.

Rachel smiled. At least everyone else could enjoy Mark's embarrassment. "I'll be right back. You can change in the servant's quarters so you don't have to climb the stairs."

As soon as she left, both Will and Jim looked at him with carefully blank faces.

"Don't say it," Mark said, still blushing furiously.

"Make a note," Will told Jim. "No glassware when the Captain is near a beautiful woman."

"I believe the problem is that she's his wife," Jim said.

She *was* his wife. It was as if Mark realized that startling fact anew. He sat back down in his chair, his wet shirt and pants chafing against his skin. "This is going to be a disaster."

Rachel came back into the kitchen, and this time Mark remained seated. She gave him a shy smile and handed him the clothes. Mark limped into the servants' quarters with his metaphorical tail between his legs and changed his clothes. When he emerged, he set the pile of stained clothing on the counter and smiled sheepishly.

"Would you gentlemen like some dinner?" Rachel said.

"You don't have to ask me twice," Will said. Jim nodded as well.

Mark sat down at the table again as Rachel put on her apron and got to work. *Listen and observe.* She was comfortable in the kitchen, working with thoughtless ease and putting part of a turkey on a spit over the fire, then wrapping potatoes in leaves to roast among the cinders.

"Can you cook?" she said.

Jim nudged Mark in the ribs, and he shook himself out of his trance to answer her question.

"I can do a fair amount over a campfire, but I've never cooked in a home kitchen before." There had always been servants to do that for him. "Perhaps you can teach me."

"I'd like that," she said over her shoulder.

Silence fell after that, made all the more uncomfortable by his very annoying sergeants looking at him expectantly. Conversation. He was supposed to make conversation, something he had never excelled at. Hannah was important to Rachel; she would enjoy talking about her sister.

"Hannah seemed to be feeling better today," Mark said. "Do you think she'll make a full recovery?"

Will gave him a silent round of applause before Rachel turned to face him.

"I do," she said. "She's always been healthy. It was the same fever that took our mother this year, though, so it made me nervous."

"That must have been difficult."

"It was." She turned back to the turkey. A piece of her hair had come loose from its knot at the base of her neck, and Mark was fascinated by the way it curled and glinted in the firelight. "How long have the three of you worked together?"

"The Colonel put our unit together a few months ago, but before that the three of us were in the same division in the cavalry," Will answered. Thank goodness someone else was contributing to the conversation where Mark was lacking in creativity.

"I see," Rachel said. "Father takes particular pride in the Partisan Corps. It must be more pleasant work than being in the main body of the army."

Mark made a face. "I don't know if any of it is pleasant, but it's a way to end the war more quickly."

"It's more efficient," Jim added. "We kill fewer men, and we can solve problems more swiftly than pitched battles."

Rachel poked at one of the potatoes with a set of tongs. "I'm all for it, then. I've been trying to convince my brother to switch over, but he's always tried to set himself apart from my father."

Mark was familiar with that particular need.

"And my father said you are to stay in this area for a few weeks?"

"Yes," Will said. He looked at Mark with his eyebrows raised. Mark saw the silent question in his eyes — could he trust Rachel enough to tell her more?

"You'd have all of our thanks if you rid us of those redcoats," Rachel continued. "They've already begun taking supplies from our store. It's only a matter of time until they do worse."

If Rachel believed that, then why had she brought them more supplies?

"There was a British encampment outside of Middletown a few months ago," Jim said. "They burned several buildings in the town before we could stop them."

"I fear they may do the same here," Rachel replied. "Eventually."

"Hopefully we can stop that from happening," Mark said. He wanted to reassure her as best he could, but how much could he promise her? With that many enemy soldiers, removing them would be complicated.

"I hope so too," Rachel said. "But my father said that he hasn't any more men to spare right now, and the main body of the army is still occupied near Trenton."

"That is true," Mark said. "We'll have to gather more information first."

If she knew that much already, did that mean she could be trusted? Or did that mean that she had more information to give the redcoats? Mark's headache was getting worse, and he felt the fatigue of the last few days more than ever.

"You'll forgive us if we don't tell you more," he continued.

"Of course."

She looked disappointed, though. *Why* did Mark feel guilty for that?

Colonel Staples came back in the kitchen door, and Rachel smiled at him. "I'm cooking part of a turkey and some potatoes if you'd like to stay for dinner, Father."

The older man shook his head. "I must return to camp. Rachel, the south fence is in need of repair. Perhaps Captain Johnson can do that for you."

"I'm perfectly capable of repairing a fence, Father," she said.

"I'm happy to help," Mark put in. "I'd like to be useful."

"Of course you would." The Colonel waved, then left without another word.

Rachel turned back to her cooking, but there was a stoop to her shoulders that hadn't been there a few moments ago. Colonel Staples didn't say goodbye to his daughter with any affection, which was surprising to Mark. He seemed to respect his daughter at least, but why the strain between them? Perhaps he could ask Rachel about it. After a few minutes of silence had passed, Will spoke the words that none of them wished to voice aloud.

"Does he always take his leave so abruptly?" He asked Rachel.

"Yes," Rachel said, not looking away from the fire.

"Oh." Will said, then they fell into silence again.

Once they sat down to supper, Mark found that his appetite was gone, though he hadn't eaten since breakfast. Too many thoughts were swirling through his mind, and his stomach was in knots.

"Captain?" Will asked, his eyebrows raised. "Are you all right?"

Will knew Mark too well. He knew very well that Mark was not all right. Rachel looked across the table at him with concern. Couldn't he get through one meal without worrying everyone around him?

Mark took a bite of his warm, flaky bread. "I'm fine."

CHAPTER 8

Rachel tried to act natural through the afternoon and evening, but her heart ached. Saying goodbye to her father was always painful, and today was no different. Mark's men were lovely, but she was glad when they left for the night. Normally after a day like today, she'd curl up with a book in front of the fire and savor the silence. But now there was a man living in her house. They'd secured the animals for the night and cleaned the kitchen, and Mark was sitting on the edge of her bed, taking the bandages off his hands.

"I like your men," Rachel said. "I can see why you are so loyal to them, and they to you."

"They've become like brothers to me," Mark said.

"I suppose you'll be glad to get back to them after your furlough."

He met her eyes. "I will."

Now why did that bother her? She admired his devotion to his work and his chosen family. She didn't *want* him to stay here any longer than he needed to. Did she? That was a thought to examine another day. Rachel took off her apron and the pockets she wore tied around her waist. Next would come her dress, but Rachel hesitated.

Mark would see her undress. The two nights they'd spent together, she'd slept in her clothes. And now he was her husband. Cheeks burning, she unlaced her bodice and took her skirt off, hanging them on a peg on the wall. Once she was down to her chemise, she put on a dressing gown and wrapped it around herself.

She braided her hair for bed and cleaned her teeth. Unable to resist, she stole a glance at Mark in the looking glass. He was undressing as well, folding his borrowed clothes neatly and setting them on a chair in the corner of the room. He glanced over his shoulder at her, and his cheeks darkened when he met her gaze. Interesting.

"What will you do while you're here?" Rachel finished with her hair and climbed into bed.

"Rest my knee," he said over his shoulder as he brushed his own hair. Mark finished his nighttime ablutions and blew out the last candle. He was warm and solid lying next to her. They'd never discussed their sleeping arrangements, but it made no sense to sleep apart, especially during the winter.

"Did you imagine your wedding night would look like this?" Rachel said.

"I never intended to marry, so I didn't give it much thought."

"I never intended to either."

There was a pause between them, where Rachel heard his deep breathing and the sound of the wind in the trees outside.

"We can be friends at least, can we not?" Mark finally said.

"We can."

"Then you must not make any more deliveries to the redcoats' camp. I didn't tell your father what you did. Keeping that secret is a conflict for me."

"I see that." Rachel had no intention of stopping her work, but his request was reasonable.

"You still won't tell me your true purpose in delivering those supplies to the redcoats?"

"No."

"Fine." His voice sounded heavy, tired now. "Good night."

"Good night," she whispered, her stomach in knots.

***

"Twenty-five shirts," Rachel murmured in her sleep. "That's not enough. Need to..."

Mark woke up with a smile on his face. Rachel had her face buried against his side, and she continued to mumble to herself, though her words made little sense. It was still dark outside, but it must be morning, for Mark felt well-rested for the first time in weeks. He also had a strange feeling in his heart and mind. He didn't wake up and look for danger, or hurry out of bed to leave a hiding place.

Rachel hadn't mentioned any pressing appointment this morning, so Mark savored the feeling of her against him and lay in bed, watching her. Her blonde braid already had pieces trying to escape. The collar of her white chemise had stretched to one side, leaving one of her shoulders bare. Unable to help himself, Mark moved his fingertip over her smooth skin. Rachel shivered slightly and burrowed closer, her face against his ribs. Heat radiated from that point, and Mark, well, Mark was baffled. Was it wrong that he was so attracted to a woman he didn't quite trust?

When his stomach and his bladder wouldn't allow him to stay in bed for a moment longer, Mark threw the covers back and climbed out of bed. He shivered against the morning chill and dressed quickly, tying his hair back. Rachel needed her sleep too, so he left her in bed. Before he left, though, he covered her bare shoulder with a warm quilt. Downstairs, Mark started a pot of coffee. He wasn't much of a cook, but he *could* make coffee.

"How long have you been up?" Rachel's sleepy voice from the doorway made him turn. She was wearing a brown dress today with white flowers on it, and she'd put her hair into some kind of knot at the back of her neck. He wanted to kiss her good morning – once hadn't been enough – but there was distance between them now, put there by their circumstances.

Mark belatedly remembered she'd asked him a question. "Not long. I slept well."

She gave him a soft smile and poured herself a cup of coffee, adding milk. Conversation. Mark needed to make conversation. Hopefully he wouldn't be as awkward as he had been the day before.

"Did you sleep well?" he said.

"Better than I have in weeks."

"Good. I was going to make breakfast," Mark said. "What do you usually eat?"

"Porridge," Rachel said. "Not terribly exciting, but I ration food during the winter. Especially with the redcoats nearby."

There was nothing Mark could do about that at the moment. One assignment at a time.

"Teach me to make porridge, then."

Rachel grinned at him, and his heart lurched. "Truly?"

"Of course. I'd like to be useful."

"Does your knee hurt today?"

"Yes, but less than yesterday."

"Good. Well." Rachel set her coffee cup down. "You've gotten the fire going, which would be the first step. I keep my oats in a container over there —" she pointed to a side table in the kitchen with labeled containers. "Next we heat some water."

Rachel handed Mark a bucket. "Go and pump some water, and we'll heat it over the fire before we add oats."

A quarter of an hour later, Mark sat down across the kitchen table from his new wife, and sampled the very first porridge that he'd made himself. Rachel had been a patient teacher, and it was strange how good it felt to accomplish such a small thing.

"Delicious," Rachel said. "You're a natural. Do you ever have porridge in the army?"

Mark shook his head. "They don't give us oats. We get some flour if we're lucky. Every soldier becomes an expert at creating all manner of dishes with flour and water."

"I suppose this porridge is a luxury, then. What did you eat for breakfast growing up?"

"Uh - not porridge," Mark said. "Meat, potatoes, pastries. Tea."

"I suppose with a Tory father you had lots of tea."

"I never acquired a taste for it. Even if it wasn't patriotic, I would prefer coffee."

"I have a secret to tell you." Rachel leaned over the table, bringing her face very close to his. "I prefer tea."

"No!" Mark said. "You're not fit to be an American."

"I'll do fine," Rachel said. "Perhaps after the war it won't be so absurdly expensive and we'll be able to drink it again."

She said the words so casually. Mark never thought about the future, if he could help it. He kept his mind fixed on the present – it was too dangerous to dream of anything else. For the first time, though, he allowed himself to imagine it. More mornings like this – making breakfast together and drinking coffee as the sun painted the kitchen in golden rays. What would that be like?

Rachel finished her bowl of porridge and brought it to the wash basin.

"What's next?" Mark said.

"Dishes, then we feed the animals."

Fortunately, Mark knew the rudiments of caring for animals since he had spent more time in the stables than in his own home when he was a child. He fed the horses and pigs while Rachel fed the chickens and milked the cow. By the time they'd finished that, it was mid-morning, and Mark was sweating despite the cold.

"You do all of this yourself?" he asked Rachel.

She lifted the bucket of milk onto the kitchen counter. "You get used to it."

"I'm glad I can help."

"While you're here."

The words were spoken lightly, but Mark stopped, holding the basket of eggs Rachel had given him. "I'm not leaving yet."

"No, but you will soon." Rachel tilted her head to meet his eyes. "I'm not upset, Mark."

"I know." Mark's emotions confused him, and he didn't examine them for now. He searched for a change of subject. "Will we go into town today?"

"If you think it's wise," Rachel said. "It would help us diffuse any rumors that Ezekiel Elliott has spread."

Mark shook his head. "I wish he would have minded his own business."

"He's a good man," Rachel replied. "Abigail, his wife, is my friend. Ezekiel is –" Rachel bit her lip. Mark wanted to run a fingertip over her bottom lip, soothing the sting from her teeth.

"Ezekiel has a keen sense of what is right and proper in the eyes of society. He loves Abigail and treats her well, so I can't find fault with him."

"But because of him you had to marry a practical stranger."

Rachel shrugged. "True."

They put the milk and eggs away. Rachel went into the servants' quarters and came back out with a cane. Mark balked at first. Any sign of weakness was to be avoided, and walking with a cane made him look weak. His father had trained him from a young age that any weakness would be punished if it wasn't hidden. He stared at the innocuous piece of smooth wood as if it was a snake.

"It won't hurt you," Rachel said. "In fact, it may help you not to be recognized if we encounter any regulars. That, and your – your beard."

She looked down at her boots, a pretty blush coloring her cheeks. Mark hadn't bothered to shave in the last few days. Did she like the way he looked?

Mark took the cane from her and tested it out. It *was* easier to put his weight on the cane than his bad knee. And if the cane could help him avoid suspicion, then it was all the better. He put his borrowed cloak and boots on and helped Rachel with her cloak, pulling her hair out from beneath it when it got caught in the collar of her cloak.

Her hair was soft, and Mark pulled his hand away before he could enjoy the sensation too much.

"Who are we going to see today?" Mark said as Rachel locked the door behind them.

"Granny and her husband first. Then we'll go to Ezekiel's store."

Fortunately, Granny lived in a modest home just to the west of Rachel's. It was painted green with white trim, and Granny waved from the doorway as they approached. She welcomed them in with warmth and cheer, ushering them into a sitting room that was appointed in creams and browns. A Black man sat in a chair by the fire, a book open in his lap. Rachel approached him and kissed the top of his gray hair.

"Morning, Mr. Greene."

"Good morning, Miss Rachel." He closed his book and stood. "This must be your new husband that Violet's told me all about."

"It is. Mr. Samuel Greene, this is Captain Mark Johnson," Rachel said with a smile.

Mark shook the older man's hand, his grip firm despite his age. Mr. Greene looked to be about fifty, and his clothes were faded with wear. "Pleased to meet you."

"Are you hungry?" Granny said. She sat across from her husband and pulled some sewing into her lap.

"We just ate breakfast," Rachel replied. "We thought we'd do some visiting around town."

"Good idea," Granny said. "Dispel those rumors before they can take root."

"Do you need anything from the store? We're going there next."

"Samuel?" Granny said.

"Nothing, thank you," Mr. Greene said. "Come back and see me, Captain, so I can get to know you better."

"I'd be happy to," Mark said, his heart warming toward the older man at his instant welcome.

Rachel took his arm as they walked down the shoveled footpath through town, waving to a few people. One or two waved back, but for the most part people just stared. Freehold was laid out like any other New England town Mark had visited; there was a common in the middle of town, with a church building just to the north of it which seemed to preside over the other buildings. Everything was coated in a fresh layer of snow from the other night, and Mark felt his spirits lifting just from being outside.

"Why wasn't Mr. Greene at our wedding?" Mark said as they walked. "He seems like a good friend."

"He is," Rachel said. "He's like an uncle to me. Mr. Greene, he –" She fiddled with the ends of her scarf. "He doesn't leave his property."

Strange. "Why not?"

Rachel met Mark's eyes. "That's not my story to tell. But you're welcome to ask him about it; he'll tell you."

Curious. But it would be disrespectful to ask more questions of Rachel.

"I'll ask him the next time we see him," Mark said. "He seemed so – ordinary."

"What is ordinary anyway? The more I get to know people, the more I realize that being ordinary is an illusion."

Mark, who worked desperately to appear ordinary, agreed with that statement. But it didn't comfort him. They walked slowly, Rachel staying close to his side. Near the church was a log building with light spilling out the windows.

"Mr. Elliott has owned this store for a few years now," Rachel said. "If there's gossip to be found, it'll be here, usually started by the man himself."

They stepped inside and were hit with the smell of cinnamon, and a few other spices that Mark couldn't identify. Six people stood scattered among the shelves, and they turned their heads to look at Rachel and Mark as they stepped inside. Mark leaned heavily on his cane, already sore from the walk across town. Mr. Elliott gave them a thin-lipped look when they entered the store. Mark wanted to know what exactly the redcoats had been taking, but this probably wasn't the day to ask about it. Not when the other man's distaste was so obviously written across his face.

Rachel took his arm and guided him to one of the shelves, which held a selection of wooden kitchen implements. "Act natural," she said in a low voice. "Soon people will see that there's nothing to gossip about."

An older woman with dark hair and a deep frown approached them after a few minutes, and Rachel tensed beside him.

"Miss Rachel," she said.

Rachel inclined her head. "Mrs. Elliott."

Mark looked back and forth between the shopkeeper and the woman who must be his mother.

"My son has shared the most disturbing news with me," she said, not taking her dark eyes off of Mark. "I thought you could share the truth with me."

"The truth?" Rachel said, her voice weak. "The truth is that –" she cleared her throat.

Mark wanted to race to Rachel's rescue, but what could he say? Anything he said could make the situation worse, and he didn't want that.

"Mrs. Elliott, this is Mr. Mark Johnson. My husband. We were trapped in a bad situation together, and we married to make the most of it."

"I see," the woman said. "I'm disappointed in you, Rachel."

"It's nice to meet you, Mrs. Elliott," Mark said, inclining his head. "It's good to know that the people of Freehold are full of kindness and Christian charity."

He took Rachel's hand and led her out of the shop.

Once they were back at home, Rachel finally relaxed. She had never in her life been the subject of town gossip (with the exception of making it to twenty-five years of age without marrying), and she didn't enjoy it. The way people had looked at her in Ezekiel's shop – people she'd known her whole life – as if they believed she had been ruined. And Mrs. Elliott had all but said the words. Mark eased himself onto one of the chairs at the kitchen table and grimaced. His steps had grown heavier the longer they'd walked.

Rachel sighed, wanting to sit down herself. But she had too much to do. She'd need to prepare the delivery of clothing for Lieutenant Feldman's troops. Her stomach turned at the thought of making a delivery, but she had told Hannah she would.

How could she do that, though, with Mark at her heels? Rachel crossed her arms, thought for a moment, and had a brilliant idea. She went out to the back of the house and hauled in the tub they used for bathing.

"What are you doing?" Mark said.

"I could use a bath, couldn't you? And it might help with your knee."

Mark's eyes went wide. "A bath?"

"Yes," she said. "I know things are rough in the army, but surely you have heard of bathing."

That actually made him laugh. "Yes, I have heard of it."

"I would ask you to haul water with me, but I don't want you to hurt your knee more."

The process of heating water for the bath was tedious, but Rachel told herself it would all be worth it in the end. Mark sat at the table, leaning his head on his hand, looking like he could fall asleep. When the tub was finally full of steaming water, Rachel pulled a cake of soap and a few towels out of a cabinet.

"Why don't you go first?" she said, trying not to sound too eager. "I'll leave you in peace."

Rachel didn't wait for Mark to undress, but went out to the barn.

"Take your time, Mark," she said to herself. One of the horses tilted his head to look at her as if he was trying to understand what she was saying. She stroked his head.

First she checked the wagon, making sure it was none the worse for wear after its trip with the Continentals. Once she was confident that she wouldn't break a wheel or a harness strap on the road, she moved a few bales of hay. Behind them was a wooden box that she and her friends had filled with clothes and boots for the soldiers. Granny had retrieved the clothes yesterday after the wedding and stored them in Rachel's barn. Lastly, she got out a sack of fabric that would be a special surprise for any redcoats she encountered. Hopefully Rachel could make the delivery the next day. As long as her husband didn't catch on to what she was doing.

Feeling more prepared now, Rachel went back into the kitchen, her eyes catching on Mark's broad – and bare – shoulders. Heavens. They were paler than his hands, neck, and face, but they were impressive nonetheless. She closed the door behind her and cleared her throat.

"I'd better get out," Mark said, not turning his head. "It'd be a shame for you to have a cold bath after all the work you did."

"Yes, it would." Goodness, he was leaning forward now, and – he was getting out of the bath, water sluicing off his body.

Rachel stared. Heaven help her, she stared. His back was riddled with scars, but they didn't detract from his beauty. Mark wrapped a towel around himself and went to stand closer to the fire.

He looked over his shoulder at her, which snapped her out of her trance. It was funny that Mark had acted so uncomfortable around her at times, but seemed perfectly comfortable bathing in front of her. Perhaps that was a product of living in a camp with dozens of other men.

"Rachel?" he said.

"Yes?" She'd been staring at the spot where his lower back met the thick towel wrapped around his waist.

"Do you want to bathe too?"

"Yes, of course." Rachel needed to pull herself together and stop staring. Mark (mercifully) put his borrowed shirt on and sat in front of the fire, combing out his hair.

If she didn't get in the bath soon, the water would be cold. She took off her cloak, hat, and mittens, and hung them up by the back door. Sitting in one of the kitchen chairs, Rachel unlaced her bodice. Mark wasn't looking – was she disappointed by that? – just staring into the fire and occasionally combing his hair. He didn't intend to watch her bathe, did he? And yet he wasn't moving. Surely he would leave the room soon enough. Any gentleman would. Rachel dropped the last of her clothes and practically jumped into the water. It was still warm. She ducked her head under, and came up with a sigh.

Mark still wasn't looking at her. In fact, he seemed frozen in place. The tips of his ears were red. Rachel felt a particular sort of victory at seeing that he wasn't unaffected by their circumstances. After washing her hair and cleaning all of the travel dirt off of herself, Rachel leaned against the edge of the tub, resting her chin on her crossed arms.

"Mark?"

"Yes?" His voice was strained.

"Are you going to finish getting dressed?"

"After I'm dried off."

He was sitting so close to the fire that his hair was almost dry, so Rachel didn't believe his excuse for a second.

"All right."

Mark dropped his comb with a clatter on the wood floor. He picked it up quickly, glanced at her, turned even redder, then looked away again. Perhaps he would be more comfortable if she put some clothes on. Rachel climbed out of the tub.

Once she was dried off, she wrapped herself in her dressing gown and pulled a chair up to the fire opposite Mark. Rachel took her own comb and untangled a section of her hair.

"I'll get dressed," Mark said. He limped out of the room, loose shirt hanging off his shoulders and towel around his waist.

Interesting. Rachel put her lustful thoughts aside and picked up a bucket. The tub full of bathwater wouldn't empty itself.

CHAPTER 9

Being in a house with Rachel was addling Mark's brain. That was the only reason he was seriously considering the topic that she'd brought up. He dressed in his own clothes – bless Will and Jim for bringing him his things – and tied his hair back. Soft rustling downstairs meant that Rachel was starting on supper. Mark didn't know that he could sit across from her and make polite conversation without doing something foolish like kiss her again. In truth, he wondered if he would fail as a husband. He'd never had any instruction, or seen an example of a healthy marriage. Sitting on the edge of the bed, Mark ran a hand through his hair. Fear gripped him; fear that Rachel would see who he really was, how he really struggled. Fear that he would disappoint her. Fear was no excuse, though. Mark would do what he always did; he would improve himself.

"Who can I speak to?" Mark said to the empty room. "Someone who loves and cares for his wife." Perhaps Mr. Greene would be a good place to start.

"Did you say something?" Rachel called from downstairs.

"Just talking to myself," he called back.

Colonel Staples had asked him to find out about supply deliveries. Granny might know about that as well. Mark finished getting dressed in his outdoor clothing – it felt so good to have a pair of boots that fit his feet again – and made his way down the stairs.

"I'll be back shortly," he said to Rachel, who was fully dressed again.

She looked like she wanted to ask where he was going, but she refrained. "All right."

He pressed a quick kiss to her cheek, because it seemed the right thing to do, then left, leaning heavily on his cane. It'd probably be better if he rode to Granny's house, but it was foolish to go through all the trouble of saddling a horse when it was only a stone's throw away. The sun was sinking below the horizon, and candles lit in window panes made the houses of Freehold look warm and inviting. Like home, almost. Whatever "home" meant. Hit by a sudden wave of nervousness, Mark stood on Mr. & Mrs. Greene's doorstep, studying the wooden door. Of course, the door opened before he could even knock.

"Mark." Granny stood in her doorway, looking up at him with concern on her face. "Is anything wrong?"

"Uh, no," Mark said. He stepped inside her warm sitting room.

Mr. Greene popped his head in from the kitchen. "Good to see you again."

Both husband and wife looked at him with the same curiosity on their faces. What had he been thinking, asking people he barely knew for advice? He couldn't even make it through more than a day of being married without needing help.

"I'm sorry," Mark said. "I must go."

Then he left without another word. Any positive impression he'd made on Mr. & Mrs. Greene had probably been ruined by his strange behavior. It was full dark now, and Mark walked back to Rachel's home with his head down. Like Will had said, he would just have to muddle through on his own for now.

Mark had only been gone for a quarter of an hour before he came back into the kitchen, his cheeks red from the cold. Rachel was making stew, and though it was only vegetables and broth, the smell brought comfort. She gave Mark her best warm smile as he came in, still yearning to ask him about the errand he'd been on. But she couldn't very well ask him about his secrets when she wouldn't tell him hers. "Are you hungry?"

"Yes," he said, hanging his cloak up by the door. He took off his tricorne hat and brushed his hair out of his face. "I'm mucking this up already."

Rachel couldn't be sure she heard him right. "What did you say?"

Mark's cheeks turned red. "I said that I'm mucking this up already. Being your husband. I'm bound to disappoint you."

"You're bound to disappoint me?" Did the man think so little of himself? She'd seen him without clothes, and he had *nothing* to be embarrassed of. "How can you know that?"

"I've never seen a marriage where husband and wife treat each other well."

Rachel's heart thumped in her chest at his sincerity. She sat down next to him at the table, and leaned toward him until he looked at her again.

"I don't have any illusions of a great romance with you, Mark," she said. "I'm not looking for that in our marriage, and I don't believe you are either."

He shook his head.

"But that doesn't mean we can't enjoy each other's company. And if you do something I don't like, I'll tell you. If you'll do the same for me."

Mark gave her a long look, his brown eyes reflecting the firelight. She stayed where she was, hoping he would see the truth in her face. Rachel didn't want to fall in love with the man – it would be disastrous, she was certain of it – but she did like him so far.

"I went to Mr. Greene's house to see if he would give me any advice," Mark finally said.

"Advice?"

"On how to be a good husband. He and his wife seem to enjoy each others' company, and I hadn't seen that before."

Rachel couldn't help a smile from spreading across her face. "And what did he tell you?"

"I didn't ask him," Mark said. " I was too embarrassed."

"There's no need to be," Rachel said. "Granny's given me similar advice in the past."

He rubbed his hand over his eyes. "I'm not used to asking for help."

Rachel took one of his hands in both of hers. His hands were rough, tan, and scarred from his work, and she enjoyed the texture against her skin. He'd just removed the bandages the day before. "There's no shame in it."

The stew threatened to bubble over, so Rachel went back to it. Mark sat at the table still, watching the clock tick on the opposite wall. Perhaps delivering the supplies to Lieutenant Feldman's troops tomorrow would help her take her mind off her intriguing new husband.

Mark ate his stew with clear enjoyment, and sighed happily when he finished.

"I suppose I have no right to grumble about having vegetable stew every day," Rachel said. "When you are lucky to get a hot meal."

"I fear the winter will only grow worse for the Continental Troops," Mark said. "It's better for us in the Partisan Corps. Since we spend so much time in the forests, we can hunt more. But getting supplies to the main body of the army is difficult."

Which was why Rachel and her friends' work was so important. But she couldn't tell Mark that.

"How long do you think you'll be here?" she asked.

He took a sip of his cider. "A fortnight or so. Long enough for my men to gather information on the redcoats."

That was all? Rachel's chest tightened. It was probably best that she was keeping so many secrets from him. If she wasn't, it would be too easy to grow attached.

It was far too early for anyone to be awake, but Rachel huddled into her cloak the next morning and watched the horse plodding along in front of her. The sky was barely turning gray, and the snow made a crunching noise under the hooves and wheels, having frosted over in the frigid night. The sooner she finished this delivery, the sooner she could be home. Hopefully before Mark woke up. She took the road west toward Millstone, which passed close to the redcoats' camp, but any other way would take far too much time.

She gripped the reins, looking back and forth into the forest on both sides of the road. Two redcoats came around the corner, and she sucked in a breath. She shouldn't have come. She should have stayed home, warm in her bed, like she'd always done. The regulars walked with purpose toward her. She kept her wagon moving at a steady pace; hopefully her plan would work.They were on foot, so it made her feel marginally better when they approached the wagon and stopped next to her horse.

"State your business please," the shorter one said. His words fogged the air in front of his face, a face that looked far too young to be a professional soldier.

Rachel cleared her throat. "I'm transporting these goods to Millstone."

"Mind if we take a look?"

They would take a look no matter what she said. "Of course not. Go ahead."

She wrapped her cloak more tightly around herself and adjusted her hat. *Eyes forward. Don't look nervous. You're an innocent young lady doing some charity work.*

The regulars moved around the wagon and lifted the tarp. The wagon was filled with –

"What is the purpose of these – pieces of cloth?"

Rachel turned to face them, her face bland. "They're rags, gentlemen."

"Rags?" one of them asked.

"Yes, for women in need in Millstone. Fabric is scarce." She let the words hang in the chilly air, waiting for realization to dawn on the soldiers.

It was almost comical when it did. Both men dropped the rags they were holding and took a couple of steps back. They seemed to realize how undignified this looked and straightened their uniform coats.

"Very well. Good day to you, Miss."

Rachel nodded to the men. "Good day, gentlemen."

They continued on their way, and Rachel continued on hers. She gripped the reins tighter to keep her hands from shaking too hard. Mother's hands never shook.

Mark awoke to an empty bed just after dawn. He dressed and went downstairs, a smile on his face. The smile dropped, though, when he saw the empty kitchen and banked fire. Rachel wasn't outside either, and the wagon and one of the horses were gone.

"Blasted woman. What has she done now?"

He couldn't stand to sit around the house and wait for Rachel to return, so he saddled the other horse and mounted. If his knee wasn't hurt, he could follow her on foot much more efficiently. But this would have to do. The hoof tracks and wheel ruts in the snow lead through town and to the main road out of Freehold going west. Rachel was delivering something, but what?

Mark couldn't take the road, so he rode through the forest. When he heard voices, he stopped the horse and paused, listening. He was near a bend in the road, and beyond it, he swore he heard Rachel's voice. It was too risky to ride closer, though. So he waited. After a few minutes, he heard the wagon wheels rolling again and started to ride, more quickly this time. Unless there were other wagons on the road, he'd found his wife.

What if she was hurt? Anything could happen to someone riding alone, even a trained soldier. Had she met with any redcoats yet? The thoughts pummeled Mark's mind like fists, and he tried to shake them off, concentrating on what he *could* do instead of what he couldn't control. Once he rounded the curve in the road, two redcoats walked by, going east, thankfully too lost in their conversation to notice him. And yes – that was Rachel up ahead on the road. His first instinct was to ride up to her and confront her. But Colonel Staples had wanted to know about supply deliveries that Hannah had been a part of. Was Rachel involved too?

There was only one way to find out.

The Continental Army camp near Millstone was nothing more than a few tents scattered roughly in a circle, and a few dozen starving men. Rachel approached the camp with less trepidation than she had the redcoats' camp, but she was still nervous. Groups of men were dangerous to a lone woman, no matter which side of the war they were on. There were men everywhere, some cooking over fires, some carrying supplies, and some building fortifications.

"Good morning," she called out to the guards. "I'm here to deliver supplies. Can you direct me to Lieutenant Feldman?"

The guards pointed her toward a low ridge that bordered the camp, where two cabins stood. Rachel stopped the wagon, setting the brake, and climbed down from the seat. It was fully light now, but no warmer, and Rachel shivered as she climbed the slight hill. One of the cabins had the door open, with officers spilling out of the one room. She approached the men and cleared her throat.

A group of Continentals turned to look at her, all in mismatched uniforms and looking haggard. Her father would be ashamed. "I'm here to see Lieutenant Feldman," she said again.

"I am he." An older man stepped forward, almost as old as her father. He reminded her of Saint Nicholas, with a white beard and austere face.

"I'm here in place of Mrs. Hannah Wellington," she said.

Lieutenant Feldman stepped out of the cabin and led her down the hill, back toward her wagon. "Pleasant day," he said. "You can see we're in the midst of planning a campaign. We've had a rough couple months of it, what with enlistments expiring and nobody believing in the Cause anymore. I can't tell you what your deliveries have meant in terms of keeping our spirits up."

He paused on the slope to catch his breath, his cheeks red. "Is Mrs. Wellington all right?"

"She took ill, but she's nearly recovered. I am her sister. Miss – Mrs. Johnson."

"Pleased to meet you. And thank you for all of your help. Truly, as I said, I don't know what we would do without you. I don't know where you find all of the materials, but the clothes and boots have been invaluable to my men."

At least Lieutenant Feldman didn't require much from her in the way of conversation. Her wagon was already emptied, the soldiers around it reveling in the clothes she had brought. A few of the women in camp were putting the menstrual rags into crates to be used later. Five or six soldiers sat in the snow, putting socks she'd brought over bare feet. The joy on their faces moved Rachel's heart. They would've had a long and cold winter if not for the work Mother had begun.

"As you can see, my men are grateful as well," Lieutenant Feldman said. "I've prepared a list of more supplies we need, if you and your friends can arrange that by year's end. If you can't, that's fine too, of course – it's just that some of them don't have shoes and –"

"I'm sure we can," Rachel said with more confidence than she felt. Production and delivery would be all the more complicated by the redcoats nearby.

He handed her a list, and she tucked it into one of her pockets. She climbed back onto the wagon seat and waved her goodbye to the Continentals, who smiled and waved in return. Lieutenant Feldman was talking to another one of the soldiers now, telling him where he should put all of the materials. As she drove away, guilt curdled in her stomach. She hadn't told Mark where she was going; she hadn't even left him a note. It had to be close to nine o'clock in the morning by now, and surely he was awake. Would he be worried about her? She didn't want to lie to him about where she'd been, but what was the alternative?

She studied Lieutenant Feldman's list as she drove. Rachel had enjoyed delivering those clothes, found great satisfaction in it. She felt better now that she was on her way back home. But guilt over deceiving Mark was ruining that satisfaction. And she had no idea what to do about it.

Once Mark saw Rachel delivering supplies to what must be a Continental camp (judging by the general disorganization and lack of uniforms), a few of his questions were answered, but so many more questions were raised. Did she deliver supplies to both sides? She didn't *seem* like a Tory. Why would she be, with her father and brother in the Continental Army? If she was helping the Continentals, why hide it? She'd made no mention of her trip to Mark, and she'd left before dawn. Colonel Staples' assignment echoed through his mind. There was something much bigger going on here, and Mark could use his time with Rachel to find out about it.

But she couldn't know.

CHAPTER 10

On the way home, Mark rode more quickly, arriving early enough that he could put his horse away and make breakfast. When Rachel came into the kitchen, it was half-past eight, and Mark greeted her with a bland smile.

"Have a successful outing?"

She hesitated, her brown eyes raking over his face. "I did."

"Good," Mark said. He helped her with her cloak and hat.

Rachel poured herself a cup of lukewarm coffee. "I thought I'd dip some candles today, if you'd like to help."

"I would," Mark said. Perhaps some gentle questioning could get him some of the answers he sought. Then again, he didn't want Rachel to suspect his true motives.

After they cleaned the kitchen of any food and cooking implements, Rachel instructed him on the rudiments of dipping candles. It seemed simple enough. They heated the tallow together and Rachel instructed him how long to cut the wicks, which he set to work doing. After they worked for a time in comfortable silence, Mark realized that he must be boring her. Conversation. Women appreciated conversation.

"Is Hannah continuing to improve?" Mark asked.

"I think so," Rachel said. "Her husband Isaac is supposed to return any day now – he usually takes a furlough this time of year – so it will be of comfort to her when he does."

"Do you like Isaac?"

Rachel frowned at him. "Do I like him?"

"Yes, your brother-in-law. Do you get along with him?"

"I do." She laid a row of wicks over a wooden rod, then dipped them into the tallow over and over again, setting a rhythm with the process. "We've all known each other since childhood. He and Hannah always seemed meant to be together. Isaac is a good balance for her."

"How so?"

Once that group of wicks was finished, Rachel set the newly-dipped candles to dry and started on another row. Mark was doing a satisfactory job cutting wicks, apparently, so he continued with that.

"Hannah has always been very serious," Rachel said. "I suppose it comes from being the eldest daughter. And Isaac is – the least serious person I know. He broke his arm once, and he was telling jokes even as Granny set the bone."

Mark had heard Colonel Staples mention Isaac Wellington once or twice, wishing he would join the Partisan Corps. "I look forward to meeting him. And your brother as well."

"I don't know if Luke will return any time soon. He comes and goes at random." She bit her lower lip, and Mark remembered what her lips had felt like against his. He cut a wick too short, and muttered a curse to himself.

Rachel gave him a curious look, so he changed the subject.

"The weather was unseasonably warm today," Mark said. Was he truly talking about the weather? Surely he could do better than that. "Do you enjoy going for a ride on days like today?"

Rachel considered his question, a line forming between her brows. "I like to ride, yes. But not since the war started."

"Why not?"

"It's not safe."

That was true. Then why did she ride to Millstone to deliver supplies to the Continentals this morning? And why had she seemed to enjoy it?

"I prefer to stay at home whenever I can," Rachel said. "Or at Hannah's. Or Granny's. What about you?" Rachel said. "Do you like to stay at home?"

Mark snorted. "No. Not if I can help it."

"Oh." Rachel's shoulders sagged.

"I might, though, in the future." He certainly would if Rachel were there. "My home growing up was not – I didn't feel safe there. So I've always preferred to spend my time out of doors."

"Your father?"

Mark nodded.

"Do you feel safe here?" Mark almost gave her a pat answer, but he remembered his shaking spell from the other night. Rachel must be curious about that.

"As safe as I feel anywhere, I suppose. My own mind isn't a safe place sometimes."

Even admitting that much out loud felt strange, and Mark watched Rachel for a reaction. She didn't react though; she merely snipped the wick of the candle she was working on and added it to the pile. They worked in silence for a time.

"Is there anything I can do?" Rachel said.

"Anything you can...?" Mark had lost track of what they were talking about.

"Anything I can do to make you feel more safe here?"

"Eradicate the redcoats camped nearby?" Mark bit his lip to keep from laughing, but Rachel gave in right away, throwing her head back and laughing without reservation.

"Believe me, I would love to do that," Rachel said.

"No, I don't think there is anything else you can do," Mark said. "You've made me feel quite comfortable here. I appreciate it."

She smiled at him. Every smile of hers felt like a gift. "Good."

After they finished dipping the candles, Rachel went to Granny's house, which left Mark restless. A gentle rap at the kitchen door saved him from himself, though. Mark peered through the back window and saw Will and Jim standing on the back porch. A smile spread over his face as he opened the door.

"I am glad to see you two," he said.

"It always smells so good in here," Will said as they sat down at the kitchen table. "I don't know how."

"It's probably these." Mark pointed at the dried apples that hung from the ceiling. Growing up, his family's cook had hung dried fruit from the ceiling, and the smell reminded him of home. Mark shook off the rare moment of nostalgia and concentrated on the matter at hand. "What have you found out?"

Jim held up one of his hands and ticked out the points on his fingers. "They are well-supplied. When they aren't having supplies delivered, they are getting supplies from nearby towns." His eye was nearly healed, only a faint bruise visible against his skin.

"What is their relationship with the local citizens?"

"We've done some asking around here in Freehold and in Mill-stone," Will said. "And everyone we've talked to is too afraid to resist them."

"So they're running roughshod," Jim said.

"We must drive them out, then." Mark said the words with confidence, but in truth he had no idea how they would accomplish that. "Have you gotten a good count?"

"There are about 150 men, all told," Jim said. "We've counted anywhere from 30 to 50 horses."

"Have you learned anything on your end?" Will asked him, brushing his dark hair out of his face. "Has Miss — Mrs. Johnson told you what she was doing in the redcoats' camp that day?"

"It looked like she was delivering supplies to them," Jim said.

Mark's cheeks burned. How could he answer that? He was always forthright with his men. But he felt loyalty to Rachel as well, even though he'd only known her a few days.

"She – uh, she hasn't told me any more about what she was doing that day. But I am watching her movements."

Mark looked around the kitchen, expecting his wife to appear at any moment. "She's given me no cause to mistrust her."

"Apart from what she was doing the day you met her?" Will's eyebrows rose.

Mark twisted his hands in his lap. "Yes, apart from that."

Both men looked at him intently, and he met their eyes. "I'm choosing to trust her. You should choose to trust me."

"As long as you know what you're doing," Jim said.

"I hope I do," Mark replied. He changed the subject. "What does Colonel Staples say?"

"He said he couldn't spare more men yet. Perhaps in another few weeks."

They hadn't dealt with a situation like this before. They'd removed smaller groups of redcoats before, but never a camp this large and well-supplied.

"Do we know where their supplies are coming from?" Mark's voice rose at the end of that question as he thought about Rachel.

Jim shook his head. "We haven't found a pattern yet, but we are keeping track. Tom is doing excellent work at that. He can hide in places none of the rest of us can."

Tom was the youngest and smallest member of their unit, and Mark smiled at the thought of the lad hiding out for hours. "He's perfect for that. How are the others getting along? Are you all quartering in nearby towns?"

"Where we can," Jim said. "Don't worry about us, Captain. You rest."

"You're no good to us with a bad leg," Will added.

That was what Mark was afraid of.

His men stood to leave. "We must deal with these redcoats quickly," Jim said. "I fear what will happen if we don't."

They left as quietly as they had come, and Mark fought the urge to beg them to stay. He knew how to be a Captain. He didn't know how to be a husband.

"Isaac has returned!" Hannah greeted Granny and Rachel as they sat in Granny's sitting room that afternoon. She came in the front door, cheeks flushed and looking healthier than Rachel had seen her in a week.

Rachel set aside her work and hugged her sister. "I'm so happy for you."

Every time Isaac returned on a furlough, it was a mix of good and bad. Rachel liked Isaac and he was a good husband to her sister, but when he left, Rachel had to console Hannah. Hannah sat down in a chair and pulled out several cloth bags that she'd brought with her. Granny poured her a cup of coffee and handed it to her. They sat in a circle in front of the fire, their work spread out around them.

"Are you hungry, Miss Hannah?" Mr. Greene popped his head in from the kitchen.

"No, thank you."

"I see then. I'll let you ladies have your fun." He went back to puttering around the kitchen, humming as he worked.

"Why are you here, and not with him?" Rachel said.

"He was exhausted and wanted to sleep," Hannah replied. "I told him I'd be here, and not to worry about me."

"He doesn't know what we're doing, does he?" Rachel said.

"Of course not," Hannah said. She turned to Granny. "How far along are we?"

"Nearly done with the first batch," Granny said, gesturing to the rifle balls that were cooling on trays on the floor. They caught the light from the late afternoon sun and filled Rachel's heart with pride. She and her friends had tried several ways of making defective ammunition, but these were the most promising so far.

"And have we tested out your new method of heating the metal?" Hannah said.

"I did this morning," Granny said. "I loaded one into Mr. Greene's old pistol." She shook her head. "Near ruined the thing and got powder all over my face. So I'd say they work."

Hannah clapped her hands together. "Excellent."

"We're stamping them with this star imprint," Granny continued, holding up one of the bullets, which had a star the size of Rachel's fingernail stamped into it.

"So we can tell which ones to deliver where."

Rachel picked up the next tray of bullets and a metal file she'd been using. "It's brilliant, Granny," she said.

"I'm full of brilliant ideas." Granny tucked a gray curl behind her ear. "Do you have the list from Lieutenant Feldman?"

Rachel pulled the list from her pocket, where she'd carefully kept it hidden from Mark the last few days. She unfolded it and handed it to Granny, then picked up the first bullet. Her part of the process was to file off any imperfections left behind by the mold. Granny took out her spectacles and read over the list. "This all seems fairly standard." She handed the list to Hannah who read over it as well.

"What should we work on next?" Rachel asked Hannah.

Hannah frowned, perusing the list. "Stockings. Those will arouse the least suspicion, especially as Rachel and I have men underfoot now. Then we can move on to the boots if we can get the leather for them."

Every woman in the room nodded, and Rachel mentally tabulated how much yarn she had at home and where she could acquire more.

"Lieutenant Feldman's men appreciated the clothes, though?" Hannah said.

"They did. Several of them were barefoot."

Granny clucked her tongue. "Poor things. I wish we could do more."

Rachel often had the same thought, but she shook it away. "Perhaps we can add to our group of Couriers in the future, but our work is enough for now."

"You're right," Granny said.

Once they finished molding and smoothing the bullets, Hannah counted them into bags of one hundred.

"Now for the delivery," Hannah said. "Charity can take them and distribute them among her mother's weapons shipments if we can get the bullets to her."

"One defective bullet for every ten?" Granny frowned.

"Every bit counts," Rachel said, quoting her mother. "This is something we can

do, and we don't know the difference it might make."

"We should inform Lieutenant Feldman that if he comes across any bullets bearing this Mark that they shouldn't use them." Granny held a bullet with the star stamped in it up to the firelight. "We'd hate for any of them to get hurt."

"Rachel, can you deliver these to Charity on Monday?" Hannah asked her. "I would, but I've got Isaac underfoot now."

"And I have Mark in my home," Rachel replied. "He's *always* there."

"You poor woman," Granny said with an exaggerated pout.

Rachel looked around, fear growing in her chest. Surely they didn't expect her to make another delivery, did they? Not when Mark was already suspicious of her. But the thrill she got from a successful delivery was addictive, and she wanted to prove she could be brave. Both to her friends and to herself.

"I'll do it," Rachel said. "But I don't want to sneak around Mark any more. We'll have to come up with a way for him to be involved somehow."

Hannah's lips thinned. "We work with Charity because her brother is a Tory and well-known for manufacturing ammunition. She has direct contact with dozens of redcoat officers, and it's the most efficient way to get these bullets into the rifles of our enemies. Mark can't know any of that."

"I won't tell him," Rachel said. But still, it didn't sit right. Mark had been nothing but forthright with her.

Granny got up to throw another log on the fire, and Rachel glanced out the window of the cabin.

"I must go," she said, standing. "It's getting dark." She hated to leave the company of her friends, but nobody went out after dark these days if they could help it.

Once they'd packed away and hidden any evidence of their work, the group dispersed. Rachel made sure she had her pistol and at least one dagger within easy reach, put on her cloak and hat, and made her way across the fields to her house.

After Will and Jim left, Mark saddled one of the horses and rode into town. He did have an assignment to complete, after all. Rachel had said that Ezekiel's store was the best place for town gossip, so Mark would start there.

A bell tinkled as he entered the store, and every person in the place turned to look at him. He gave what he hoped was a friendly nod.

"Mr. Johnson," Ezekiel said, frowning at him. The man had blonde hair neatly tied back, and looked to be a little younger than Mark. " Can I help you find something?"

Mark approached the counter, not hiding his limp. Going out in public still felt risky – the redcoats might recognize him – but it was necessary.

"Oh, not really," Mark said. He leaned against the counter and surveyed the room. There were three people from town in the store, all studiously avoiding looking at him.

"Busy today?" he asked Ezekiel, trying to keep his voice casual.

"Somewhat."

There didn't seem to be a chance of Ezekiel warming up to him any time soon, so Mark asked the question he'd come in to ask, heedless of what the man thought of him.

"Have you had any regulars come in?"

"Not since earlier in the week."

"What do they usually take?"

Ezekiel frowned. "Why do you wish to know?"

"I'm merely curious. There's a Continental camp near Millstone, and I wondered if they were stealing from the Continentals too."

The other man glowered at Mark. "Can't say I know anything about that."

Very well. The man didn't trust Mark yet. And he was probably wise not to. Mark stretched his lips into a smile. "I like to help with the war effort wherever I can. I can't fight with this knee."

That much was true. He didn't want word spreading around town that he was a Continental soldier. Not yet, anyway.

"If you stay around long enough, you'll find ways to help, I'm sure," Ezekiel said.

The man pulled a leather volume off a nearby shelf and opened it up, studying the rows of figures inside. Mark was being dismissed. Well, that was fine. Getting sensitive information wasn't done in a day, especially from strangers. Mark would just have to win Ezekiel's trust.

Rachel mulled over the secrets she kept from Mark as she turned the roasted chicken above the fire. It was one thing to deliver supplies to Lieutenant Feldman's troops. But going to Charity's house would require a whole day of being gone. She didn't want to hide that much from Mark. Two saddle bags full of bullets needn't be conspicuous. In fact, she could bring Mark along with her (if he wanted to go), and Charity could slip out and retrieve the bullets at any time.

The chicken was golden and fragrant, so Rachel pulled it off the spit and set it on a platter to rest. She tried not to eat meat too often

– it would be a long winter, after all – but having some in a stew on the Sabbath was lovely. Mark came in the back door and greeted her with a warm smile. She found herself smiling right back.

"I went to Ezekiel's store," he said.

"Ah," Rachel said. "Did you want to incite more curiosity from everyone in town?"

Something in Mark's eyes shifted. Before Rachel could inquire about it, Mark changed the subject. "Is that chicken?"

"It is. And I'm roasting some potatoes and cabbage." Rachel poked at the bottom of the fireplace, where the potatoes were roasting. They were nearly done.

Mark patted his stomach. "You'll make me never want to leave."

Rachel stilled, the poker in her hands. Did he mean that?

"I meant – well…" Mark opened and closed his mouth like a fish. He was blushing again, and Rachel shouldn't find it so appealing.

"Of course I wouldn't *want* to leave," he finally said.

"But you must do your duty," Rachel finished for him. She understood that duty well.

"Yes. I must."

They finished preparing supper together, and Rachel tried to eat her chicken slowly, but it was far too delicious. Mark ate heartily as well and it was all they could do to save enough meat for a stew the next day.

"I thought I might visit my friend Charity on Monday," Rachel said, cutting herself a piece of potato. "Would you like to come?"

"Where does she live?"

"Millstone. It's about five miles west of here. I was going to ride there in the morning and probably come back in the afternoon, provided the weather's decent."

"Would you like me to come?"

Rachel blinked. There was nothing but sincerity on his face. She'd expected him to be much more concerned with where she went and what she did. So far, though, he seemed willing to afford her an unexpected amount of freedom.

"I'd like that. You might like Charity."

Mark smiled, his eyes warm in the candlelight. "I probably shall, if she's your friend."

After supper, Rachel retired to the sitting room with a new book that Granny had loaned her. Mark finished cleaning the kitchen and came to stand in the doorway, shifting from foot to foot, watching her.

She positioned herself in her favorite chair by the fire and pulled a woolen blanket over her lap. "Would you like to borrow a book? My father has dozens of them in his study that you might find interesting."

"No, thank you," Mark said.

Still, he didn't move from his place. Did he not like to read? That was an unsettling fact to learn about one's new husband. Well, that was sad for Mark. But the new book called to Rachel, and she opened the cover, savoring the smell of the worn pages.

"You don't mind if I read, do you?" Rachel said.

"Of course not. I suppose I'll retire, then. Goodnight."

"Goodnight."

Much to her dismay, Rachel couldn't concentrate on the words on the page yet. Not until Mark's uneven footsteps disappeared into the hallway upstairs.

"What are you so excited about?" Rachel asked Mark on the walk to church the next morning.

She was tired; she hadn't slept well. Once she'd gone to bed the night before, Mark had moved toward her in his sleep, tucking her against his side. It had been very distracting, and Rachel hadn't been able to sleep, finally falling asleep after hours of laying awake. He'd been awake and made breakfast before she pried herself out of bed, and now he was fairly bouncing with his cane along the packed snow path.

"I enjoy church," he said simply.

Rachel felt guilty. Church was fine – she supposed she enjoyed it too – but it wasn't anything to get excited over. Sometimes it was just several hours that stood in between her and reading her book. But Mark's simple pleasure in going to meeting was endearing. The doors to the white building were open, and light and warmth spilled out into the cold morning. Rachel took Mark's arm as they made their way through the crowd. Most of the people in town would've greeted her with at least a nod, but it looked like Ezekiel had spread what he'd seen around town. Rachel smiled brightly and pretended that it didn't hurt that hardly anyone looked her way. There was nothing they could do about it but brave their way through. Hannah was already sitting in the family pew next to Isaac, who stood up to embrace Rachel. She pulled back and looked up at her brother-in-law. His light brown hair was pulled back and he looked dapper in his brown waistcoat.

"You're looking well," she told him.

"As are you," Isaac said. "My wife has told me the strangest thing: you, Rachel Staples, have finally chosen a man to marry."

"This week, actually," Rachel said. Mark stepped up behind her, and the men shook hands. "Mr. Mark Johnson, meet Isaac Wellington. He's married to Hannah so we must tolerate him."

Isaac's warm laugh echoed through the church, and he covered his mouth as people stared.

"Your brother sends his regards," he said.

Rachel's heart leapt. "Is he all right?"

Isaac nodded. "Had a scratch on his shoulder in our last engagement –"

"He means a bullet wound," Hannah said.

"--but he's fine now," Isaac finished.

Rachel tried to find the calm that had visited her in the church, but it was gone now. In its place was the icy tightness in her chest when she thought about her younger brother being shot.

Hannah squeezed her arm. "Rachel's a bit squeamish about these things, you know," she told Isaac. "We'd best not give her more details."

She didn't have the heart to correct her sister. "As long as he's all right. Will he be home any time soon?"

"I don't believe so," Isaac said. "It was hard for me to get away. Enlistments are expiring and good soldiers are scarce right now."

"But you'll stay until the new year, won't you?" The hope in Hannah's voice tugged at Rachel's heart.

Isaac took his wife's arm. "Of course I will."

"Isaac," Ezekiel said as he and Abigail filed into the pew behind them. "Good to have you back."

"Good to be back. I only wish I could spend more time at home."

Rachel saw the sadness flash across Hannah's face at the mention of Isaac leaving, but her sister quickly covered it up again. Which of course made Rachel sad that Hannah would have to go through that again.

"I doubt you've heard what Rachel and Mr. Johnson did this week?" Ezekiel said.

Abigail stood silent next to him, sympathy all over her face. Isaac looked between the four of them, his lips pressed together. "I've heard several wild stories. I'm sure none of them are true."

"I assure you, I saw them," Ezekiel said. "In fact, I think it best that we move, Abigail."

Rachel's heart died a little bit inside her chest when Ezekiel turned to leave. Abigail couldn't work with her any more; would Rachel be able to see her friend at all from now on?

Mark's hand gripped Ezekiel's arm before the other man could move. "That's not necessary. We were caught in an unfortunate predicament, but we have married, which should please even the most sanctimonious people in town."

"I only meant –" Ezekiel said.

"I know what you meant," Mark replied. "I would hope Mrs. Johnson's character speaks for itself. There's no need to malign her more than you already have."

Ezekiel went pale, snapping his jaw shut. Mark let go of his arm and stepped back, putting his arm around Rachel. He turned them around so they faced the front of the church, as if he didn't care what Ezekiel decided to do. He kept his arm around Rachel, though, only dropping it when they rose for the opening hymn. How was Rachel supposed to concentrate on the sermon now?

CHAPTER 11

"I don't know how you convinced her to marry you," Isaac said as they entered Rachel's kitchen after church. "You're a soldier too, aren't you?"

"I am," Mark said. "But we're keeping it quiet around town."

"Rachel, are you aware that this man is a soldier?" Isaac called over to her. He seemed like a nice enough man, and Rachel clearly viewed him as her own brother. He was about as tall as Mark, with light brown hair and scars on his face that marked him as a soldier who'd seen many battles.

"Yes." Rachel gave him a quelling look. "I am aware."

"I need to hear this story," Isaac said.

And Mark told it. For what felt like the dozenth time in the past few days. But Isaac was a good listener and reacted appropriately in all of the right places.

"The Partisan Corps, eh? You all have quite the reputation."

"Truly?" Rachel said.

Isaac nodded. "Luke doesn't want to be any part of it, of course, because he's stubborn, but I would love it."

"Why?" Hannah said.

They filled their bowls with stew and their mugs with cider, and Rachel slid onto the bench next to Mark. It felt right to have her next to him like that.

"Fewer pitched battles," Isaac said.

"When Luke was young, all he wanted to do was fight," Rachel said. "He forced us to play soldiers all the time."

"He joined the militia when he was fifteen, but Father allowed it," Hannah added.

"Were you that way, Mark?" Rachel asked.

That was an excellent question. "No. I don't suppose I was. Not until after my father died."

"I'm sorry to hear that," Isaac said.

"Don't be," Mark took a bite of his stew, and the flavor of the vegetables and chicken burst across his tongue. "He wasn't a good man."

Thankfully they sensed his hesitation and changed the subject, talking of Isaac's adventures in the last few months.

"Who's for backgammon?" Hannah asked when they had cleaned up the dishes.

Rachel grinned and followed her sister into the sitting room. Mark happened to enjoy backgammon – perhaps he could take a turn –

"Don't even try it," Isaac said, following him. "They'll be at it all afternoon. You and I can sit on the sofa and watch the battle."

Rachel and Hannah set up the backgammon board on a side table by the fire, apathetic to the men's presence, and began to play. The competition was fierce and Mark found himself transfixed, watching this different side of Rachel with a foolish grin on his face.

"You like her, don't you?" Isaac said softly as Hannah and Rachel broke into a loud argument about checker movement and who was correct.

Mark shifted in his seat. Dare he admit it, even to himself? "I think I do."

"A finer wife you couldn't find," he said. "I think of her as my own sister. I grew up with them, you know."

Rachel and Hannah settled their argument and play resumed, so Mark closed his mouth before he could ask Isaac more about what Rachel had been like growing up. The fact was that Mark did like her, more and more every day, and the thought terrified him. What was more, he could see himself living here, with Rachel and her family, having many more Sundays like this. The last game ended in another argument, and the women stood and put on their cloaks.

"What are you doing?" Mark said. Isaac didn't look surprised. He merely put on his own cloak as well.

"A duel," Rachel said to him. "To decide the winner."

"A duel?" Mark said. Surely they were joking.

Isaac laughed at him. "It's not what you think. Come outside and see."

"Do you need a second?" he asked Rachel as he put on his own cloak.

Her hearty laughter made his insides feel warm. "Not at all. I intend to win."

Rachel and Hannah led the men out the kitchen door and through the fields to where the Staples' land met the forest. Isaac carried the supplies, and Mark limped along beside him, looking adorably confused. Rachel would wager that Mark was rarely confused, so it was entertaining to see him so baffled. They reached the two dead trees they used as targets, and Rachel took stock of the area, noting the wind speed, any sounds or smells that could distract her, and, most importantly, how she could hit her target better than her sister.

"This is better than I was imagining," Mark said. "But not much."

Was he *concerned* about her? Rachel's heart lifted at the thought. "We'll be fine. I've been doing this since I was four."

"Four?" Mark's eyes went wide.

Hannah hastened to explain as Rachel finished setting up. "Our mother was terribly ill when she was carrying Luke. Father was at his wit's end trying to entertain us, so our duels were born."

Rachel had forgotten about that. For as much as she had trouble with her sister, they had always had each other.

"They know it's not actually a duel," Isaac said.

"It's just what Father called it when we were small," Hannah continued. "And the name remained."

Rachel dusted the snow off of their targets while Hannah drew a line in the snow with the toe of her boot. Rachel was nervous. Why was she nervous?

She wanted to impress Mark. Admitting it to herself was embarrassing, but denying it was fruitless. That was all right, though. She could be his friend and care about what he thought, without having any affection for him. Couldn't she?

Rachel finished with the targets and walked over to where Hannah was pulling a leather case out of its carrier. Hannah handed her one of the cases and opened one herself. Good. The neatly-polished row of knives looked clean and sharp. They traded cases, as was their practice, and stood behind the line Hannah had drawn.

"I don't need a second," Rachel said to Mark, who was watching with interest on his face. "But you could hold my knives for me if you'd like."

He stepped closer, and Rachel felt his warmth from several feet away. "Your father taught you to throw knives when you were *four* years old?"

Rachel laughed. "We used wooden ones for years until we learned to throw properly. He didn't teach us with real knives until much later."

Mark didn't look reassured.

"Are we going to settle this like women, or are we just going to talk about it all day?" Hannah said, raising her eyebrows.

Rachel tilted her chin up. Hannah always won, but Rachel still tried. Having Mark's eyes on her made it difficult to concentrate, but she remembered what Mother had said. She took several deep breaths and ignored all but the target. The wooden knife handle was cool in her hand, and she tested its weight, flipping the knife a few times to get a feel for it.

A *thunk* told her that Hannah had thrown her first knife, but Rachel didn't look. She didn't want to see how far ahead her sister was. Instead, she looked at her target again, and when she felt calm enough, let her first knife fly. While not her best throw, it was satisfactory. Rachel worked her way through her five knives, hitting near the center of the target with each one. It wasn't until she finished that she looked over at Hannah's.

"Rachel," Hannah said slowly. "I do believe you've won."

"Truly?" Rachel hardly ever won. But, as she looked back and forth, it was true. Her knives were clustered much closer to the middle of the target than Hannah's.

"Well done, Rachel," Isaac said.

She looked to Mark, who was grinning at her. Her heart seemed like it was about to beat out of her chest, and not because she was nervous. Hannah shook her hand and conceded the victory for the day.

Isaac put his arm around Hannah as they walked back to the house. "After that, I believe I shall spend some time alone with my wife. She'll need some consolation, you know."

Hannah blushed, and Rachel felt a stab of jealousy. But she didn't let it reach her face; she was happy for her sister, truly.

"We'll see you soon," Hannah called as she and Isaac walked toward their home.

Rachel went in the back door before Mark, and directed him where to put the knives so they were out of the way.

Mark limped over and sat at the kitchen table. He looked natural in her home. He'd gotten along well with Hannah and Isaac – he fit so well into her family. Rachel wasn't sure how she felt about that.

"How often do you do that?" He said.

"Duel?"

"Yes."

Rachel leaned against the kitchen counter. "Once a month. Maybe twice."

"I'm impressed."

She warmed under his praise.

"Do many women you know practice with knives?" he asked.

Rachel considered his question. "Every woman I know is proficient with at least one type of weapon. We must be."

"Because the men are all at war?"

"Yes. Even before the war, though, my mother taught Hannah and I to keep ourselves safe. This country has never been a safe place."

Surely Mark knew that. He was looking at her so intently that she felt the need to keep talking.

"Mother favored the knife because it is light and can be concealed easily. Father may have begun our training, but Mother made sure we practiced every day."

He stood and came toward her, towering over her, his eyes dark and intent. His breath smelled like apples from the cider they'd had earlier. Rachel froze, meeting his gaze.

"You're a wonder, Rachel Johnson." His voice was low, and he ran the back of his finger down her cheek.

Rachel was just wondering what he would do next when he stepped back. She gripped the counter behind her with both hands. He was standing a few feet away from her now, his chest heaving under his shirt and waistcoat. Rachel's heart was pounding and she couldn't have moved from that counter if she tried.

Mark cleared his throat. "Should we have some supper?"

If Mark had wanted to kiss her, he would have. Did she want him to? She'd certainly enjoyed kissing him before. Mark Johnson was a man that deserved to be kissed, and kissed frequently. But she'd told herself she wouldn't pressure him, and she wouldn't.

"Yes," Rachel answered briskly. "Supper. Before we lose the light."

She and Mark put together a simple supper for themselves and ate in silence at the table. By the time they finished, it was fully dark and time to light some candles. They sat together on the sofa in the sitting room. Rachel was tired but content from the day, and Mark's warmth at her side was a comfort.

"I'm glad you're here," she found herself saying. "With me."

He put his arm around her and pulled her against his side. "I'm glad as well."

Her eyes were drifting closed when Mark spoke again. "I never thought I'd have this."

"Have what?"

"Be a part of a family like this."

Rachel sat up to look at him. His face was partially shadowed by the firelight, but he looked happier than she'd ever seen him.

"That is – it feels like I am part of a family now. I know I'm not, not truly..."

Rachel took his hands in hers. "You are, Mark."

When that seemed to reassure him, she leaned back against his side. "Your family wasn't very pleasant, was it? What about your mother?"

"My father – well, I told you what he was like. The woman who raised me was not my mother. My true mother was a servant in the household who my father took advantage of. She fell pregnant, and my father sent her off to New York City as soon as I was born."

Rachel's heart clenched. "What happened to your father's wife?"

"When my father died, she went back to England to be with her family. She made it clear that she wanted nothing to do with me."

"How did you find your mother?"

"She'd written letters to my father – I found them in his effects. Letters begging to come see me." His muscles tightened underneath Rachel's head, and she wrapped her arms around his waist.

"I found her, and set her up in my father's house. She lives there now, mistress of the place."

That made Rachel smile. "I'll bet your father would've hated that."

"Absolutely."

"What's your mother like?"

Mark laughed softly. "She's the kind of woman that could go through what she did and come out a kinder, softer, and stronger person for it. She's the best person I know."

"Perhaps I'll meet her one day."

"I hope you will." Mark pressed a kiss to the top of her head. "I think she'd love you."

"Are you all right?" Mark asked her for what felt like the fifth time.

It was the next morning, and they were getting ready to ride to Charity's house.

"Yes, I'm fine." Rachel was trying to hide her nerves as she saddled her horse, but she was failing, apparently. How could Mark see through her so easily?

They mounted their horses and rode out of Freehold. It was mid-morning, so they got a few curious stares, but Rachel smiled brightly and waved. Hopefully nobody would be too suspicious. All of the defective bullets fit in their saddlebags, and two riders on horseback were less likely to attract attention than a woman driving a wagon. Rachel told herself this as they rode, willing the nerves to subside.

"Riders ahead," Mark murmured to her about a mile outside of town.

"How do you know that?" Rachel saw nothing but snow and trees.

"Listen."

Rachel listened, but she didn't hear anything out of the ordinary. It wasn't until the group of ten redcoats rounded the corner that she recognized the gentle clanking of their bridles and the horses' soft footsteps on the snow.

"Good morning," the man with the most decorations on his uniform said. "Where are you headed?"

"Millstone," Mark answered. "To visit a friend of my wife's."

The man rode up between them. "I'll just take a look, and you can be on your way."

He flipped open the leather flap on Mark's saddlebags, and pulled out the canvas sack of musket balls.

"What do we have here?"

Having Mark with Rachel was a small comfort, for the redcoat addressed Mark instead of her. Mark didn't know what they were delivering, however – Rachel had packed the saddlebags the night before – so he raised his eyebrows at Rachel.

Meeting the soldier's eyes, Rachel cleared her throat. "My friend's name is Charity Marshall. Her brother, Jonathan Marshall, supplies His Majesty's troops in Millstone and the surrounding area. Perhaps you've heard of her?"

"I haven't," the man said.

Rachel shrugged, trying to look unaffected, though her heart was pounding. "We were trying to help His Majesty's Cause. I have more musket balls in my saddlebags as well."

Perhaps if she was forthright, they would let her and Mark go. The soldier frowned, looking between her and Mark again. Mark was pale, but his face was expressionless.

"Is this true?" he said to Mark.

"My wife doesn't lie," he said, looking right at Rachel with anger and disappointment in his eyes.

Rachel swallowed hard.

"We'll just take these, then," the redcoat said. "Since you're so keen on helping His Majesty's troops."

And Rachel could do nothing but sit there and study her gloved hands as the redcoats took all of the musket balls that they'd worked so hard to make, along with the extra food and supplies Rachel had packed.

"Good day," the redcoat said when they finished. He clucked his tongue and his horse walked again.

Tears formed in Rachel's eyes, and she wiped them aside with her hand. To his credit, Mark didn't say a word at first, though he was frowning at her. And he still looked pale.

"I don't suppose we should go to Charity's," she said. She turned her horse around and rode back toward Freehold.

"All right," Mark said.

Rachel let herself cry frustrated tears all the way back to Freehold, which was unfortunately only about twenty minutes. Once they were back in town, she tilted down the brim of her hat so she wouldn't have to meet anyone's eyes.

"I'll take care of the horses," Mark said. "You go inside."

Fortunately Rachel went inside before Mark said something he'd regret. As it was, he was barely holding his frayed emotions together. Both horses pranced nervously, and Mark took a deep breath. There was no need to make the horses unsettled. No good would come from that.

"It's not your fault," Mark whispered to them, patting both of their flanks. "I need to speak to my wife about what she is not telling me."

Grooming and caring for the horses settled Mark's nerves as it always had, and as he went through the motions, he thought about Rachel. His wife. The woman who he was coming to care for. His hands were still shaky, but he felt more steady than he had a quarter hour before.

Today she had intended to deliver musket balls to the redcoats. Hadn't she? Unless she was lying to the redcoats. Which was a definite possibility. Mark didn't want to jump to conclusions, but it was a good reminder that there was a great deal Rachel wasn't sharing with him.

By the time the horses were cared for, Mark felt marginally calmer. Calm enough to have a rational discussion with his wife. She was sitting at the kitchen table with a cup of coffee warming her hands. She'd poured him a cup too, from the looks of it. Mark took the coffee and sat across from her. Rachel had stopped crying, but her eyes were still red and she looked pale. Pity stirred in Mark's chest, the desire to take care of her.

"Tell me I'm not wrong about you," Mark said gently. "I believe you are loyal to the Cause and would never work against the Continental Army. I trust you, Rachel, though perhaps I shouldn't. Tell me my trust isn't misplaced."

"It's not," Rachel said. "All of what you have said is true."

"And yet you intended to deliver musket balls to a woman who supplies the redcoats? Or were you lying to the regulars?"

"I did." She met his eyes, not saying any more.

"You can't tell me any more about it?"

Rachel shook her head, and frustration built in Mark's chest. "What am I to do with you, then?"

"I don't know," she said softly, more tears forming in her eyes. Mark hadn't meant to make her cry, but she was hiding information from him.

Colonel Staples had given Mark an assignment, and he would see it through. That assignment meant that he had to continue observing Rachel and her sister. He'd just have to keep his heart safe from her. Mark finished his coffee and set his cup in the washbasin.

"I'm going to go for a walk."

Rachel watched him go, and didn't do anything to stop him. In truth, she couldn't blame Mark for being suspicious. And she couldn't tell him the truth of what they were doing, not without betraying her friends. She sipped at her coffee, her heart aching. When her coffee didn't solve all of her problems, she stood and went to Father's study.

Charity would need to know not to expect bullets from them any more, nor a visit from her. It had taken them weeks to accumulate enough scrap metal to make those musket balls. It was of small comfort, though, that at least the bullets had gotten to the redcoats.

Rachel got out a pot of ink, a pen, and a sheet of paper, and scratched out a note.

Dear Charity,

I regret to inform you that I can no longer visit as planned. My gifts for you were stolen, and I must find time to make more. Come see me when you can.

with love,

Rachel

She replaced the ink and pen, sprinkled pounce on the words so they wouldn't smear, and sealed the letter. Mailing that letter was something she could accomplish, then she would put herself together and find something to do. Rachel was five steps in front of the house when Mark came up behind her, hobbling on his cane.

"Going into town?" He didn't meet her eyes.

"Yes, I was going to mail Charity a note explaining my absence."

"I'll come with you."

"That's not necessary."

Mark took her arm, ignoring her indignant huff, and started the walk. Rachel would understand if he was furious with her, but he just seemed frustrated, and she wasn't sure what to do about that.

A few people walked to and fro, and occasionally they saw a horse or wagon pass by. Six redcoats walked in pairs through town in different places; they weren't in a group, but it seemed that they watched each others' movements. Reverend Alder was coming out of Granny's home when Mark and Rachel passed by, putting his tricorne hat back on top of his thinning hair.

"Do you mind if I join you?" he said. He also walked with a cane, leaning heavily on it. He'd been a soldier himself in his younger days, and Father had told her that he'd had his knee injured by a stray bullet. Rachel had never had the nerve to ask the older man about it, though.

"Of course not," Rachel said. She took Reverend Alder's arm on his other side, and they continued their walk.

"So how are you two getting along?" the minister asked. "There was a great deal of talk about you at first, but I think the rumors have died down."

"Good," Mark answered. "Mostly everyone has been kind."

"Except for a certain shopkeeper?"

Rachel stretched her lips into a smile that didn't quite feel real. "He'll come around. I hope."

"Well, good."

They met two of the regulars who walked down the path toward them, and Rachel drew closer to Mark.

"Good afternoon," one of the men said. Rachel had a difficult time telling them apart with their powdered wigs, but she didn't recognize either of the men. "Reverend Alder, we'd like to speak to you please."

The minister let go of Rachel's arm and stepped in front of her. Rachel's heart melted at the chivalrous gesture.

"How can I help you gentlemen?" the minister said.

Mark was radiating with tension beside her, his jaw hard, but he hadn't moved from Rachel's side.

"We need to use the church for a training exercise tomorrow. Surely you don't mind."

"I do mind, in fact." Reverend Alder stood up straighter. "I have meetings in the church that day, and those must take precedence."

The redcoat shifted his feet. "This was more of a notification than a request. We'll be using the church whether you approve or not."

Both soldiers stepped closer to Reverend Alder, and Mark dropped Rachel's arm, planting his feet next to the minster. And then something remarkable happened: Mark became Captain Johnson before her eyes. It wasn't any one change, but the air around him seemed to shift from the power radiating off of him.

"I'm sure that's not necessary," Mark said to the officers, apathy on the surface of his voice but iron underneath. "You won't need the church. Find somewhere else to conduct your training exercise."

Perspiration trickled down Rachel's brow, and she wiped it away with her gloved hand. She was both intimidated and – warm. So warm, watching him stand alongside Reverend Alder. Both redcoats looked between Mark and the minister, their eyes comically wide.

"And who are you?" one of them asked.

"Nobody of consequence." Then he tipped his tricorne hat and took Rachel's arm again. "Good day, gentlemen."

Tugging Reverend Alder along with her, Rachel followed Mark down the path, leaving the redcoats staring after them. As they walked, Mark became the man that Rachel knew again: his shoulders relaxed under his jacket and he smiled at her. Rachel thought she might combust.

"That was remarkable, young man," Reverend Alder said softly when they were out of earshot.

Mark shrugged. "One of them was picking at his thumbnail, and the other rocked back on his heels with every word that was said. They were following orders, not giving them. It was easy to deter them."

"Do you think they'll try to use the church anyway?" Rachel said, her voice breathy. She needed to get a hold of herself.

"I'm not sure," Mark said. "They could still, Reverend. You should be prepared."

"I hope this doesn't come back on you," Reverend Alder said.

"I doubt it will."

Rachel hadn't even thought of that; she'd been too busy lusting after her husband. What if word got back to Sergeant Neumann? Mark hadn't done anything but speak forcefully; still, the redcoats often needed little reason to be cruel.

"Reverend," Mark said. "I've been meaning to ask you...do you know of any Continental troops that are stationed nearby?"

The minister appeared to think for a minute. "Lieutenant Feldman's would be the closest group. They're about ten miles away, out west past Millstone. Why do you want to know?"

"I was curious," Mark said.

Rachel's face heated. Why was Mark asking about Lieutenant Feldman's troops? Perhaps he was just making polite conversation. There was no way he could know what she was doing, could he? And after what he had seen this morning, he had every reason to be suspicious. Rachel may not tell Mark what she was doing, but he might discern the truth for himself.

When they returned home that evening, Mark couldn't put it off any longer. He had to ask Rachel to trust him. Again.

Over a supper of stew and bread, Mark broached the subject. "Will you please tell me more about your work?"

Rachel set her spoon down, her eyes not meeting his. "I'm sorry. I can't. I promise you there is a reason for this secrecy. It's for a good reason. Do you want to tell me why you were pale when we encountered the redcoats on the road this morning? Or why your hands were shaking?"

The breath seemed to freeze in Mark's chest. He looked down at his hands.

"I didn't think so," Rachel said. "Perhaps we both have our secrets."

She went back to eating her stew. So Rachel was stubborn. Well, Mark was stubborn too. He would find out what his wife was up to, whether she wanted him to or not.

CHAPTER 12

"Good morning, Rachel."

Abigail's soft voice drew Rachel out of her thoughts the next day. "Morning." She set aside her knitting and stood to greet her friend.

"I thought I'd go to the store, and make sure everything's running smoothly. Care to join me?"

Rachel could think of five different reasons that that was a bad idea, and all of those reasons were Abigail's husband. "Are you sure that's wise?"

The sadness on her friend's face made Rachel almost regret her words, but not quite. She didn't want to incur Ezekiel's wrath any more than she already had. Rachel hated for anyone to be displeased with her.

"I miss you," Abigail said simply. "I thought we could do this together. And Ezekiel is on an errand, so Henry is watching the store."

"All right," Rachel said. "We can."

She took off her apron and hung it on a hook, then put on her cloak, hat, and mittens. Rachel wasn't sure what to expect when

Abigail sought her out like this, but she missed her friend too much to say no.

"I'll say goodbye to Mark on our way out. He's in the barn."

With a quick wave to Mark, Rachel walked with her friend across the melting snow in town. Today was a gray, dreary day. The sky looked like it wanted to pour forth snow but it couldn't quite muster up the effort.

"I wanted to apologize," Abigail said, her voice gentle. "I didn't mean for things to go the way they did with Ezekiel last week."

"You mean when you walked in on Mark and I?" Frustration still burned in Rachel's stomach. The matter could have been resolved easily if Ezekiel hadn't magnified it.

"Yes," Abigail said. "I tried to dissuade him from spreading the news around town, but you know what he's like when he sets his mind to something."

Rachel searched her words carefully. "I'm sure he thought he was doing the right thing."

"I'm just sorry you had to pay the consequences. I know you didn't want to marry."

"I didn't have any issue with marrying," Rachel said. "It was marrying a soldier that I didn't want to do."

"I see," Abigail said. "Well, I'm truly sorry. I hope we can be as we once were."

"I don't know if we can," Rachel said. "Ezekiel doesn't trust me. I don't want to come between you and him."

Abigail took her arm. "Give him time. He'll come around eventually."

"I hope he will. I miss you too," Rachel said.

The store smelled comfortingly like cinnamon, as it always did. Henry, one of the clerks, greeted Rachel and Abigail warmly and they perused the aisles. Abigail and Ezekiel wanted to have a baby, so Abigail was looking at the baby things with a dreamy look on her face. Rachel hadn't given much thought to children — perhaps that was a conversation she should have with Mark.

"Hannah seems happy now that Isaac is here," Abigail said in a low voice. "It seems that she's gotten over her sickness."

"She has."

"It must be nice to see Isaac in such good health."

"It is." Rachel said. She didn't need to burden Abigail with all of the complicated emotions that Isaac's return brought. Ezekiel came into the store sometime during their conversation, and Rachel hid behind a barrel of molasses. There was no need to antagonize him.

"She seems to come alive when he returns."

The bell over the door rang as three redcoats walked into the store. They approached the counter.

"Good day," one of the soldiers said. "We need some supplies. We'll help ourselves, thank you."

Ezekiel tilted his chin up, his cheeks pink. "Then you'll pay for those supplies. I'm running a business here."

Henry stepped to the door and crossed his arms, as if daring the redcoats to argue. Several seconds passed where nobody spoke. At last, one of the soldiers approached the counter and pulled out a bag that jingled when he lifted it.

"Very well," he said. "But you'd do better to be more hospitable in the future. Our sergeant will hear about this."

"You go ahead and tell him," Ezekiel said.

Rachel didn't breathe again until the regulars had left the store with their goods. She and Abigail went to the counter. Ezekiel was pale and had a sheen of perspiration on his forehead. Henry patted the other man's shoulder, while Abigail went to his side. "That was brave of you," Abigail said.

"Perhaps." He shook his head. "Perhaps it was foolish."

Rachel gave the man her best attempt at a smile. "Good day, Mr. Elliott. Henry."

They walked back toward Rachel's home, and Rachel's stomach was in knots.

"I wish there was something we could do," Abigail said.

"There might be. If we can get them to leave somehow –"

Abigail covered her ears. "Whatever you decide to do, I'm all for it. But know that I can't be a part of it."

"You're right I'm sorry." Rachel hated this feeling of powerlessness that came with being a woman in 1776.

Rachel came home from her errand after only a quarter of an hour. She looked subdued as she took off her cloak and poured herself a cup of coffee.

Mark cleared his throat. "Did you have a good time with Mrs. Elliott?"

"No." She sat next to him at the table. He wanted to put his arm around her and pull her to his side, just because he could, but he couldn't read her mood.

"Why not?" Mark kept his hands to himself. For now.

"We went to Ezekiel's store, and three regulars came in."

He gave in to his impulse and wrapped an arm around her. "And?"

"They tried to take some supplies from Ezekiel without paying. He stopped them."

"How?" Mark couldn't imagine Ezekiel stopping trained soldiers from doing anything.

"He told them they had to pay for what they took, and Henry, his assistant, blocked the doors."

Mark removed his arm and turned to face her. "You were there for this?"

"Yes."

"That was brave of him."

"I'm not sure if it was brave or foolish." Rachel looked at her coffee, not meeting his eyes.

"What should he have done? Let them steal from his store?"

"They're enemy soldiers. That's what they do."

Rachel's casual acceptance of that made Mark's heart sink. Did she truly think there was no point in resisting the redcoats? Is that what she thought of his work? And what about her own work in helping with the Cause? That was what made this all the more confusing for Mark.

"By resisting them outright, he's made himself a target," she said.

"If he doesn't resist them, who will?"

"You!" Rachel said. "You're prepared to do that. You're a trained soldier. I've never seen you fight, but you look like you could kill a man with a teaspoon. Ezekiel walks with a limp when the weather gets cold. Resisting those redcoats will only go poorly for him."

Mark was so frustrated it overshadowed any pleasure at the compliment. "I pray it won't."

"I'm going upstairs."

She walked away without giving Mark a chance to reply.

There was a knock at the kitchen door that made Mark frown. Hannah, Isaac, or Granny would have just come in. He peeked through the kitchen window and saw a tall, thin man standing on the doorstep, looking stern. That was Ezekiel Elliott. What did he want? Mark opened the door.

"Ah, Mr. Johnson. Good afternoon."

"Good afternoon," Mark said, unable to hide the curiosity from his voice.

"May I come in?"

The man didn't seem openly hostile, merely polite and detached, so Mark stood aside.

Mr. Elliott sat down at the kitchen table. Apparently he was here on a social call. Years of training on how to make a guest feel at home returned to Mark's mind.

"Would you like some coffee?"

Ezekiel nodded. "Yes, with sugar please."

Mark poured him a cup, his own hands still cold from working in the barn. "We haven't any sugar, I'm afraid. Rachel says it's hard to come by."

"Ah." Ezekiel said, disapproval in his voice.

Mark sat across from the other man, warming his hands with his own cup of coffee.

"Perhaps you're wondering why I'm here."

"I am." Mark didn't see any reason to hide that.

"I came to give you a warning."

Mark's defenses went up and his shoulders stiffened. "A warning?"

"A poor choice of words, perhaps. More like a caution."

"About what?"

"Your wife."

"What about her?" Mark ground out.

Ezekiel's hazel eyes met his. "You should know why I don't allow my Abigail to spend too much time with her any more."

If this man said one ill word about Rachel —

"Miss Staples — Mrs. Johnson — is involved in some work that I believe is dangerous. I don't want my wife involved."

"What kind of work?"

"She and some of her friends — her sister and Mrs. Greene, that I know of. There may be other women involved; I'm not sure. They deliver supplies to the Continental Army. They ride all around the countryside, risking their lives. I admire their dedication to the Cause, but it's much too dangerous for women to be involved in."

Mark took a hearty sip of his coffee, hoping it would stop his mind from spinning. "They deliver supplies?"

"Yes."

"To the Continental Army."

"Yes."

"How long have they been doing this?"

"At least a year," Ezekiel said. "I believe the late Mrs. Staples was involved as well."

Mark sat back in his seat, staring into his coffee cup. Well, this was enlightening. Hope and pride blossomed in his chest, as well as satisfaction. That answered Colonel Staples' curiosity about the matter, and made Mark's assignment much easier. But if Rachel had kept this a secret from him, it had to be for a reason. His long silence was probably suspicious, so Mark looked at Ezekiel again.

"And your wife was involved?"

The other man nodded. "For a brief time. When she told me what she was doing, however, I had to put a stop to it. It was far too dangerous."

"I see," Mark said, irritation rising in his chest. "Tell me, do you and Mrs. Elliott have children?"

"Not yet."

"Do you intend to?"

"Yes," the other man said with a smile.

"Childbearing is dangerous, is it not? Probably more so than delivering any supplies. And yet you have no issue with that."

"That's not the same at all."

Mark paused, getting a hold on his anger and trying to see things from the other man's point of view. He could see how Ezekiel would be worried about his wife. But to forbid her from doing work that helped the Cause? Mark had seen Rachel handle a pistol and a knife. She knew how to protect herself if need be. Surely Abigail was the same? Looking at the set in the other man's jaw, though, Mark saw that no argument of his would change Ezekiel's mind.

"Thank you for the warning." He tried to make his voice calm and even.

Ezekiel studied him a moment longer. "I feel it is my duty. Your wife is a fine woman, but she –"

Mark held up a hand. "Reconsider any words you speak about my wife."

Jaw clicking shut, Ezekiel stood. "Good day, Mr. Johnson. I'll see you at church on Sunday."

Ezekiel left the kitchen without another word, and Mark sat at the kitchen table, his mind reeling. He'd watched Rachel deliver supplies to a Continental camp and he'd had his suspicions, but he hadn't wanted to assume. *And* she hadn't told him about it. Why not? Surely she didn't think he would react the way that Ezekiel had, did she? Then again, perhaps she did. In any case, Rachel had chosen to withhold that information for a reason, and until she trusted him enough to tell him on her own, he wouldn't bring it up. It did make his assignment from her father much simpler, though...and more complicated. Rachel hadn't told her father, so to tell him would be a betrayal of her trust. Besides, he only had the word of Ezekiel Elliott and his own suspicions. Mark would just have to watch his wife more closely.

Rachel was quiet when they went to bed that night. She lay beside him in bed, not saying much. She turned over onto her side, gave him a perfunctory pat on the shoulder, then went to sleep. Mark lay awake for a long time, watching the candle burn down and trying not to imagine all the danger that could befall Rachel in her work.

CHAPTER 13

The next day, Rachel went back to Granny's to spin yarn. The sitting room had all of the furniture pushed towards the walls to make room for the spinning wheels, which hummed along in a comforting rhythm. Rachel's mind wouldn't be set at ease, though, especially not after her conversation with Mark. Her thoughts finally demanded that she voice them out loud.

"Something has to change," Rachel said. "The redcoats must leave. And we should make them leave."

Her friends looked at her with blank faces.

"What can we do, though?" Hannah said. "We're doing all we can. It would be foolish to do more – we are treading a line as it is."

A month ago, Rachel would've taken her sister at her word and dropped the matter. But she couldn't. not now. "There must be something we can do that doesn't involve force."

"Some of our friends in Boston have had success with misinformation." Granny tapped her finger on her chin.

Her husband was upstairs asleep, and she looked tired as well.

"Misinformation," Hannah said.

"Yes, gaining the trust of enemy soldiers and giving them false information. I don't feel the need to be friends with any of the regulars, though," Granny said.

"Nor I," Rachel said. "But it could be something we can do. That was the purpose of delivering the supplies to them in the first place, was it not?"

"I wouldn't go that far," Hannah said. "That was so that they would allow us to make our other deliveries without growing suspicious."

Rachel's mind was turning. It was risky, but Granny's idea might be their best.

"How would we spread false information?" she said.

"Charity would be the one to speak to," Granny said. "She has a connection to the British officers through her mother's business. Perhaps she knows some of them already."

The thought of befriending some of the officers – or being friendly with them at least – made Rachel's skin crawl, but it was something they could *do* to help.

Granny took a dainty sip of her coffee. "You're looking awfully thoughtful over there, Rachel."

"We'll continue to think about this," Granny said. "It's not a bad idea. It might just need refining."

Hannah turned to Rachel, who had stopped her spinning wheel again. "In the meantime, we have work to do."

Mounting a horse was tricky with Mark's knee the way it was, but he made it work. He made sure he was bundled against the cold and that the house was locked up, and he set off. Even being outside for ten minutes lifted his mood. He rode around the edge of Rachel's property and followed the road northeast of town. Eventually he dismounted and led the horse in the direction his men said they'd go. They'd set up camps in small groups in the hills outside of Freehold, and Mark found the first one because he knew what to look for.

"Captain!" Jim poked his head out of the cave when Mark whistled. "What are you doing here? Is everything alright?"

"Yes," Mark said. "I have another assignment for you."

Jim raised his dark eyebrows, huddling in his cloak against the cold. Mark made sure his horse was sheltered from the wind, then followed Jim into the cave.

"The regulars have stolen supplies from the store in Freehold. At least once."

"Don't they do that everywhere?" Jim replied. He rooted through one of the bags laid against the wall of the cave, and offered Mark an apple.

Mark shook his head. Their supplies were scant enough without Mark eating them. "You've been watching their shipments. Do they have any regular deliveries that we could intercept?"

"At three o'clock some afternoons, a single rider will come or go with full saddlebags," Jim said. "We could relieve him of whatever he is carrying."

While Jim was among the more cautious of his men, Mark could tell by the gleam in his dark eyes that he was excited about the prospect.

"Could we do it discreetly?"

"If we timed it so that he was still a good distance from the camp."

"Excellent," Mark said. "Do you have a man to spare that can take the redcoat back to the Continental camp once we've relieved him of his cargo?"

Jim nodded. "Will can go."

"Will you meet me at my home after dark?" Mark said. "If all goes well."

"Of course," Jim said. "Happy to do it, Captain. Now, get back home before you're missed."

Feeling much better about his life than he had an hour ago, Mark mounted his horse again and rode home.

Home. He was beginning to think of Rachel's home as his own.

Rachel fed the animals once she returned, and working in the quiet barn was comforting. One of the horses was missing – hopefully Mark had taken it and it hadn't been stolen. Rachel refused to check the house to see if Mark was there. That would be admitting to herself that she cared where he was. And she did. Far too much. She was so lost in her thoughts that she jumped when Mark led the missing horse into the barn.

"Oh, you're here. I didn't expect to see you."

"Well, I live here, so –" Rachel finished brushing down one of the horses and moved to the next.

Mark climbed off the horse he had taken, landing gingerly on his bad knee. She wanted to ask him where he'd been, but that would hardly be fair given the secrets she kept from him.

"I needed some fresh air," he said.

"It's above freezing today – or it feels like it, at least. I'm sure it was nice." Now Rachel was babbling, and his steady regard made her even more nervous.

"A few of my men might stop by tonight," he said. "If they successfully complete an assignment I've given them."

"All right," Rachel replied. She liked his men, and she felt safer with all of those soldiers around. It was odd. "They're welcome to stay for supper if they'd like."

The shy smile he gave her made her even more nervous. "I'm sure they'd love that."

It wasn't until after dark that Jim and two other men that Rachel didn't recognize came in the door.

"Good evening, Mrs. Johnson," Jim said.

"Evening," Rachel said. "Who are your friends?"

"This is Tom Jones —" he gestured to the slight man with dark hair who was barely taller than Rachel. "And Dr. Edward Smith."

Dr. Smith had auburn hair and was about Jim's height. All three men were dressed for the cold and looked relieved to be inside.

"Will should be along any minute," Jim said. "Hopefully."

Mark came in from the sitting room, smiling. He placed his arms around Jim and Tom's shoulders. "Was the assignment a success?"

Jim grinned, his white teeth standing out against his tanned skin. "He was carrying saddlebags full of money."

"What type of money?" Mark said.

What were they talking about? They seemed comfortable discussing it in front of her, so she poured some cider and invited the men to sit around the kitchen table.

"Continental currency," Mr. Smith said.

"Coins or paper?" Mark asked.

"Coins. Silver, we think."

Mark clapped his hands together. "Excellent. If you leave it here, I can give it to Ezekiel in the morning. Or Rachel can."

"Ezekiel?" What did stolen silver coins have to do with Ezekiel?

Jim must've seen the confusion on her face. "That Captain said that the regulars have been robbing Ezekiel, and he asked us to help."

"So you stole money from the regulars?"

Mark regarded her, his face giving nothing away. "We're giving the money to someone who needs it more."

"You did this?" Rachel said, moved.

"It was the right thing to do."

She wanted to hug the man, but this wasn't the time for that. "Yes, it was."

"Would you come with me to deliver the money to him tomorrow? He might trust it more if it came from you."

"And there's no way this can get anyone in trouble?"

Mr. Jones shook his head. "We were careful."

Rachel sat down at the table and put her head in her hands. Mark had ordered this? And his men had been able to accomplish it in a day?

A warm hand rested in the middle of her back. "Are you all right?" Mark's voice was soft.

Rachel brushed away the few tears that had escaped. "I can't believe you did this."

"That's what we do, Miss Rachel," Jim said, frowning.

Rachel's heart warmed at that thought. As much as she resented her father's role in the war, the Continental Army did some good as well.

"I don't understand," Ezekiel said. "*Where* did this money come from again?"

He was standing at his doorstep, looking pale. Mark's stomach twisted. Would he truly not accept the money? Or would he insist on knowing where it came from? Mark had thought he was doing the right thing, but if it exposed him and his men, then it could backfire.

Rachel took the purse of money from Mark's hands, and handed it to Ezekiel.

"We all care about you and your store," she said. "Please let us help you. By helping you, we're helping ourselves. Surely you would let us do that."

Ezekiel frowned. "Who is 'we'?"

"The donors wish to remain anonymous," Rachel said. "They are merely following our Lord's directive to do good deeds in secret."

That seemed to be the key to easing the frown from Ezekiel's face. He finally accepted the money, handing it to Abigail.

"Well, give them our thanks."

"We will," Mark said.

When they were well away from the Elliotts' home, Mark put his tricorne hat back on his head. "I don't know how you do that," he said to Rachel.

"Do what?"

How could he explain how amazing she was? "Speak to people like that. I thought he would refuse that money with his last breath."

"I've known Ezekiel since we were children." Rachel tucked her cloak around herself with her gloved hands. "He's very religious. That's the key to speaking to him."

"I'm still impressed."

"I am too," Rachel said. "With you."

Her praise made his heart swell. "Truly?"

"Yes. I never could have gotten that money so quickly."

"My men are good at what they do."

"I'm beginning to see that."

Mark was nervous. In the past few years, he had rarely been this nervous outside of combat situations. This was not combat; this was a friendly dinner with Mr. & Mrs. Greene. He'd been looking forward to it all morning, but now that it was time and they were standing at their doorstep, Mark's hands were sweating.

Mrs. Greene opened the door and embraced them both. "Going to come inside for more than ten seconds this time, Captain?" she said.

Mark laughed, and his nerves eased. Mr. Greene approached them, a broad grin stretching across his face. He embraced Rachel and shook Mark's hand. "Glad you could come."

Once they were seated around the dinner table, Rachel and the Greenes talked about town gossip, and Mark was pleased to find that he knew enough people in town to follow the conversation.

"We might be having a Christmas party in a few weeks' time," Rachel said. "Of course you're both welcome to come."

That was news to Mark. A Christmas party sounded lovely, though he supposed he would be gone by then. He tried not to dwell on that.

Mrs. Greene took her husband's hand on top of the dinner table. "I believe we'll have to decline, honey. But thank you for the invitation."

Rachel gave a wry smile. "That's all right."

"You know I wish I could, Miss Rachel."

"Maybe someday," Rachel said.

"Maybe."

Mark cleared his throat. "If you don't mind me asking, Mr. Greene, why can't you come to the party?"

"I prefer to stay home," Mr. Greene said. A frown appeared between his gray eyebrows. "You know I'd love to come if I could, Miss Rachel. I don't mean to hurt your feelings."

"Of course not," Rachel said, taking the older man's hand. "We're all doing the best we can, and that's all anyone can ask for."

Mark's heart ached. Here was a man who couldn't leave his home, yet the people in his life loved him despite that vulnerability. He and his wife adored each other, and Rachel doted on him as if he were her own grandfather. A lump formed in his throat. Could such a thing be possible for him? The conversation turned to other matters, and Mark ate his dinner thoughtfully. All in all, it was a lovely meal, and Mark wished he hadn't been so intimidated to visit with Mr. & Mrs. Greene before. But they were clearly very important to Rachel, so he desperately wanted them to have a good opinion of him.

CHAPTER 14

That night, after they got into bed, Rachel laid a hand on his chest and propped her head on her other hand, lying on her side.

"Did you not enjoy the dinner with the Greenes?" There was a note of uncertainty in her voice.

"I loved it. I see why they are family to you."

She smiled softly. Mark touched a fingertip to her soft bottom lip, then let his hand fall. He needed to tell her about his struggles. But it was terrifying. All his life, he'd been taught that any vulnerability was a weakness that would be exploited and punished. That need for invulnerability had served him well in the army. But he didn't want to be invulnerable and alone any more.

"I need to tell you something," Mark blurted out.

"All right."

Surely she could feel his heart pounding beneath her palm. Mark's throat was dry, so he took a sip of cold water from the cup on the nightstand.

"I wasn't going to take a furlough because of my knee. Well, not only because of my knee."

She watched him, her eyes dark, listening intently. That gave Mark the courage to continue.

"I needed a respite from my assignment because I'm having difficulties with my – with my mind."

"With your mind?"

"Yes. Being a soldier has changed the way my mind works, and it – it scares me. I freeze up sometimes, or start shaking. You saw that when we first stayed at Hannah's house."

Her fingertip rubbed gentle circles on his nightshirt.

"I thought you were cold." There was no judgment in her voice, only curiosity.

"I was. That was part of it. But a large part of it was fear. Sometimes I'll start shaking. Sometimes I can't sleep. I have episodes where I feel like I might die."

He cleared his throat. The words were difficult to say, but it felt like a wound was being drained. Now that he'd started speaking, he couldn't stop.

"I don't know how to get better," he said. "I don't know if I'll ever get better. I don't know if I can go back."

Tears formed in Rachel's eyes, and she sat up, pulling him to her. "Oh, Mark," she said softly.

Mark leaned against her chest, tears falling from his own eyes. He let them fall, hating the vulnerability and feeling so relieved at the same time. Rachel put one arm around him and stroked his back with the other one. Her touch was soothing, and Mark closed his eyes and breathed in her scent. This was his wife, and she wasn't repulsed by his weakness. She cared for him in spite of it. After a while, Mark sat up, studying Rachel's face. She was still crying.

"Did I upset you?" he said.

Rachel dabbed at her eyes with a handkerchief. "No. I'm glad you told me."

"You are?"

"Yes. I'd noticed some of what you said, and it concerned me. Now that I know, we can face it together."

That seemed too good to be true. "You're not ashamed?"

"Of course not. I know what you've been through – well, not firsthand, but I have an idea – and of course it has affected you. It's affected every soldier I know in different ways."

"Including your father."

"Yes, including my father. But my father has never told me about his difficulty. He denies it."

"I see," Mark said.

Rachel took a shuddering breath. "That was why I didn't want to marry a soldier."

Mark felt her words like a blow, but she crawled into his lap.

"Not because of what you struggle with," she said. "But because I've seen so many soldiers refuse to ask for help. And their families pay the price."

She was very close to him now, her small body pressed up against him, and Mark tried to sort through her words.

"So you don't regret marrying me?" Surely she would now.

Rachel tilted her chin up, bringing her face close to his. "Not at all."

She didn't kiss him – he didn't give her the chance. Mark met her eyes, looking into them for a moment. He wanted to kiss her – he'd been wanting to for days. Her breath smelled of cinnamon from her tooth powder. She was all softness and warmth in his lap. Mark finally took her lips and sighed against them, putting all of his relief, all of his growing care for Rachel into the kiss. Instinct took over and he stopped worrying about what tomorrow would bring. At last he pulled back, his entire body alight, and smiled down at her. She smiled right back. Mark wanted to keep kissing her – he wanted to do far more than that. Was she ready, though?

Rachel rested a hand over Mark's pounding heart again, and smiled up at him. He looked dazed, but he smiled back. Rachel wanted a real

marriage with this man. She wanted to see what they could be like together if they didn't hold back.

"I have something to tell you too," she said. He'd been brave enough to be vulnerable with her; surely she could do the same with him.

"You've asked me what I was doing at the redcoats' camp the day we met," she began.

Mark sat up straighter underneath her. His cheeks were flushed and his lips red and puffy from her kiss. It was distracting, but Rachel continued.

"I was delivering bullets to the redcoats. You may have seen that. But what you didn't know was that they were defective bullets."

"Defective? How so?"

"Granny developed a different way to structure each lead ball. It will combust in the barrel of a rifle or musket when fired. If it works, it will ruin the gun and cause a small explosion."

"That's...brilliant," he said.

Rachel's heart lifted at his encouragement. "We delivered those bullets under the false pretense of 'helping' the redcoats. To gain their trust so we can make our legitimate deliveries in peace. I deliver supplies to the Continental Army on a pretty regular basis, so we didn't want them to interfere with that."

"I knew about the supply deliveries to the Continentals."

Rachel lifted her head, meeting his eyes. "You did?"

He nodded. "Ezekiel Elliott told me about them. He thought he was warning me."

"Why didn't you say anything?"

"I wanted you to tell me on your own. Ezekiel has this misguided notion that your work is too dangerous for his wife. And yet they want to have children." Mark shook his head. "I let him say his piece, then asked him to leave."

Rachel couldn't stop the smile from spreading across her face. "You did?"

"I did. I think your work is admirable."

Rachel's heart was beating so fast now she had to lay against Mark's chest again just to take it all in. He admired the work they did. He didn't want to stop it. She could have her work *and* her husband.

"Your father suspects you."

Now *that* was news.

"He'd spoken to Lieutenant Feldman, whose regiment is among our most successful in this whole region. Your father wanted to know why. The lieutenant didn't name any names, but he said that there were women in Freehold who had been supplying them for several months."

Rachel groaned, hiding her face in her hands.

Mark continued. "Your father suspected Hannah was involved with the deliveries, and he wanted me to find out more."

"What have you told him?" Rachel said through her fingers.

"Nothing yet. I haven't spoken to him since. This was when we first married."

Frustration curdled in Rachel's stomach. If Father found out, he had the potential to stop the Couriers if he was worried for their safety.

"Do you want him to know?" Mark said.

"No."

"Then I won't tell him."

Rachel dropped her hands. "But he's your commanding officer."

"And you are my wife. You're more important to me."

At the simple conviction in his statement, tears sprang to Rachel's eyes. No man in her life had ever put her before the Cause, never made her feel more important.

"Thank you," Rachel whispered.

"You're welcome." Mark tilted her chin up, kissing her again. They'd kissed before, but this time was different. There were no secrets between them now, and Rachel poured all the love that was growing in her heart into that kiss.

The next morning, Mark tidied the kitchen with a smile on his face. Everything was different now. His entire world felt as if it had opened up. For the first time in his recent memory, he looked forward to the future. Rachel was feeding the animals, so once he finished cleaning, he started some stew for dinner. He was learning where everything went, and such a small thing was satisfying. There was a knock at the front door. Rachel had said that Mrs. Greene might come by to take some yarn, but Mark checked out the front window nonetheless.

Sergeant Neumann stood on the front stoop, flanked by two of his men. Mark's heart beat faster. What did they want? Had they somehow discovered who he was? If he let them stand out there, they'd only grow more suspicious. His beard had grown out quite a bit in the last weeks, he was dressed completely differently, and he leaned on the cane. Hopefully that would be enough. Mark opened the door, a polite smile on his face.

"May I help you?"

Sergeant Neumann tilted his head. "Do I know you?"

"I don't believe we've met."

"Oh. Well, we won't disturb you. We'll just go around the back to your barn."

What did they want in the barn?

"I'll walk you back there myself."

He led the men around the outside of the house – there was no way they were setting foot inside his home if he could help it – and kept a tight grip on his cane. If it came to it, he and Rachel could fight three soldiers. Hopefully it wouldn't come to that, though.

Rachel looked up from her work, pitchfork in hand. Mark went to her, putting himself between her and the redcoats.

"Miss Staples?" Sergeant Neumann said. "Who is this?"

Her hand gripped his arm. "This is my husband Mark Johnson. Mark, this is Sergeant Neumann."

"Pleased to meet you, Mr. Johnson." Sergeant Neumann said. "I didn't realize you were married."

"It's recent," Rachel said. "Can we help you?"

"My men and I are getting hungry," Sergeant Neumann said. "So we've come for your assistance."

His men went into the stalls and led the cows and pigs out of their warm hay.

"You don't mind, do you?"

It wasn't a question. Mark gritted his teeth. "Not at all."

The redcoats led the animals out of the barn and through the back fields. Sergeant Neumann gave a wave as he disappeared from sight. Rachel sank onto a bale of hay and put her head in her hands. Mark sat beside her and put his arm around her shoulders.

"He didn't recognize you," she said softly.

"I thought he might for a moment, but he didn't."

"The beard and the cane are enough of a disguise, then," Rachel said.

"It seems so."

Rachel stood. "I suppose I don't need to clean out those stalls now."

Her thin lips were pinched, and she hung her pitchfork on its hook on the wall. The horses were looking around the barn, confused that the other animals were gone. Rachel patted one of them on the flank.

"I'm going inside," she said. "I'll need to check the cellar and see how we can make do for a while."

Mark tried to unclench his fists, but failed. "Will we have enough to eat?"

"For now."

"Why don't we just buy another cow and a few pigs?" The words were out of Mark's mouth before he could call them back.

Rachel's face said it all, and heat rose to Mark's cheeks. Working in the army was harsh compared to how he had grown up, but he *had* grown up without worrying about getting through the winter.

"Even if I had the money, which I don't," she said. "Animals are much too dear to just buy some more. People that have them aren't willing to part with them. And I don't blame them."

He let her walk back into the house alone. The anger that burned in his stomach demanded an outlet. He picked up the pitchfork and set to work on the now-empty stalls.

"We've come together tonight to share what we have," Reverend Alder said.

Rachel sat squeezed between Mark and Hannah on the minister's sofa that evening. Reverend Alder had sent a message earlier that day, inviting Rachel and Mark over after supper. Apparently he'd done the same thing to every Whig in town. Everyone in the room looked at the minister with rapt attention. If they were like Rachel, they'd had a very discouraging day after the redcoats had taken their animals.

"Who was robbed today?" the minister said.

Nearly everyone's hands went up.

The minister adjusted his spectacles. "If we're to get through the winter, then, we'll need to share what we have. Who still has their chickens?"

Rachel raised her hand, along with about half the people in the room.

"If you can," Reverend Alder said. "Keep your hand raised if you are willing to share eggs with your neighbors who no longer have chickens."

Only a few hands went down, and Rachel's heart swelled with pride. They would make it through if they all took care of each other, and the minister's idea to share was brilliant.

"All right then. Who still has their cows, and is willing to share milk?"

Rachel took note of who she could ask if she needed milk. It was humbling to have to ask, but she and Mark needed to eat. The meeting went on like this for a few minutes, with priority given to those who had small children or the elderly to care for. Reverend Alder kept order until the emotions of everyone in the room grew too high.

"I didn't let them take anything," James Bell, the blacksmith, said. "I leveled my rifle at them and told them to get off my property."

"What did they do?" Mark said.

Mr. Bell frowned at Mark. "I don't believe we've been introduced."

In fact, throughout the meeting, Rachel had noticed more than one curious stare directed Mark's way. The room fell silent.

Mark used his cane to push himself to his feet. "Mark Johnson," he said.

"And who are you? You've married Miss Rachel, haven't you?" Mr. Bell said.

"They were married last week," Ezekiel Elliott put in.

"Can he be trusted?" someone in the room said.

"He can," Rachel said, making sure her voice was loud enough to carry through the room.

"If you have any more questions for Mr. Johnson, you're welcome to ask them after this," Reverend Alder said. "In the meantime, we should all disperse to our homes. We've gathered long enough to attract suspicion. If you please, leave in small groups, not all at once."

There were murmurs of assent throughout the room. When Rachel and Mark finally left, she was exhausted and looking forward to going to sleep. It was completely dark and very cold as they started the walk back home. The hairs on the back of Rachel's neck stood up as they walked. She kept one hand on her dagger in her pocket and the other tucked into the crook of Mark's arm.

"Are you all right?" he asked softly.

"I don't like being out after dark."

"That's fair. We'll be home soon."

"I feel safer with you," she said.

Mark's lips quirked. It was true, though. There were some advantages to having a husband. Once they were inside the house, Rachel breathed easier. She and Mark closed the house up for the night, then walked up the stairs together. Mark had fit effortlessly into her routine, and it was nice to have someone around to share the load. Mark sat down heavily on the bed once he got to their bedroom.

"Is your knee all right? It seems to be getting better, but then I've noticed you limp more at the end of the day."

"Slowly," he said. "But I still need to rest more than I am."

"Your hands have healed," Rachel took one of his palms and ran her fingertip along the pink skin. "Though you'll have some scars."

"They have." His voice was rough. He went to what was becoming his side of the room and undressed efficiently. Rachel hurried through her nighttime routine, took off her outer clothes, and climbed into bed in her chemise.

After the last candle was blown out, Rachel lay beside her husband. She was exhausted and wide awake at the same time.

"Do the Whigs in Freehold always gather like that?" Mark said softly. "I've never seen anything like it."

"We have at different times, but not recently. It helps us to feel less – well, less helpless."

"I'm sure," Mark said.

He rolled over onto his side as he did when he was preparing to go to sleep. All of the nervous energy buzzing through her veins demanded an outlet; maybe tonight Mark could be that outlet.

"Mark?" she said. "Do you think we could –"

His soft snores broke through her halting words. Rachel sighed. She was determined to explore her curiosity about what she and Mark could do together. A different night, perhaps.

The smell of smoke yanked Mark out of an uneasy sleep. That was smoke, wasn't it? He sat up in bed, dislodging Rachel.

"'S'wrong?" she asked.

Mark swung his legs over the side of the bed and went to the window. Flames glowed in the night sky, consuming six buildings in town.

"Get dressed," he told Rachel.

CHAPTER 15

Rachel lit a candle and went to the window after him, then, having apparently drawn the same conclusion he did, hurried into her clothes. Once they were dressed, they raced downstairs to look out the kitchen window. The barn and chicken coop were unharmed. That was a small consolation when there were other fires to be put out. Mark helped Rachel with her cloak and put on his own, then they walked around to the front of Rachel's house, extra buckets in hand.

"Where to first?" he asked her. She knew the people in town; she'd be able to tell where they'd be the most helpful.

"There." Rachel pointed. "Ezekiel & Abigail's store."

She took off at a run, and Mark hobbled along behind her as best he could. As they got closer to the burning buildings, the noise of chaos grew louder: dogs barking and children crying and adults screaming. It reminded him too much of a battlefield. When they got to the burning store, Mark tried to assess the situation with his soldier's eyes. The store wasn't near any other buildings, so there wasn't a high risk of the fire spreading. That was a small mercy.

Rachel set to work filling buckets with snow and setting them near enough to the fire that the snow would melt.

"I'll do this if you can throw the water," Rachel said.

Mark picked up the first bucket. The illumination from the fires cast an eerie orange glow over the town that made Mark's skin crawl. With each bucket he threw, he looked back at their home, making sure it was still unharmed. They carried on that way until the fire was out. Only the frame of the store remained standing. Mark stood back to catch his breath. Rachel wiped her sleeve across her forehead. It was almost dawn by now.

The Elliotts' home was nearby, not aflame, thankfully. Mark had been so intent on putting out the fire that he hadn't seen past the store.

Mrs. Elliott sat on the front stoop, cradling her husband in her lap. His head was bleeding heavily and she pressed a cloth to the wound. Blood stained the snow all around him. Rachel raced toward her friend, but Mark – well, Mark froze. The blood staining the snow seemed to take on a life of its own, swirling around him and blurring his vision. He was transported back to every other time he'd seen such a sight.

Mark blinked. He couldn't afford to freeze like that every time he saw blood. He forced himself to step closer to Mrs. Elliott, and he took off his cloak to wrap it around her shoulders.

"Let's get him inside," Rachel said.

Ezekiel was still unconscious, so Mark carried him to the small blue sofa by the fireplace inside. Rachel led Mrs. Elliott by the arm. Once they were inside, Rachel raked up the fire. Mrs. Elliott was pale and drawn, staring into the fire. Mark lay Ezekiel on his sofa and propped up his head. The wound was still bleeding, and the sight of it made Mark's skin clammy. He hoped he wouldn't be sick. Always competent, Rachel came in with some towels and a basin of water. She set them down and got to work cleaning the wound. Mark picked up a candle and held it up to give her better light. His hands only shook a little.

"It'll need stitching." Rachel wiped her hands on her apron. "We need a needle and thread."

Unable to get a word past his lips, Mark stood there, holding the candle, his hands quivering. Rachel picked up a clean cloth and pressed it to the wound. Ezekiel groaned.

"I'll get it," Mrs. Elliott finally said. When she returned to the room, she handed the needle and spool of thread to Mark.

Rachel looked at Mark expectantly, and, not wanting to let her down, he held the needle up to the firelight and threaded it. Mark had stitched wounds a dozen times before. But this time was different. He managed to thread the needle and tie off the end, but every time he got too close to the wound, his hands shook harder and bile rose in his throat. Mark swallowed hard and stepped back.

"Rachel, I can't –"

"I can." Mrs. Elliott came in, tear-tracks streaking her face. She gave Mark a wan smile and got to work. Rachel picked the candle up where Mark had set it down on a side table.

As soon as he was free, Mark stepped out the back door and shut it behind him. He rubbed a handful of snow in his face, trying to get his panic under control. Leaning against the wall of the house, he looked at the dawn sky still tinged with smoke and flame. This was Sergeant Neumann and his men, Mark had no doubt. Ezekiel had paid the price for his resistance. His hands stopped shaking after a few minutes, but he still couldn't find it within himself to go back inside. Fatigue and despair settled on Mark like a damp blanket that he couldn't shake off.

The door next to him creaked and he felt Rachel's presence at his side. She placed her hand in the crook of his arm.

"Abigail got the wound stitched and bandaged, and she's done all she can for the moment."

"Good," Mark said.

"Are you all right?"

"No, I'm not." It was no use pretending any more; Rachel had seen his weakness. He wouldn't blame Rachel if she thought less of him because he couldn't stitch up a wound, couldn't help when he was needed. If he was this upset over one wound, how would he ever go back to the battlefield? It was one thing to tell Rachel that he struggled, but for her to see it firsthand was shameful to Mark.

Rachel's arms went around his shoulders, and she buried her face in his neck. Mark gave in to his impulse and wrapped his arms around her, pulling her flush against him. She felt so *good*, so alive in his arms. He rested his cheek on her head and breathed her in. She smelled like a campfire.

"Let's go home," she whispered in his ear.

Mark pulled back, unwilling to release his hold on her. "The other buildings –"

"We've done enough," Rachel said. "Others can help. We'll come back later and check on Ezekiel."

She took his arm and led him back home. They made sure the horses and chickens were safe, then went back inside. It was full daylight now, but Mark wanted to crawl back in bed and sleep the day away. They washed the soot from their faces and arms, then Rachel took his hand.

"Let's go back to bed."

He didn't have the heart to argue, so he followed her up the stairs and took off his soot-stained clothes, changing into fresh ones. Rachel did the same thing and climbed into bed beside him. The bedroom was bright, and Mark didn't know if they'd sleep at all, but it felt good to lay down in a warm, safe place. They sat next to each other, backs against the headboard, and Mark tried to calm his racing thoughts. Rachel had been quiet for the last few minutes, and he pulled her against his side, needing her warmth.

"Thank you for your help," she said softly. "I couldn't have done that without you."

"I could have been more helpful." Mark couldn't keep the self-reproach out of his voice.

Rachel folded her fingers around his. "I can't pretend to know all that you have gone through. Sometimes I think I know what the soldier's life is like, with my father and brother being who they are. But I don't, not really. And your reaction to Ezekiel's injury tells me that you've seen things you wish you could forget."

"I have," Mark said. "I don't like to speak of it."

"Perhaps you *should* speak of it," she replied. "Not to me if you don't want to. But you should."

Mark didn't respond to that. He wasn't sure what to think. "You're not upset with me?"

She turned toward him, her dark eyes studying him intently. "Why would I be?"

"Because I –" the words were hard to force through the emotion clogging his throat. "Because I couldn't help Ezekiel."

"Come here," Rachel said. She pulled on his arm until he lay down sideways with his head in her lap.

Her soft fingers combing through his hair felt strange at first, but soon the pressure at his temples eased.

"My father has nightmares, you know," she said.

"Colonel Staples has nightmares?"

"He does. Whenever he's home. Almost every night. It might be one of the reasons he's hardly ever home. Even when my mother was ill, he preferred to be away."

"What does he do about them?"

"Nothing." Rachel's hand stilled. "He denies that they even happen."

Mark chewed on his lower lip. "That's not very helpful."

"It's not. It's not good for him, or for any of us."

"It's hard to talk about these things," Mark said.

Her hand resumed its slow movements through his hair. Though they were discussing a painful topic, Mark's eyes drifted closed.

"I know it is," Rachel replied. "I'm here for you, though, Mark. You should know that."

Those words eased something in Mark's heart, and he smiled as he drifted off to sleep.

Rachel held Mark until he snored softly, then eased him onto his pillow. Her heart ached for him, but she was *so* relieved that he'd shared his struggles with her. Lying down beside Mark, she closed her eyes and tried to sleep too, but the room was too bright, even with the curtains drawn. Mark grunted in his sleep and pulled Rachel against him, tucking her to his side. Would Ezekiel survive his injury? What did this mean for Abigail? And how would they replace everything at the store?

Rachel was trying to be brave, but at times like this it felt futile. How many hours had she spent puzzling over how to drive the redcoats away? It was no use trying to sleep. She eased herself out of Mark's arms and stood up. There was something she could do.

Two hours later, she had retrieved the defective bullets from Granny and sat at the kitchen table, making sure they were packed carefully in their canvas pouches.

"What are you doing?" Mark stood in the doorway of the kitchen in his stockings, looking rumpled and all the more handsome for it.

"I'm going to deliver some more bullets to the redcoats." To his credit, Mark didn't blink when she said that. "You should go back to sleep."

"Can I come with you?"

"No." Rachel straightened her spine and met his eyes.

He frowned. "I don't see why not."

"So far the regulars still trust me. I believe they do, in any case. So you can't come. They might not trust *you*. There's also still the chance that they'll recognize you."

Rachel bit her tongue to keep from saying more. She needn't explain herself any more than she already had.

"Fine," Mark said. "When will you be back?"

"In an hour or two," she replied. "It's a simple delivery. I don't even need to take the wagon."

She gathered up the canvas pouches and settled them into her apron pockets for now. Mark didn't look happy with what she was doing, but he would have to be all right with it. She stood on her tiptoes and pressed a quick kiss to his lips, then went out to the barn to saddle her horse.

Mark was *not* all right with this. He waited until Rachel was out of sight before dressing, saddling a horse for himself and riding toward the regulars' camp, taking the discreet route, of course. Six buildings in Freehold were burned-out frames, and people still gathered around them, despair and anger hanging over the town like a cloud. There was nothing more that Mark could do about that at the moment, though. He needed to make sure his wife was safe.

Rachel rode her horse with easy grace, a knitted cap on her head and her hair in a loose braid to one side. Mark watched from the forest as she rode into the redcoats' camp, dismounted, and gave one of the guards the bags full of bullets. She climbed back on her horse and rode away without incident. Still, Mark's heart was pounding and he had to restrain himself from riding after her. When Rachel was most of the way back to her home, Mark rode up beside her. Rachel shook her head.

"I told you to stay home."

"I felt like going for a ride." The levity in his tone didn't make her smile. In fact, she looked more upset.

When they were home and putting their horses away, and Rachel wouldn't meet his eyes, Mark rested his hands on her shoulders.

"Rachel, look at me. I'm sorry that I didn't respect your wishes. I wanted to keep you safe."

Tears shimmered in her eyes. Alarm bells went off in Mark's mind.

"This is why I didn't want to tell you about my work."

"I haven't mentioned it to anyone. I told you I wouldn't." Didn't she trust him by now?

"Yes, but by following me you could have exposed me. Or cast doubts on my innocence. What if the redcoats had caught you and decided to take you prisoner? Again?"

Mark shuddered at the thought. The truth was, though, that at the time he hadn't given it one moment of thought because he couldn't stop worrying about his wife.

"What was the last assignment you did before you came to Freehold?"

That was a strange question, but Mark answered it automatically. "We were out near Long Branch. We were intercepting scouts that were getting too close to a Continental encampment."

"And what if I had followed you there, on my own, even after you'd asked me not to?"

A potent mix of anger and fear churned in Mark's stomach at the thought of Rachel out there alone. "That would be unacceptable."

Her blonde eyebrows lifted toward the brim of her knit cap. "How is this any different?"

As much as Mark wanted to protest that it was *very* different, Mark couldn't argue with her. He'd seen how competent Rachel was. The woman had rescued him from a camp full of enemy soldiers and could throw a knife with astonishing accuracy.

All of Mark's bluster went out of him with a sigh, and he pulled Rachel to him. "I'm sorry."

"I forgive you," Rachel said. "Just don't do it again, or I'll have to start keeping secrets from you."

"I won't," Mark said. Anything was better than secrets between them. Even trusting that his wife could handle herself when he wanted nothing more than to keep her safe.

"Mark? Rachel?" Isaac came in the kitchen door later that day, dressed for the outdoors and carrying a rifle.

Rachel came in from the sitting room. "Is everything all right?"

"As much as it can be right now. I came to see if Mark wished to go hunting. With so many cows and pigs taken, everyone will need the extra meat."

"I'll go," Mark said. "Can I borrow your rifle?"

"Of course." Rachel squeezed his arm. "I've work to do anyway."

Mark looked like he wanted to protest, but he didn't. Good. He was learning. Once the men had all they needed and were off to hunt in the forest, Rachel got to work. Abigail's home was her first stop.

"How is he?"

Abigail glanced back at her husband's still-sleeping form. "He awoke for a moment or two, then went back to sleep."

"Have you had a chance to rest?"

"I – I don't think I could."

Rachel shook her head. "That won't do. At least go upstairs and change your clothes. I'll sit with him."

"If you're sure." Abigail stood and staggered up the stairs.

Ezekiel's face looked pained, even in his sleep. His hands were clasped over his chest. The head wound was his only injury that they'd seen, but the man might not survive it.

"I know we don't always get along," Rachel whispered to Ezekiel. "But I'd be sad if you died. So try to push through this, all right?"

He didn't respond, but Abigail came down the stairs a few minutes later. She looked like she'd washed up and changed her clothes, but exhaustion still hung heavily on her. Rachel stood.

"If you won't sleep in your bed, can we set up a bed for you on the floor at least? Then you can rest by Ezekiel's side."

"We can do that," Abigail said. Relief poured through Rachel.

Together they set up the extra straw mattress next to the sofa, and Rachel helped Abigail pile the bed high with quilts and pillows.

"I'll bring supper by later," Rachel said. "You just rest."

Abigail snuggled down into her makeshift bed, her eyes drooping. "I'll try."

Her friend was asleep by the time Rachel left, locking the door behind her. Rachel went to Hannah's next. She was still exhausted from the night's ordeal, but the walk did her good. And concentrating on other people besides herself.

Hannah looked up from where she was dipping candles in her sitting room and gave Rachel a gentle smile.

"Your house is still standing," Rachel said by way of a greeting.

"Yours is as well," Hannah said.

Rachel nodded. "We helped take care of Ezekiel. There's not much left of his store."

"All of the other buildings that were burned were Whig families or businesses." Hannah looked back down on her work, cutting the wicks of her batch of candles. "They killed Mr. Bell and burned down his shop."

"They killed him?" Rachel repeated dumbly.

"Remember the other night – Mr. Bell said that he resisted the redcoats when they tried to take his animals?"

Now that Hannah mentioned it, Rachel did remember that. Her stomach sank. "Mr. Bell has a wife and four children."

"They'll need all of our help," Hannah said. "I'll give Mrs. Bell some of these candles when I've finished them."

"And I told Abigail I'd bring her supper." Rachel put her head in her hands. "That means I have to *make* her supper."

"I've some extra stew and bread you can take over," Hannah said.

"Thank you."

Rachel sat down in Hannah's extra chair in her sitting room, the fatigue of staying up most of the night weighing on her. Mr. Bell was a good, kind man who'd never had a cross word for anyone, even when Hannah had broken three wagon wheels in a week making supply deliveries. That same feeling of frustrated helplessness came over Rachel again. "Hannah, we have to do something."

Hannah set the candles in a wooden box. "We have to trust the Continentals to do their jobs."

"That is taking too long," Rachel said. "We can do something about these redcoats *now*, ourselves."

Hannah frowned. "You're not still considering using misinformation, are you?"

"I am," Rachel said.

"I don't like it," Hannah said. "It's dangerous."

"Well, so is staying in our homes right now. If we're in danger, I would like to be making progress."

A desperate voice inside Rachel's mind still wanted her elder sister's approval, but Rachel reminded herself that she didn't need Hannah's permission to try to help with the Cause.

"I won't take any drastic action before discussing it with all of you first," she said with more resolve.

"Fine," Hannah said. "And what about Mark? I saw the way he was looking at you the other day."

"I, ah..." Rachel shifted her weight. "I told Mark about us. About our work."

"About the Couriers?"

"I didn't tell him who was involved. I told him that the bullets I delivered to the regulars' camp the day we met were defective. He knows that I'm on the Continental side; everything I do is to help the Cause."

There was a long pause between them, and Rachel tried hard not to fill it.

"What did he say?"

Rachel let out a long breath. "He was impressed. And he thinks we should work together."

"Truly?"

"Yes."

Tears formed in Hannah's eyes. "I – I can't believe you did that."

Could Hannah blame her? "He won't tell anyone," Rachel insisted.

"How can you be sure?"

"I can't," Rachel said. "But hasn't he proven himself to be trustworthy by now?"

Hannah shook her head, a few tears falling to her cheeks. "Rachel, this could ruin everything. What if Father finds out?"

Father might already know, but this wasn't the time to point that out. "I had to tell him. I want to have a real marriage with Mark, and I didn't want those secrets between us."

"Are you saying that Isaac and I don't have a real marriage?"

"Not at all," Rachel said, regretting her words. "But I couldn't hide the work from him any longer."

Hannah wiped at her tears with a handkerchief. "I see."

Even that small acknowledgement was a victory for Rachel. "It'll all work out," she told Hannah, hoping that was true. "You could tell Isaac, you know. I truly believe you could."

"I'm not so sure." Hannah's words were barely audible. "I hope you know what you're doing, Rachel."

Rachel hoped she did too. But Mark had chosen to trust her with his secrets; she wanted to do the same.

CHAPTER 16

"Has Hannah recovered from her illness?" Mark said as he and Isaac walked out of town, rifles over their shoulders. Mark's knee still ached, but it felt good to get outside and away from the sadness of Freehold.

"She has."

"Good."

The snow was thicker on the ground in the forest, and Mark's knee ached as they walked. Frustration burned in his stomach. "I can't go far because of my knee."

"That's fine," Isaac said. "I hate to be away from Hannah for too long."

"You must miss her when you're gone." Mark was already dreading leaving Rachel.

"I do," Isaac said.

They went to the south of town, where the forests were more peaceful, and no hint of redcoats were to be seen. Mark found a rock to crouch behind, made sure Rachel's rifle was loaded and ready, and waited. Isaac did the same, several feet away.

Waiting for the animals to get used to their presence, Mark let his thoughts wander. Hannah had known about the delivery Rachel made the day they met. So was Hannah involved as well? And if she was, did Isaac know? Surely Hannah had told her husband about their work. Hadn't she? Mark had seen the way Mr. Elliott was with his wife. Ezekiel had even warned Mark. So where did Isaac fit into all of this?

Mark's curiosity finally got the best of him, and he questioned Isaac on their walk back to town. He adjusted his grip on the cloth sack that held the rabbits he'd killed. "So, does Hannah do any work for the Cause?"

Isaac frowned at the question. "I don't believe so."

"Ah." Mark kept his voice light. "I was just curious."

"What made you curious? Did she say something?"

If Isaac didn't know, then Mark couldn't be the one to tell him.

"Rachel has been making extra stockings for my men. That's all." Mark tried to change the subject. "How much longer do you have on your furlough?"

"Another two weeks or so. I'm due to report back after the new year." Isaac frowned. "When do you go back?"

"Colonel Staples wants me in Freehold until we rid the town of that camp of redcoats."

"Any luck so far?"

Mark shook his head. He hadn't heard from his men in a few days, and the fires were a definite step back. "We're still stuck."

"Best of luck to you," Isaac said. They reached the edge of town, and he walked the opposite direction. "I'll see that my rabbits get distributed to people who need meat, if you and Rachel can do the same with yours."

"I will."

Well, that was interesting. Hannah Wellington hadn't told her husband about her work. Why?

Rachel walked toward Mark when he got back to town, waving at Isaac as he passed. She kept her hat tilted down and took Mark's arm. "Are you all right?"

"Hannah told me that Mr. Bell died. The regulars killed him and burned his shop."

Mark could feel the sadness radiating off of her, and he didn't know how to fix it. "Mr. Bell the blacksmith?"

Rachel nodded.

Anger filled Mark's chest, anger that had subsided when he'd been out in the woods away from Freehold. "I'm sorry. We'll do what we can to help his family."

That seemed to help a little, and Rachel leaned against his shoulder as they walked. Back home, Mark helped Rachel take her cloak and hat off, and hung them by the back door.

"I had an interesting conversation with Isaac."

"Oh?" Rachel glanced at him. She was still sad and distracted, but Mark's curiosity couldn't wait.

Mark unlocked the front door and helped Rachel with her cloak. "He doesn't know about the work that you and Hannah do. He has no idea."

Rachel fiddled with the string of her apron.

"Why?"

"Hannah has chosen not to tell him. So you must not either."

"I hate to repeat myself, but why?"

Rachel sighed. "Did you know that Abigail Elliott used to work with us?"

"Yes, Ezekiel mentioned it to me."

"Then you'll understand why Hannah hasn't told Isaac. And why I didn't tell you for so long."

"I suppose I should be flattered." But Mark couldn't help but think that Isaac deserved to know.

"You should." She studied him for a few moments. "You won't tell him, will you?"

"I won't," Mark said. "That's between the two of them."

Mark sat next to Rachel on the sofa, and she wrapped her arms around his waist. "You're the only man who knows what we do," she said. "Besides Mr. Greene, that is."

"I suppose there's no risk of him telling anyone."

"No, and Granny trusts him implicitly." She lifted her head, met his eyes, and groaned. "Not that I don't trust you."

"Rachel," he said. "It's all right. We've had a long day." He kissed the top of her head. "We'll work this out together."

And they would. Wouldn't they?

After finally getting a full night of sleep, Rachel felt more clear-headed the next day. She was no less frantic to *do* something, though. Mark was meeting with his men, so she saddled one of the horses and rode to Hannah's.

"I have an idea," Rachel said. "And you're going to hate it."

Hannah laughed. "You don't know that."

"Oh yes I do."

"Fine, tell me what this idea is of yours." Hannah was spinning wool into yarn, and her foot kept its steady rhythm. She was always doing something for the Cause.

"Misinformation," Rachel said.

"You *still* like that idea?"

"I do," Rachel said.

"What false information would you give the redcoats?"

"I'm not sure yet." Undaunted, Rachel continued. "But that's not the point. Not yet. The point is to get them to trust us. Mark and myself. I was thinking we could have some of the officers over for supper."

Hannah's foot stopped moving, and the spinning wheel slowly came to a stop. "Surely you're joking."

"I'm not. I know it sounds foolish, but –"

"Of course it sounds foolish!"

Tears pricked the back of Rachel's eyes. When it came to her sister, Rachel always became smaller, and she was tired of it. She took a deep breath.

"I came here to tell you my intention," Rachel said. "Not to ask for your permission. Excuse me."

Then she got back on her horse and rode away without waiting for her sister's response.

Once the hurt passed, Rachel was filled with something akin to the way Mark made her feel – a desperation of sorts. Her body felt warm despite the cold outside. Her heart beat faster, and she felt the need to urge her horse into a gallop. She didn't do any of that, though. Instead, she turned her horse down the road to the redcoats' camp.

Mark's rear end was asleep. They'd been hiding for hours, bundled up and camouflaged. Some of his men were in trees, but Mark was in the same position he had been weeks ago when he'd first watched the camp. He crouched behind a rock, one leg straight against the cold ground to save his knee from further harm. They'd been observing the British camp and their movements since dawn, and so far everything they'd learned had been discouraging. The redcoats were well-fed, well-supplied, and moved about their day with ruthless efficiency. Mark and his men needed to take action. The people of Freehold wouldn't survive the winter if they didn't.

"Captain," Jim said in a low voice, pointing to the entrance of the camp.

A lone figure rode a horse into camp, and Mark couldn't tell who it was except for the shock of blonde hair that stood out against her brown cloak.

Panic raced through him. That wasn't – that wasn't her, was it? It couldn't be. Mark looked around at his men in the trees, and all of them were staring at the woman with rapt attention. She rode into the camp, past the guards, and climbed down off of her horse. Mark wasn't close enough to hear what she said, but she dropped the hood of her cloak and followed Sergeant Neumann into a tent. That was Rachel. His men looked at him. Mark shook his head, clinging to his composure. The last time they'd been here, Mark had been impulsive. He wouldn't be today, no matter how upset he was.

"Captain, we know how that looked," Will said when they returned to the cave. "You need to talk to your wife."

Mark put on his cloak over the leathers he had worn to hide in the woods. He nearly tore the fabric in his haste.

"She's not working with them, is she?" Jim said.

"She wouldn't do that," Mark said, meeting his sergeants' eyes.

Will & Jim looked like they believed him, but every other man in that cave looked wary. Mark couldn't afford such doubts as the captain. He needed to speak with his wife.

Rachel sat in her kitchen later that day, sipping a cold cup of coffee and trying to stop shaking. She'd done it. She'd talked to Sergeant Neumann and invited him to bring a few officers over for supper. Would they come? Rachel wasn't sure. But at least she'd done her part. Mark came in the back kitchen door, looking disheveled and all the more handsome for it. He took off his cloak, and she saw that he was wearing his leathers underneath instead of the shirt, breeches and waistcoat he'd been wearing lately.

"Were you successful?" she asked. She wasn't sure what, but she knew that he and his men had been up to something today.

"Somewhat," he said. He didn't look at her, just moved to pour himself a bowl of vegetable soup from the pot in the fireplace. He sat down across from her and ate his soup with his usual efficiency. Once he finished, he set the bowl aside and pinned Rachel with his dark gaze. The man was downright intimidating when he wanted to be.

"Rachel, what were you doing at the British camp today?"

Nerves stirred in Rachel's stomach. She'd been impulsive, and Mark might be angry with her.

"I, uh – I invited Sergeant Neumann and some of his officers over for supper in two night's time."

His eyebrows rose. "Why?"

Rachel couldn't bear to have a repeat of the conversation she'd had with her sister. "I thought we could use misinformation to draw them out of their camp. Perhaps. This could pave the way for that, building on the work I did when I delivered the defective bullets."

Mark leaned his head on his chin, studying her. Rachel squirmed in her seat.

"What would be the purpose of this supper? What kind of misinformation would you spread?"

"I'm not sure yet. Perhaps nothing yet. But if we could build trust with them, maybe –" Rachel swallowed hard. What had she been thinking?

It had been *so* foolish to ride off to the British camp alone. And now she'd invited them to supper?

"Rachel," Mark said. "Come here."

She stood and crossed the table to stand in front of him. Mark took one of her hands and pulled her into his lap, then wrapped his arms around her. A few tears fell, and Rachel wiped them aside.

"You're not angry?" she said in a small voice.

"I wish you had told me," he said, his warm voice fanning over her hair. "But I think it's a good idea."

"You do?"

"I do," Mark said. "Nothing else we've tried yet has worked. And it's a lower risk than trying to fight them. How can I help?"

Rachel kissed him, unable to contain her growing love for this man who supported her. Mark smiled at her when she pulled back.

"You can help me get ready."

CHAPTER 17

"We can seat ten if we need to," Rachel was saying. "I believe that will be enough room. What do you think?"

Of course, Mark was watching her mouth move. "I – uh – yes. I agree."

"Is there anything I'm not thinking of?"

"Well, you said you'd be removing anything valuable and storing it…where will you do that?"

"Granny's, I think. Mr. Greene dug out their cellar long ago so there's plenty of room down there."

"Good. Should I have some of my men nearby in case we need help?"

Rachel bit her lip. "That's not a bad idea. I trust that they can remain undetected."

"They can."

"I think that will work then. And we'll make the redcoats vegetable stew. They should eat the way we do since they stole our animals. Don't you agree?"

Mark grinned at her. "Excellent idea."

Mark's hands were shaking as he opened the front door to find Sergeant Neumann standing on their doorstep. Only Sergeant Neumann.

"Good evening, Mr. Johnson."

Mark cleared his throat and stepped aside. "Good evening," he said mechanically. "I thought Rachel invited more of your officers."

"Yes, but I thought it would be best if I came alone."

Sergeant Neumann followed Mark into the sitting room, where Rachel had a tray prepared with coffee. Mark leaned heavily on his cane and hoped the other man didn't recognize him.

Once they were seated in the sitting room, Mark and Rachel on the sofa, and Sergeant Neumann on a chair, Mark tried to look anywhere but the man's red uniform coat. Why had he agreed to be in the same room as a redcoat, and to try to be polite? This whole affair had been Rachel's idea, and he hoped she had a plan, because Mark had no idea what to do.

"Are you from Britain, Sergeant?" Rachel asked, sipping her coffee.

"Call me John," he said. "Using my rank all the time is tedious."

"Are you from Britain, John?" Rachel asked again.

"No – I'm from Trenton actually."

"And when did you become a soldier?" Mark said, trying for casual interest. "I've always admired you soldiers myself. I never could fight, with my knee being the way it is."

He gestured with his cane to his knee.

"I'd always trained with the militia," he said. "But I joined His Majesty's troops when the war began." He laughed. "My father hated it."

Mark met the other man's eyes. They had more in common than he'd originally thought. The thought was disconcerting. But Mark remembered the state of those prisoners in the British camp, remembered Mrs. Elliott's tears as she cradled her husband. Sergeant

Neumann may be just a man doing his job, but Mark would do well to remember that they were on opposite sides of the conflict.

"Supper is ready," Rachel said when there was a break in the conversation. Mark helped her carry the bowls of vegetable soup to the table, and they ate for a time in silence.

"This is delicious, Mrs. Johnson."

"Thank you," Rachel said. "It's difficult to make palatable food in the winter."

"I understand that," Sergeant Neumann said.

Mark wanted to make a comment about how he and his men were starving all of the towns around them so they could have fresh meat, but he bit his tongue. The conversation flowed, mostly between Sergeant Neumann and Rachel, and Mark did his best to contribute.

"Do you have a regular weapons supplier, Sergeant?" Rachel said at one point.

"Not besides you." The other man didn't meet either of their eyes, so perhaps he was lying.

"My friend Charity's brother, Jonathan Marshall, supplies rifles to the redcoats in Millstone and the surrounding areas. Perhaps you've heard of him."

"I have," the sergeant said. "But I've never met him in person."

"I'll have Charity invite you all over for a demonstration," Rachel said. "Perhaps next week. Her brother does exceptional work."

Mark looked back and forth between the two of them, his heart pounding. Did Rachel have a plan that he didn't know of? In any case, Mark was intrigued.

"Thank you for a lovely evening," Sergeant Neumann said when he left.

"You're welcome," Rachel said.

When the man had left, Rachel wrapped her arms around Mark and rested her head against his chest. "I was so nervous."

"I was too." In fact, now that the Sergeant had left, Mark was exhausted.

They tidied up and went to bed. Mark didn't have many words left to say, and Rachel was thoughtful too.

"Did you accomplish what you meant to with that supper?" he asked when she climbed into bed next to him. "I'm curious how Charity will come into this."

"I believe so. But we won't know until we can test it out."

"Test what out?"

Rachel rested her chin on his chest, smiling at him gently. Warmth filtered through Mark's chest that this woman was his, and that she'd chosen to trust him.

"I wondered if I could borrow some of your men."

"I have some news," Mark said the following Monday.

He hadn't seen them in a few days, but after Rachel's idea the week before, Mark was eager for their help. His men looked tired, and guilt filtered through Mark that he got to sleep in a comfortable bed with Rachel while his men slept on the ground in a cave.

"Out with it, Captain," Will said.

"I found out what Rachel was doing in the regulars' camp the day I met her."

The cave went silent, every man staring at Mark with open curiosity.

"She was delivering bullets to the redcoats. But they were defective, designed to disintegrate inside the barrel of a rifle or musket."

His men looked like they were struggling to grasp the brilliance of it, so he spelled it out for them. "Rachel was seeking to sabotage the enemy by gaining their trust but delivering them defective supplies."

Jim cleaned his spectacles on his shirt. "I like it."

"I do too." Mark couldn't help the pride in his voice. "So I thought she might be able to help us with our work."

"How so?" Will said.

Mark sat them down and laid out the plan that he and Rachel had discussed.

"We can't rid ourselves of 150 redcoats that way, though," Will said.

"No," Jim put in. "But it's a start. And it's much wiser than trying to attack the camp."

"When can we do this?"

"I'll discuss it with Rachel, but we thought tomorrow or the next day."

Jim gave him a brisk nod. "Let us know when and where, and we'll be there. We'll even wear our uniforms."

"You brought them with you?" Mark said.

"We weren't sure when we would have an occasion to use them," Will said. "It turns out that we do already."

Mark walked toward the entrance to the cave.

"Captain," Jim said. "If this goes poorly, your rank could be at risk. This is unconventional, even for us. Colonel Staples might not be pleased."

"I know." That was the thought that was churning Mark's stomach. But Rachel had chosen to trust him; he needed to repay her trust in kind.

"I don't know how you do this," Granny said the next day. "I'm so nervous my hands are shaking."

"That's the beauty of gloves," Rachel replied. "They hide the shaking."

They walked toward the redcoats' camp; it was an unseasonably warm day, and Rachel enjoyed the fresh air. She tried to, at least. But she was *so* nervous. Not only was she putting herself at risk, but Granny as well. Granny had insisted on coming, though, knowing that this was a bolder plan than what they had done before.

Rachel waved to the guards at the entrance of the camp, her face more serious than the usual bright smile she wore at the camp.

"What do you need, Mrs. Johnson?" one of them said.

So they recognized her by now. Good. "I need to speak to Sergeant Neumann, please."

They looked at each other, then at Rachel and Granny, and apparently not seeing a threat, waved them through the entrance. A few curious stares followed them as they walked through camp, but nobody approached them. Granny clung to Rachel's arm, and Rachel tried to be brave so Granny wouldn't need to be any more frightened than necessary.

"Sergeant Neumann, we wish to speak to you."

The other man looked up from a letter he was reading. "Mrs. Johnson. Back again so soon? How can I help you?"

"We were taking a walk in the forest and saw a small party of Continentals. I thought you'd like to know."

"How do you know they were Continentals?"

"They were wearing blue and red uniforms, and were all armed heavily and had rucksacks," Rachel said. "They were camped around a fire. There were about ten of them in all. Wouldn't you believe they were Continentals?"

Sergeant Neumann looked between her and Granny, pursing his lips.

"Sergeant," said the man beside him, also an officer, judging by his uniform. "You're going to believe the word of a young woman and a –"

"Finish that sentence, Lieutenant," Sergeant Neumann said. "I dare you."

That quieted the man quickly. Sergeant Neumann looked at Rachel again. "If you tell me exactly where you saw them, I can send a few of my men after them."

Rachel described the location that she and Mark had agreed on. If Mark and his men weren't where they said they'd be, then it would make Rachel look foolish at best and deceitful at worst.

"Best of luck, Sergeant," Rachel said. "We're going back home. We don't want to be out with such dangerous men around."

"Probably for the best. Good day, Mrs. Johnson." Sergeant Neumann was distracted and already issuing orders to his men, so Rachel and Granny walked as fast as they could out of the camp without looking suspicious.

"Do you think he believed us?" Granny said as they walked back.

"I'm not sure." She took her friend's hand. "But you were brave today."

"By standing next to you?" Granny scoffed.

"Yes." In fact, it moved Rachel almost to tears. "With Hannah not telling Isaac what we are doing, I've felt guilty for trying to work with Mark's men."

Granny tugged the hood of her cloak over her head, covering her purple headscarf. "This is a good idea, honey. Don't doubt yourself. Hannah's your sister, but she has her own fears to work through."

Granny's words were comforting, but Rachel still felt uneasy about the whole matter. Perhaps that was a good thing, though. She'd always tried to keep the peace between herself and her sister, and often it came at the expense of Rachel acting on her own ideas. If only growth didn't come with so much discomfort, though.

"Remember," Mark said. "Don't make this look too easy."

They'd set up a campfire in the middle of a clearing, the location that he and Rachel had agreed on, and his men were wearing their uniforms, looking like they hadn't a care in the world. Mark was dressed in his usual clothes – he couldn't be a part of this – but he was going to watch. And hope it went all right.

"We'll do our best." Will rubbed his hands together.

Jim was fiddling with the campfire, making sure there were strong branches that could be easily used as flaming weapons. "We'll be careful," he said over his shoulder.

Mark hid himself in the trees while his men braced for the attack. Three redcoats came into the clearing about an hour later. Either Sergeant Neumann didn't believe Rachel, or he was so confident in his men's abilities that he didn't feel the need for more. Mark wasn't sure which reason he preferred. It was over quickly, with the three redcoats bound and gagged.

"We'll bring them back to the main Continental Camp this afternoon," Will said, dusting off his hands.

Mark clapped Will on the shoulder and congratulated his men on a job well done. He walked back home to find a very anxious Rachel pacing the kitchen. She looked at him with wide eyes when he came inside.

"Well?"

"It worked."

She grinned. "It did?"

"Sergeant Neumann sent three men, who we easily captured and took back to our camp."

"And when those men don't return to their camp?"

"I have more men waiting to take care of any more redcoats Sergeant Neumann sends. That idea was brilliant, Rachel."

"We won't be able to execute that same plan again, though," Rachel said. "We'll have to think of something else."

"The important thing," Mark said, putting his arm around her shoulders, "Is that your idea worked."

"And perhaps with us working together, we might have more success than we would have apart."

Encouraged by the success of their plan, Rachel saddled a horse the next day to ride to Charity's. She'd never heard back from the note she sent Charity, and perhaps Charity could help them by getting to know Sergeant Neumann and his men as well. Mark was with his men, helping them since Will and Jim were taking the captured redcoats back to the Continental camp.

Rachel tilted her face back to enjoy the sunlight as she rode, allowing her hose to set a leisurely pace. The roads were relatively dry today, and it should be a short, easy ride to Charity's.

A redcoat approached her on the road, as if summoned by Rachel's relaxed mood to ruin her day. He was all alone, but he was tall and imposing (it seemed that all of them were tall and imposing). He held a hand up as he was walking by, and Rachel stopped her horse, her heart pounding.

"How can I help you, sir?"

"What are you doing?" So this man wasn't one for pleasantries. That was fine. Rachel kept her dimwitted smile fixed on her face and ignored the perspiration beading on her brow.

"I'm going to visit a friend."

"Alone?"

"Yes."

She met the man's eyes, but he didn't seem to blink. Fear was clawing up her spine now, and she tried to keep her hands steady, gripping the reins in her lap. The man walked around to the back of her horse and lifted the flaps of her saddlebags. He took the spare food and canteen of cider she had and tucked them in his pockets.

"It's not fitting for a woman to be out alone," the man said, coming around to face her again.

Rachel couldn't think of a response for that, so she just smiled at the man. When he moved along without another word, Rachel let out a long sigh. That had been far too close.

"You look pale," Charity said when she greeted Rachel in her sitting room. "What's wrong?"

Charity and Rachel didn't see each other as often as they liked, but Charity's mother and Rachel's mother had been lifelong friends, so Rachel had grown up visiting back and forth with Charity. Less so since the war started, unfortunately.

"I encountered a curious soldier on my way here," Rachel said. "It was fine. Is your brother here?"

Jonathan Marshall happened to be on the other side of the war, so they couldn't have a frank conversation if she was nearby. Charity frowned. "He's out. Are you sure you're all right?"

"Yes, I am." Perhaps if she told Charity that she was fine, then Charity (and she) would believe it. "Did you receive my note?"

"I did," Charity said. "I've been busy, as I'm sure you have been too. I heard about the redcoats that have been making a nuisance of themselves. Is everyone all right?"

"Abigail's store was burned down. And Ezekiel was injured."

Charity sat down on her plush sofa, her blue eyes wide. "How? What happened?"

"It was last week," Rachel said. She told Charity what had happened in Freehold, from Ezekiel refusing to give away items from his store to the redcoats burning down buildings of Whigs in town.

One of Charity's servants brought in a tray of tea, and Rachel poured herself a cup, too rattled to feel guilty.

"But you were unharmed?" Charity said.

Rachel nodded. "The redcoats think I'm on their side."

"I see," Charity said.

"Which brings me to my next idea. I believe you can help."

"How?" Charity took a dainty sip of her tea.

"Perhaps your brother could invite some of these redcoats over for a demonstration of your rifles."

"All right," Charity said.

A plan was forming in the back of Rachel's mind, but she couldn't quite grasp it yet. As she moved forward, perhaps the path would become clear.

"I'm not sure when yet, though," Rachel said.

"Send me a note. Call it a Christmas party, and give me a date, and I'll send an invitation."

"Thank you."

Charity leaned forward, her dark hair curling over her shoulder.

"Now, my dear friend, you've been here a quarter of an hour and you've yet to tell me that you are married. You married a *soldier*."

"You talked to Hannah." Heat crawled up Rachel's cheeks.

"Of course I talked to Hannah. *She* had the courtesy of sending me a letter when all of this happened."

Rachel didn't have a good excuse for why she hadn't told Charity about Mark. "I'm sorry."

"That's all right." Charity waved a hand. "But I'll need to meet him, you know. You must care for this man if you're hiding him away."

"I do," Rachel said. She really did. Despite her efforts to keep her heart safe, she was falling more and more in love with Mark every day. And when he left – not if, but when – she would pay the consequences for that.

"I trust your judgment," Charity said. "If you think he's a good man and he's worthy of you, then I wish you the best."

Rachel hadn't known how desperately she needed to hear those words from her friend. "Thank you," she said.

"Of course. Now get home safely. Would you like an escort?"

Rachel stood. "No. I can get home in a little over an hour without the wagon encumbering me. It'll be fine."

"If you're sure."

"I am." If she had an escort, that would only raise more questions. It was best that she travel alone.

"Very well." Charity kissed her cheek. "Safe travels."

Mark was wide-eyed and frantic when she returned home.

"I left you a note!" Rachel said. "I thought you were helping your men!"

He pulled her into his arms and squeezed her tight, and she savored the scent of campfire that always seemed to cling to his clothes.

"I was still worried," he said at last.

"I went to Charity's." She didn't tell him about the unsettling soldier she had encountered. There was no need to worry him more.

Mark stepped back, resting his hands on her shoulders. "You're pale."

He couldn't read her so easily, could he?

"I'm merely cold."

"Rachel." There was a slight growl in his voice. "I thought we'd agreed to no more secrets."

"We did." He turned his Captain look on her, and she gave in. "Fine. I encountered a redcoat on the road, and it was unsettling."

Mark's blunt fingertips squeezed her shoulders, and he pulled her closer. "Did you recognize him?"

Rachel shook her head. "He was closer to my father's age, and tall and very strong. He searched my saddlebags and...well, that was it. I'm sure it was nothing."

"It was not nothing," Mark said. "You have instincts for a reason, Rachel. I know you've been taught to ignore what you think and feel, but you need to listen to that voice in your mind that tells you if a situation is unsafe. Ask any soldier and they'll tell you the same." .

"I'm new to this, though," Rachel said. "I've only made a few deliveries. I'm sure I'll grow more accustomed to the danger when I'm more experienced."

"Perhaps. But you know as well as I how dangerous this country is. It's good to be cautious."

He pressed a quick kiss to her lips. "Come. Let's sit by the fire."

CHAPTER 18

Rachel and Mark were repairing a section of fence a few days later when her father rode up, his dark cloak billowing out behind him.

"I heard about the fires last week," Father said without preamble. "Are you all right?"

Rachel's heart squeezed. She lifted her hand to her brow to shield her eyes from the brightness of the snow.

"We're fine, and the house is unharmed."

"They took some of the animals, though," Mark said.

Father's lips pressed together into a thin line. "Perhaps I'd better come inside."

Once they were situated at the kitchen table with warm mugs of cider, Rachel leaned against Mark's side. Mark put his arm around her. Having Father here was always unsettling to Rachel's emotions, but she was glad she had Mark with her this time.

"I see you two are getting along," Father said.

"We are," Mark replied.

"What have your men discovered in the past weeks? What must we do to move this group of redcoats away from Freehold?"

Mark's deep inhale raised his chest against Rachel's ear.

"My men have been recording the times and dates of their supply deliveries and what they spend their days doing. We know that there are about a hundred and fifty men. And apart from stealing supplies from Freehold and Middletown, they mostly stay at the camp. They are led by a Sergeant Neumann, who is ruthless."

"And Rachel? What do you think?"

"Me?" Rachel said. Was he asking *her* for her opinion?

"Yes. I know you have friends, connections of your own. What is your opinion on how to accomplish our goal?"

Father's eyes, cold and blue, looked into hers. He had never been an affectionate man, which stopped hurting her feelings (mostly) years ago. Colonel Staples had many failings as a father. But he was asking her for her opinion, and that meant something.

"I, uh – I think that using misinformation to draw some of the redcoats away from the camp would be helpful."

"We can't afford to combat them with force right now," Father said. He set his mug down and leaned back in his chair. "It's a good idea if you can manage it."

"Will you help too?" Rachel said.

Father shook his head. "I am needed in New York tomorrow. General Washington is planning something – well, something significant right after Christmas, and I'm to help organize it."

Rachel knew better than to ask her father what General Washington planned, but her heart sank at the thought that he wouldn't come to help. "Very well. I'm going to go talk to Ezekiel Elliott, and check on Mrs. Bell – pay my condolences. Best of luck to you both."

He stood, and with a cursory nod of his head, was gone again.

"He's...efficient," Mark said.

Rachel had started on supper and Mark was finishing the fence when Colonel Staples appeared again. Mark could avoid being seen if he wanted to, but Colonel Staples had the uncanny ability to appear out of nowhere.

"I thought you'd left," Mark said. "Rachel thinks you did."

"How fares your assignment?" the older man asked, ignoring Mark's barbed comment. "Have you found out if Rachel and Hannah are involved in delivering supplies to the Continentals?"

Mark pursed his lips. "I don't know all the details. But they are not being taken advantage of. They are advancing the Cause. If you want to know more, you'll have to talk to your daughters yourself."

Colonel Staples studied Mark intently, and Mark met his commanding officer's eyes.

"You've come to care for Rachel, haven't you?"

Mark didn't hesitate. "I have. Very much."

"Good," Colonel Staples said. "Do you think I should talk to my daughters about what they are doing?"

"I don't know, sir."

"You can assure me they are helping the Cause?"

Mark nodded.

"Then perhaps I don't wish to know," the older man said. "I trust you to look after them. While you are here."

Which probably wouldn't be long, if they were successful in somehow driving the redcoats away. Mark's heart sank at the thought of leaving. But what else could he do?

Mark was with his men again, the next day, and Rachel was inspecting his work at finishing the fence. It'd be hard to adjust to doing all this work when Mark left.

When he left. Rachel had kept herself so busy in the last week that she'd not thought of Mark leaving. She loved the man; there was nothing she could do about that now. She'd just have to lose herself in her work when he left. Perhaps that would provide enough of a distraction.

She saw the soldier coming across the back fields after a few minutes of working by herself. He wasn't wearing his uniform today, but she recognized him as the one she'd met on the road on the way to Charity's. Rachel's heart pounded. *Breathe.* She had a hammer in her hands. It wasn't the best weapon, but it would do in a pinch. Perhaps he was coming to apologize for his rudeness to her the other day. Doubtful, but Rachel didn't want to assume the worst just because he was a redcoat.

Then again, Mark had told her to trust her instincts, had he not? The first thing her mother had taught her about fighting was to do everything she could to prevent a fight. So Rachel pasted her best dim-witted smile on her face and gripped her dagger in her pocket.

"Good day...Mrs. Johnson, was it?" He stepped closer to her.

Rachel took a step back, but he followed.

"How can I help you?"

"My lieutenant sent me here to check on you. To remind you that we're watching you. Sergeant Neumann might trust you, but not all of us do. And if we see or hear of you doing anything untoward..."

He had her hair in his grasp before Rachel could take a breath. He pulled her toward him and placed his lips close to her neck. Rachel froze, feeling like an animal in a trap. If she struggled, he would only pull her hair harder. She couldn't aim her knife at this angle.

"If we hear of you doing anything untoward," he repeated. "Well, you won't like the results. You left town last week. Where did you go?"

Rachel kept her voice calm. "I went to Millstone."

He held her there for a moment, then released her as suddenly as he had grabbed her. She stumbled, and righted herself.

"It's not becoming for a woman to lie."

"I was telling the truth." Rachel couldn't resist. The blow came out of nowhere, and fire burst out along Rachel's jaw. She let out a cry and staggered, clutching the side of her face.

The man walked away as if this was something he did every day. Then he was gone again. Rachel tried to continue what she was doing, but her hands were shaking too hard for her to grip the hammer. She hurried back into the house. Mark was in the sitting room, sewing up a hole in one of his shirts.

"What's wrong?"

Rachel sank into the chair opposite of him. "One of the redcoats, the one I met on the road the other day. He came here."

Mark set aside his shirt, his movements tense. "And?"

"And he grabbed me by my hair." Her voice shook on the last few words. "And he hit me." The man hadn't broken the skin, but she would have a nasty bruise.

Mark stood, coming toward her. "Are you all right?"

"Yes, I think so." Rachel tried to force some lightness into her tone, but it didn't quite carry through.

He pressed a hand to her cheek, avoiding her injured side. He was very close to her now, his brown eyes warm in the firelight. "Are you sure?"

This tenderness was breaking her heart. He pulled her to her feet and wrapped his arms around her. Rachel sighed and sank into his warmth. Just when she was starting to get comfortable, though, he pulled away.

"I'll be right back," he said. "I'm going to take care of something."

Mark didn't stop to put on his cloak. He stepped out the kitchen door into the yard. There were footprints in the snow leading away from the fence. Good. He would have a path to follow. His hands were shaking. In the heat of the most brutal combat, he could find an inner calm that came from – he didn't know where. But now, when his wife had been threatened, he couldn't find it within himself to be calm.

The footsteps led off of Rachel's property and toward neighboring fields. Mark walked as fast as his knee would allow, stopping when he saw a man he didn't recognize, but who fit Rachel's description. There was nobody else around. Good. The regular was sizing up one of the horses, and Mark climbed over, so he was in the enclosure with him. The man looked Mark up and down with a dismissive look on his face. No matter. Mark had been underestimated before.

Mark had him by the back of the collar before the man could blink, and he slammed his face into the icy water of the horse trough. The man fought, but Mark held him down. He held the man's face underwater for long enough to make him nervous, then yanked him up by his hair. Coughing and sputtering, the man called Mark all kinds of names that he probably deserved, so Mark gave him another dunking or two until the fight went out of him and he was gasping for air. His lungs had to be burning like wildfire.

Colonel Staples had always told him to use his environment to his advantage. Who knew the frigid water of a horse trough could be so effective? Mark finally let go of the man's hair, and he fell to his knees in the snow, gasping and coughing and giving Mark the chance to strip him of his weapons.

"Don't come near my wife again," Mark said, his chest heaving.

The other man didn't acknowledge him, but he didn't challenge Mark either. Now, what to do with him? Mark stopped and *thought* for the first time in several minutes. He didn't want to make things worse for himself and Rachel. He didn't want to draw more attention to them or put anyone else at risk.

But that kind of behavior couldn't be tolerated, especially toward Rachel. Mark hadn't hurt him, but he had humiliated him and taken his weapons. Hopefully he'd scared him. By this point, the man had caught his breath, and he lunged at Mark from his position in the snow. Mark sidestepped him and grabbed him by the back of the collar again. This time he pressed the man's face into the snow, putting his good knee in the middle of his back and pulling out the pistol. Powder and bullets came from the man's belt – the man was struggling so much it was difficult to load the pistol, but Mark managed.

He finally let the man up and pointed the loaded pistol at his head. These pistols weren't the most accurate, but at this range he couldn't possibly miss. The man's face was red and he was breathing hard, but he didn't try to attack again, not with his own pistol pointed at his face.

"This is what's going to happen," Mark said. "You're going to scurry back to the hole you crawled out of. And you're going to leave my wife and I alone. Do you understand, or do I need to hurt you?"

The man didn't respond; he gave Mark a hard look. That wasn't good enough.

"Do you understand?"

"Yes." The man finally said.

"Good. Run along." Mark waved the pistol.

The man ran away in a very undignified manner – it was probably difficult to run in the snow when you were soaking wet with freezing water, but that wasn't Mark's problem – and Mark watched him go. It looked like he was heading northeast of town. Mark saved that information in his mind for later.

The knot in Mark's stomach never eased throughout the rest of the afternoon. This was a sign that an episode was coming on, and the more Mark tried to ignore the feeling, the worse it seemed to get. He kept himself busy preparing supper with Rachel, but when they sat in the sitting room after supper, he couldn't distract himself any more.

Rachel settled against his side, opening her book. Mark was usually content to watch her read, occasionally listening to comments on one of the passages or her excitement over a point in the story. Tonight, though, Mark felt cold. The cold seemed to take on a life of its own and crawl outward from his stomach to his extremities. It seemed to pull him under, and Mark couldn't think of anything else. Absently, Rachel got up and retrieved a blanket, wrapping it around his shoulders, then returned to her book. The blanket was of slight comfort, but it didn't stop his shaking. He pressed the heels of his hands into his eyelids, but nothing seemed to help.

After another minute or so, during which his shaking continued, Rachel closed her book and looked at him.

"You're not cold, are you?"

Mark shook his head.

"Come here."

She pulled his head onto her lap and adjusted his bulk so he was laying across the sofa. "If you tell me, I can help you."

Mark wasn't sure what to say to that. Her fingers in his hair felt nice, but it didn't stop the shaking.

"What was the date for the battle at Lexington and Concord?"

"What?" Mark said. What a strange question to be asking at a time like this.

"Answer the question." Authority rang in her tone, and Mark thought back in his mind.

"It was in '75. Spring. April or May, I think." That had been a turbulent time in Mark's life as well as the country's, and he hadn't been concerned with the exact date.

"It was April nineteenth. And when was the battle at Breed's Hill?"

"That was the following summer. June – June 17th."

"Good. How many men are in your unit?"

That was a much simpler question. "Thirty-nine."

"How many Captains?"

Mark laughed. "One. Me."

"How many Lieutenants?"

"We had one but he died of smallpox."

"I'm sorry to hear that. What about Sergeants?"

"Two. Will and Jim."

"Who is your favorite of your men?"

"I can't choose," Mark said. "They'd have my head if they found out."

Her gentle hand had never stopped stroking his hair, and Mark noticed it now more than he had a few minutes before.

"What is your favorite thing to do with your men?"

Mark thought through all of the things he did not enjoy about his work. Past those painful memories, though, were some good ones.

"I think – I think sitting around a fire in the evening after an assignment. Sharing whatever meager food we have and talking. We've all lived another day."

"I'll bet the warmth is comforting."

"It is," Mark said. In fact, he was feeling warmer now. That infernal cold, the cold that never felt like it would go away, was easing its grip, and Mark felt like he could breathe again.

Rachel didn't say anything for a few minutes, merely stroking his hair, and eventually he closed his eyes.

"Let's go to bed," Rachel said. "The last time we fell asleep on a sofa like this, we ended up married."

Mark looked at her to see if she was joking, and she had a wide smile on her face. He smiled back at her, and eased off of the sofa.

"My knee is feeling better," he said as he climbed the stairs.

"I'm glad." She took his hand and pulled him up behind her. They followed their routine before getting into bed, and Mark felt better. The cold had passed, and he'd been all right. Moreover, Rachel had helped him through it and hadn't mocked his weakness.

"Thank you," he said to her.

She paused in the middle of brushing her hair. "You're welcome."

Once they were in bed, he turned to her again. "Let me take care of you."

"Take care of me?" Rachel raised her eyebrows.

"Yes – I. You're always taking care of everyone: Hannah, Abigail, even your father. Me. You've taken such good care of me. Allow me to return the favor."

Her soft smile made warmth spread through Mark's chest. Once they were in bed together, he widened his legs and tucked her in front of him. She leaned back against his chest, humming content-edly. "You're right. This is nice."

"I haven't even begun yet," Mark said. She was wearing the shift that she often slept in, and her hair was braided. He lifted her hair over one of her shoulders and rested his hand on the back of her neck.

Rachel leaned forward, and Mark squeezed the back of her neck, then moved his hand up to massage her scalp, neck, and shoulders. She was tense – no surprise – and it felt good to help her in this small way.

"You were the one who was assaulted today," Mark said. "And yet you comforted me tonight."

"It was frightening." Rachel's voice was low, heavy, and her head was bent forward as Mark worked on her shoulders.

"Has that ever happened to you before?"

"No. I've been lucky."

"Well, it won't happen again."

"Mark, you can't promise that."

"I –" What could he say to that? That he would protect her, and be by her side always?

"I don't want to leave, Rachel."

The confession was easier when she wasn't looking at him.

"I want to stay here."

Rachel didn't say anything for a few minutes. Had she heard him? He worked the tension out of her shoulders and when he finished, he pulled her back against his chest because he wanted to.

"I want you to stay too," she finally said, barely above a whisper.

What would that look like? How could Mark continue to protect and care for his men, continue to advance the Cause, and not leave Rachel behind? Rachel curled up against his chest on her side, and he wrapped the blanket around her, letting her ease into sleep in his arms. He rested his cheek on the top of her head, breathing her in. Mark wasn't sure what the next few days and weeks would bring, but he knew one thing: he loved Rachel. And he couldn't leave her.

When Mark came downstairs the next morning, he had a cramp in his neck from sleeping sitting up. The sitting room was as they had left it, with Rachel's book on the sofa and the blanket she'd wrapped around his shoulders hung over the back of the furniture. She'd been kind and helped him through his episode, but he needed to do something to heal his mind from these struggles. Was that possible? Mark wasn't sure. Perhaps he was permanently damaged from what he'd seen and done. But if it was possible to get better, he wanted to try. And he knew just who to ask.

Mr. Greene opened his front door, a pair of spectacles perched on his nose. "Mr. Johnson. Can I help you?"

"Yes. I wondered if I could speak with you."

Mark wiped his sweaty palms on his breeches as he followed the older man into the sitting room. He could do this. This might help him. He wanted to get better, for Rachel's sake if not for his own.

"I've been meaning to come by again," Mark said once they were seated with coffee. He took a bite out of a piece of bread with butter that Mr. Greene offered him.

"This is delicious," he said.

Mr. Greene smiled. "Thank you. It's somewhat of a specialty of mine. Luke, Rachel's brother, likes to bake too, and I taught him everything I know."

"You'll have to teach me sometime," Mark said around another bite. "Where is Mrs. Greene?"

"Working in her shed out back. She's experimenting with – I'm not sure I should tell you."

"Rachel told me about her work, and that your wife had the idea for the defective bullets."

"Oh?" Mr. Greene's eyebrows leapt above his spectacles. "She trusts you a great deal then."

"I suppose she does." That assertion comforted Mark. "I wanted to speak to you about something else, though." Every polite bone in

Mark's body wanted to avoid the topic he must bring up, but Mrs. Greene and Rachel had both assured Mark that it was all right.

"I've noticed that you rarely leave your home."

"I don't leave it at all," Mr. Greene said. "Haven't for years, I'm afraid."

Mark sat back. There was no embarrassment or hesitation in the older man's words.

"You can ask why not. I don't mind."

"Why not?" Mark said.

"I'll tell you the full story some day," he said. "But the short version is that Violet and I escaped from our old life and began a new life in Freehold. This home is the first one that has been *mine*, and the first place I've ever felt safe. I want to keep feeling safe. So I don't leave. I can't leave."

Mark took a sip of his coffee and buttered another piece of bread, searching for the right words to say. He couldn't pretend to understand what Mr. Greene and his wife had gone through, but he admired how they'd thrived in spite of it. Most of all, he admired Mr. Greene's frank acceptance of his own limitations.

"Does it get tiresome? Never leaving?"

"Sometimes," Mr. Greene said. "But I have good friends who keep me company. And Violet and her friends are always up to something, Miss Rachel included."

"Thank you for telling me," Mark said. "I've been struggling with my own fears."

"Mr. Greene's dark eyes met Mark's and held them. "The war?"

Mark nodded. "And my role in it. I have – episodes – where I can't stop shaking."

He told him more about the night before, where Rachel had helped him by distracting him.

"Have you tried that before?"

"No, but it helped a great deal. That, and having Rachel beside me."

"I'd be lost without my Violet," Mr. Greene said.

"I won't always have Rachel with me, though," Mark said.

The older man seemed to be giving this some thought. "Must you go back to the war?"

"That's what I haven't decided yet."

Mr. Greene took a sip of his coffee. "Then I suppose that's the dilemma, isn't it?"

"It is." The fact that Mr. Greene had a rich, full life gave Mark hope, though. Perhaps he could have that kind of life one day.

They finished their coffee, talking about books and Freehold gossip. Mr. Greene didn't tell Mark what to do, but he did offer a listening ear. Mark could see more and more why Rachel loved him so much.

"Thank you for your help," Mark said when he got up to leave.

Mr. Greene shook Mark's hand, wrapping both of his hands around Mark's. Tears pricked Mark's eyes at the gesture.

"You'll be all right," Mr. Greene said. "You'll be all right."

"This isn't going to work," Rachel said to herself as she set her hammer and nails down.

The weather was tolerably warm today, so she was fixing a warped side of the chicken coop. Mark had gone for a walk, and this was a project that she'd been putting off for too long. Patching the wood wasn't working, though; the wood was too far gone. She'd have to replace the whole side.

Squawking indignantly, the chickens poked their heads out of the side of the coop.

"I'm trying to fix your home," she said.

A quarter of an hour later, Rachel had the old piece of wood on the ground and had cut down another piece to replace it, but the chickens were getting in her way.

"All of you need to go somewhere else," she said, picking up one of the chickens and carrying her into the pen where she let the horses out to roam on nicer days.

Of course, she followed Rachel right back to the coop. Putting them inside wouldn't do; Rachel had just cleaned the kitchen.

"All of you are too clever for me," she said.

Rachel went back inside, to her cellar, and looked for something, anything to keep the chickens occupied that wasn't too dear.

Ah. There were two smaller pumpkins in the corner of the cellar. Rachel carried those out to the yard with her and used a knife to carve a few holes in them. Once the chickens realized what was before them, they flocked – literally – to the pumpkins and happily pecked away at them. Rachel stood, hands on her hips, watching with satisfaction as every last chicken left the coop and crossed the yard.

Seizing her opportunity, she drove the first nail into the new piece of wood. "See, all you needed was a distraction, and you happily left your home."

A distraction. Rachel looked again at the coop, and the chickens, still occupied with their pumpkins. A plan was forming in Rachel's mind, and it was all she could do to clean up her project before she got out a pen and paper and made a list.

CHAPTER 19

Rachel was in her father's study when Mark came home. He crossed the room in large strides and pulled her into his arms. She tucked her face into the spot between his neck and shoulder, breathing him in. Few things made her more excited than a good list, and Mark Johnson was one of them.

"I need to show you something."

"All right."

Rachel swept aside the papers she'd scattered across her father's desk – she'd always wanted to do that – and laid out one of his maps. This was all of the thrill of delivering supplies, but multiplied.

Mark looked at her expectantly. "I'm intrigued."

Rachel pointed just north of Freehold to where the British camp was. She'd sketched a rough circle on the map to indicate the size and shape of the camp. "How many soldiers have your men counted?"

"The latest number is around a hundred and fifty."

"And we don't have enough Continentals at our disposal for an attack by force?"

Mark shook his head. "We want to avoid that. We tend to lose those kinds of battles, and the camp is too close to Freehold; people could get hurt."

"So the aim would be to draw as many of them out as possible, then take the camp by force?"

"If there are fewer than, say, thirty or forty of them, then my men and I can take them. We've been watching that camp for weeks."

Rachel bit her lip. "So if we can draw over a hundred redcoats out of the camp, you and your men stand a chance?"

"Yes." Mark frowned.

"Well, we don't want them to go near Freehold, so south is out." She pointed to Millstone, which was to the west, where Charity lived. "I've already spoken to Charity. She's going to invite some of the officers to her home for a demonstration of her brother's rifles."

Rachel drew a line on the map with her fingertip. "Lieutenant Feldman's camp is near Millstone. We've been delivering supplies to his troops for months; you could say he owes us a favor."

"What if he had some of his troops intercept the regulars on their way to Charity's?" Mark crossed his arms, shifting his weight.

Rachel smiled; he was still listening. "So this would take care of twenty or thirty of them, going to the west. We want them separated, correct?"

"Easier to pick them off that way," Mark said.

"There's plenty of land to the east, between Freehold and Long Branch." Rachel continued. "What could we use to draw some of them out that way?"

"A diversion of some kind?"

Rachel thought through the women she knew. "Granny is good with explosives. Would an explosion do?"

Mark raised his eyebrows. "That would do, yes. She is?"

"She's quite a genius, actually."

Mark pointed to the map. "So that would take care of another, say, ten or twenty soldiers. That still leaves far too many."

"My father doesn't have any more troops that he can spare?"

Mark shook his head. "Many of the Continentals' enlistments are expiring," Mark said. "Maybe some would like to volunteer. Perhaps Isaac knows some men he could ask for help."

"That could be what we need."

A grin stretched across Mark's face. Rachel grinned right back. "What are you thinking?"

"This could work."

"It could." There were many unknowns and they had some work to do, but for the first time, Rachel believed it was possible. They could fight back against the redcoats and avoid the bloodshed of a direct attack.

Another hour later, Rachel was exhausted. She sat in the chair behind her father's desk and rested her chin on the palm of her hand. Mark was still studying the map with his arms crossed, his mouth in a firm line.

"You're awfully thoughtful over there."

Mark looked at her, his eyes dark. "Have you ever considered joining the Continental Army?"

Rachel laughed.

"I'm serious," Mark said. "You'd make a brilliant strategist. My men and I have been trying to solve this problem for weeks, and this might be the best way to do it."

"I couldn't have thought of all of this on my own either," Rachel said, warmed at his praise. "We work well together."

Mark sank into the chair across from the desk, still studying the map. Rachel brought up a question that she'd tried to dismiss from her mind, but it persisted.

"You said last night that you didn't want to go back. Why not?"

He gave her a wry smile. "Take a guess."

He wanted to stay with her that much? "Because of your episodes?"

That brought a soberness to Mark's face. "I don't know if I'm fit for combat any more. And not just because of my episodes. Or my knee. The day we met, the day that I was watching the redcoat camp —"

"And watching me," Rachel put in.

"And watching you. That day, I couldn't stay calm. I made impulsive decisions that endangered my men and myself. I couldn't follow a plan. If I were one of my soldiers, what would I tell myself?"

"What *would* you tell yourself?"

Mark ran a blunt fingertip over the road on the map. "This war will be over someday. I have to live the rest of my life with what the war has done to me."

Rachel crossed to his side of the desk and stood beside him. "I wish more Continental officers thought like you. I wish my father thought like you."

"He does," Mark said.

"Does he?"

"With regards to his men, he does."

"I wish he thought the same way toward himself. He keeps himself busy at war because he can't live with himself otherwise."

Mark leaned his head against the top of hers. Would it be possible for him to stay with her?

As if reading her thoughts, Mark smiled. "I want to stay, Rachel. But there are my men to consider."

She took his hand. "We also have to survive the next few weeks."

"That we do."

The next day, Mark went to discuss their plan with his men, and Rachel had to discuss it with Hannah and Granny. She'd brought along a map that she drew herself, and she pointed to the different areas as she explained her and Mark's ideas.

"An explosion is very possible," Granny said.

"Could you do it safely?" Rachel asked. "Set an explosion large enough to draw their attention?"

"I think so," Granny said. "You're not expecting us to fight the redcoats off when they come running, are you?"

"Of course not," Rachel said. "We'd see that the explosion was near enough to a hiding place."

"The biggest unknown I see in this plan is the Continentals," Hannah said.

"That's where you come in." Rachel searched her sister's face. "We would need Isaac's help."

Hannah's lips thinned. "What about Father?"

"We'll ask him too. The more Continentals we can get, the greater chance we have at success. But Hannah, you have to decide whether or not to tell Isaac about our work."

"He might already know, child." Granny patted Hannah's arm.

"I've never told him. I haven't made any deliveries since he's been here either."

"True," Granny said. "Are you going to tell him?"

Hannah looked like she might cry. "I might have to."

"Would that be so bad? It worked out well with Mark," Rachel said. "In fact, Mark is helping us with our work."

"What about Abigail?"

Rachel looked around the faces at the women she trusted with her life. "Only you can make that decision, Hannah."

"What else do we need to do?" Hannah said, changing the subject.

Rachel took a deep breath. This was where it could get overwhelming.

"We need to keep delivering supplies."

"More 'special' bullets for the regulars too," Granny added. "We wouldn't want them feeling left out."

Rachel's heart warmed with satisfaction at her friends' fast acceptance of this plan. And hope stirred within her after her conversation with Mark. This could work. She could have a real marriage with Mark. They would just have to fight together for the future they both wanted. That evening, when they both returned home, Mark greeted Rachel with a kiss that made her toes curl. Pulling back, he grinned at her.

"I take it your men approved of the plan?" Rachel said.

"They want you to be a part of our regiment. What do we do next?"

"My friends suggested delivering more supplies to the redcoats in the next few days, whatever we can spare."

Mark grimaced, but to his credit he didn't complain. "What kind of supplies?"

"Probably more defective bullets. Mrs. Bell has given us some of her husband's scrap metal."

It would be a strange way to honor the late blacksmith's memory, but Rachel suspected Mr. Bell would approve.

"Can I help?" Mark said.

"Make the bullets?"

Mark nodded.

"I suppose so, if you'd like. We were going to make them tomorrow or the next day."

"Good," Mark said. "It's a way for me to feel useful without hurting my knee."

Granny came over to help Mark and Rachel make bullets, and Mark was happy to be doing something that he'd actually done before. Granny had reheated the metal in a way that made it brittle, and that combined with a hollow mold made bullets that would ruin any gun they were fired out of.

"This is brilliant, Mrs. Greene," Mark said, for what felt like the fifth time, as he held some warm bullets in his hands.

"Thank you," Granny said. "I hope they can do some damage."

"We'll find out soon enough," Rachel said. She was filing each bullet down with easy confidence, as if she'd done this hundreds of times. Perhaps she had.

Mark poured more hot metal into the mold Granny had created.

Rachel was trying to calm herself down – no matter how many of these deliveries she made, they didn't get any easier – and approached the redcoats' camp with her saddlebags loaded with defective bullets. Hopefully she wouldn't encounter the man who'd attacked her again.

"Ah, Mrs. Johnson. Good to see you again." Sergeant Neumann came to greet her at the entrance to the camp.

"You as well, Sergeant. I've brought some more bullets."

"I'm sure my men will appreciate them. Thank you."

This was normally where Rachel would let the men unload her saddlebags and she'd get out of camp as soon as possible, but Rachel lingered, looking down at the Sergeant.

"We're also working on some cloaks and blankets for you. The winter will only get colder. I should be able to bring them next week."

"Very good. Thank you."

"And my friend Charity – the one I mentioned to you – her brother would like to show you some of the rifles he makes. Would early next week suit you?"

Sergeant Neumann tilted his head, studying her. "Yes," he said at last. "You may set that up."

"Perfect," Rachel said. She'd write a note to Charity when she got home. "Expect to hear from her soon."

CHAPTER 20

Once she'd written the note to Charity and tucked it into her apron pocket, Rachel and Mark set to work cleaning the barn. Will came around the corner, whistling, his hands in his pockets. He always seemed to be cheerful.

Mark smiled at the sight of his sergeant. "Is all well?"

"We're running out of supplies," Will said.

"Are you going to the store?" Mark said. Ezekiel, with the help of several people from town, had reconstructed a smaller version of his store and they were working to get it stocked again.

"I thought about it; would it arouse too much suspicion?"

"Probably. We can go for you if you finish cleaning out the barn," Rachel said with a cheeky smile. "I have a note to send anyway."

In answer, Will picked up a pitchfork. "What happened to you, Miss Rachel? To your – " he gestured to her cheek.

Rachel reflexively put her hand over her face, covering the bruise.

"It was one of the redcoats," Mark said.

Will gripped the pitchfork until his knuckles went white. "He struck you?"

"Yes."

"Captain," Will said. He was the most jocular man Rachel had ever met, but a change came over him at that moment. When his good humor left his face, he looked downright lethal.

"I took care of him," Mark said.

"Oh," Will said, eyebrows raised. "All right then. Well done, Captain."

Will got to work scooping hay, and Rachel put on the cloak that she'd hung on a peg on the wall. When they reached the store, there were a few people browsing the sparsely-restocked shelves.

"I'm sorry we don't have much," Abigail said. "We've only been able to replace what people have donated. Everyone's lean right now."

Rachel put her arm around her friend, leading her away from Mark. "How are you doing?"

Abigail was pale and drawn, with dark circles under her eyes. She leaned against the wall and closed her eyes for a moment.

"Sometimes it all seems like too much," she said.

"Has Ezekiel recovered?"

"Some. But I worry – I worry he won't be able to manage the store. I have to follow him around. He's trying his hardest, but he forgets. He forgets how to do basic things. He forgets what he's doing in the middle of a task. So far it's been small things, but I worry it will cause real problems."

Rachel couldn't think of anything comforting to say, so she let her friend continue.

"And our house is a mess, the barn a mess – it's all a mess because I have to be here at the store with Ezekiel all the time."

At least that was something Rachel could help with. "Let Mark and I help."

"You would do that?" she raised her eyebrows. "After Ezekiel has treated you so poorly?"

"You're my friend," Rachel said. "We might not be able to be what we once were, but we will always be friends."

Abigail enveloped her in an impulsive hug, and stepped back. "I'd better check the front. I have to review Ezekiel's account totals without him knowing I'm doing it."

Rachel laughed at the thought, then quickly sobered. Ezekiel and Abigail weren't farmers. They'd taken over the store from Ezekiel's father, and this had been their livelihood for years. What would they do if Ezekiel, a proud man, needed help?

"So we're helping with this in exchange for supplies from the store?" Will said.

"Not exactly," Mark replied. Will had heard about what had happened with the redcoats, and he'd known that Ezekiel had been injured. But Mark didn't think he knew the full extent of Ezekiel's injury. It was sobering, seeing how the blow to the head had affected the other man. That could have been Mark.

"So he can't remember anything?" Will said.

"It's not that he can't remember anything," Rachel said, tossing handfuls of feed to the Elliotts' chickens. "His memory is – fragile at the moment."

Will pursed his lips and looked between Mark and Rachel. "Isn't he the one who made you get married?"

"He didn't make us do anything," Mark said. "But he did see Rachel and I, yes."

"And spread rumors about us all over town."

There were a few beats of silence between the three of them, then Will continued. "I don't see why you're helping him."

"He's a good man, deep down," Rachel said. Mark still wasn't sure about that, but he trusted Rachel's opinion. "His wife Abigail is a good friend of mine, and we're doing this for her as much as for him. They usually share the housework and work at the store together, but right now Abigail is trying to do all of it herself."

Will held his hands up. "I see. And I'm happy to help. Anything different than watching the same group of –"

He stopped talking when Mark made a slashing motion across his throat.

"The same group of trees," Will said, looking around.

"And where are you from, Will?" Rachel asked, not-so-subtly changing the subject.

"White Plains."

Mark smiled at his friend. They'd grown up together, with Will's family becoming a second family for Mark in many ways.

"Are they living?" Rachel asked gently.

"Yes," he said. "I miss them."

Would Mark have a family to miss when he went back to the war? Was he even going back at this point? He would miss Rachel, but would she miss him? She seemed fond of him, but they'd been so caught up with the conflict with the redcoats that they hadn't *talked* lately.

Silence fell between them again, and Mark worked, methodically cleaning out the shed that housed a single cow - it was a miracle the redcoats hadn't stolen this cow when they burned down the store. The cow was very friendly, and kept nudging Mark's pockets, looking for treats, he suspected. He rubbed the cow's ear absently. After the war, would he and Rachel keep animals together? Where would they live? He thought she would like White Plains and adore his mother, but how could he ask her to leave her family's home?

The fact was that it didn't make sense to ask Rachel to leave her work, especially while the war was as vicious as it had ever been. Perhaps that could be a conversation they could have one day.

A few days later, Rachel rode with Mark to Lieutenant Feldman's camp to ask for his help with their plan. Mark had insisted on coming, but at the moment Rachel was wishing she had left him behind.

"I should be with them," Mark said to Rachel, for the fifth time in the past hour. The wagon rattled down the road behind them, and Rachel tried to be calm so she wouldn't make Mark nervous. His men were doing some scouting today, and Mark was conflicted, which Rachel understood.

Rachel tilted back the brim of her hat, facing him. "Do you want to ride back and join them? I can do this on my own."

"No." Mark sighed. "I want to meet Lieutenant Feldman. And tell him of our plan."

"And you said you wanted to avoid combat if you could," Rachel said softly. That was hard to bring up, but he'd told her that the night before, after he couldn't fall asleep for hours after one of his episodes. They seemed to be brought on by combat, or thinking about combat. Or fighting of any kind.

"You're right," Mark said. He put his arm around her and drew her to his side. When she'd met him, she never would have guessed that he was such an affectionate man. He'd seemed cold, gruff. And he still could be at times. But it felt so good to know that he could be warm and giving as well.

They made it to Lieutenant Feldman's camp without incident, and Mark's arm tightened around her instinctively when they rode past the guards. The camp looked much the same as the last time Rachel had been here, and the men looked at her and Mark with open curiosity. It was comforting to have Mark with her. Despite his fretting, she was glad that he had come.

"Mrs. Johnson!" Lieutenant Feldman stood near one of the cook-fires, eating a hard biscuit. "So glad to see you! I hope you had safe travels. I see you've brought us some more supplies. Who is this?"

"This is my husband," Rachel said. "Captain Mark Johnson."

"Pleased to meet you, Captain. Your wife and her sister have been very useful to us. We would've been in rough shape without them."

Pride stirred in Rachel's chest, and she grinned at the Lieutenant from her seat on the wagon. "Now we have a favor to ask of you in return, Lieutenant."

"I'm listening," he said.

Rachel looked to Mark. This would sound better coming from another soldier.

"If you and your men happened to march due north on Monday, you might encounter a group of redcoats," Mark said.

"How many?"

Charity had sent word to them that morning that she'd invited forty men to her home on the following Monday.

"Twenty to forty."

Lieutenant Feldman tilted his head. "What are you planning?"

"Why ruin the surprise?" Rachel said.

"Mrs. Johnson, if I'm to risk my men's lives, I'd like to know why I am doing so."

Rachel looked to Mark again, but he raised his eyebrows, refusing to speak for her.

"It will be for the Cause," Rachel said. "There will be risk, but it will pay off if you will help us." She sat up straighter and looked the man in the eye, letting her words hang in the air.

"Well then," Lieutenant Feldman said. "I think I'll do that. My men will march north that morning. We'll take our time about it until we meet up with the redcoats you've mentioned. Hopefully it all works out, whatever you're planning."

Rachel knew that their plan was a leap of faith. But she desperately hoped it worked. By the time they finished their conversation, the wagon had been emptied and it was time to ride back home.

"You did well," Mark said as they rode back.

Rachel smiled at him. "I suppose I did, didn't I?"

On the way back into Freehold, they stopped by Hannah's home to tell her of their success. The front door stood ajar, which made Rachel's senses instantly alert.

Mark handed her the reins. "I'll look inside first."

Rachel's stomach churned as she parked the wagon and tied the horses up, petting their flanks. Mark came back to the doorway. "It's Isaac."

"What happened?" Rachel said, pushing past him into Hannah's sitting room.

Groaning from the kitchen drew her in there. Hannah was holding a bloody cloth to Issac's leg, and she was pale as a sheet.

Rachel's senses dulled and she went to her brother-in-law, looking for other injuries.

"It appears to just be his leg," Hannah said, far too calmly. Rachel took a deep breath, the scent of blood in her nose and mouth. "There's a bullet. I – I can't –" Hannah's calm facade cracked, and her voice ended in a sob.

Mark shifted his weight in the doorway. "I'll get Edward. Uh, Edward Smith. He's the surgeon for my men. I'll take one of the horses."

Rachel gave him a small smile of gratitude, but he was already gone. She filled a pot with water to boil over the fire, and pulled more bandages out of Hannah's cabinet.

Isaac wasn't conscious, which might be a mercy. His face was pale and grey. Judging by the trail of blood coming in from the front door and the wads of bandages already used, he had lost a great deal of blood already.

Hannah didn't seem to want to leave Isaac's side or to speak, so Rachel watched the water, waiting for it to boil, and picked up a rag to clean up the blood on the floor.

Mark unhitched the horses from the wagon, used the wagon seat to help him mount, then rode one horse toward where his men were encamped. The other horse trotted alongside him, and Mark's thoughts raced. That was a bullet wound. How had Isaac, a soldier on furlough, gotten a bullet wound? Would he live?

If he didn't, what would that do to Hannah? And to Rachel? His heart raced, but he couldn't afford to lose his calm right now. He needed to fetch Edward, and quickly.

His men were clustered in their cave encampment, eating dinner, when Mark burst in, breathing hard from the climb up the hill. "Edward," he said. "I need your help. Now."

To their credit, his men snapped to attention instantly, and Edward was following Mark down the hill with his bag in hand within a minute. Will and Jim followed behind them on foot while Mark rode off with the surgeon in tow.

"Tell me," Edward shouted as they went down the road at a canter.

"It's Rachel's brother-in-law, Isaac Wellington. He's been shot."

"Is he a Continental?"

"Yes, but he's on furlough."

Mark couldn't see the other man's face under the brim of his tricorne hat, but the silence spoke volumes. By the time they returned to Hannah's house, despair weighed heavily on Mark's shoulders.

Edward moved to Hannah's side and went to work immediately. Rachel was scrubbing the trail of blood off the floor, and Mark grabbed a rag to help her. It would be best if he didn't watch what Edward had to do.

Rachel watched the water in her bucket turn an eerie pink as she cleaned the blood from the floor. Mark helped her, but they didn't speak. She tried not to listen to the sound of Dr. Smith performing surgery on Isaac in the next room; there was nothing she could do to help. Hannah stood next to her husband, lending her silent support.

She still wasn't sure what had happened, but that could have been Mark. That could have been Mark clinging to life on the kitchen table. Rachel had fallen in love with her husband, but he could be snatched away from her so quickly. Dread filled her stomach at the thought. But dread wouldn't help Hannah. After the floor was reasonably clean, Rachel and Mark brought a straw mattress downstairs and set it up in front of the fire in the sitting room. It would have to be a sick bed of sorts for Isaac as he recovered.

Rachel dared to look in the kitchen, and saw Dr. Smith washing his hands in the hot water Rachel had prepared.

"I extracted the bullet and sewed up the wound," he said. Dr. Smith was a quiet man, but he seemed calm and methodical in his work, which Rachel was grateful for.

"Will he be all right?" Rachel asked, because Hannah hadn't. Hannah still stood there, her eyes on her husband, looking pale and drawn.

Dr. Smith's lips thinned. He was about Mark's age, but there was a sadness about him that made him seem older; perhaps he had seen too much of war. "He might be. I was able to extract the whole bullet in one piece, which bodes well. It will just be a matter of staving off infection."

Mark squeezed Dr. Smith's shoulders. "Thank you. Let's move him to the sitting room."

While the men moved Isaac, who thankfully hadn't regained consciousness, to the sitting room, Rachel brewed some coffee. She helped Hannah wash her hands, and poured her a cup.

Rachel sat with Hannah in the sitting room while Mark rode back to camp with Dr. Smith.

"He was just trying to help," Hannah said when the men had gone. "He was only trying to help."

"Trying to help?"

Hannah nodded, looking into the fire. "He had climbed a tree;

wanted to watch the redcoats on the road. Make sure none of them came too close to us. They shot him for no reason."

That sounded like Sergeant Neumann's troops. Rage coursed through Rachel, but she sipped her coffee. They would drive the redcoats away, and soon. But would Isaac live to see it?

Mark returned, limping into the sitting room. He poured himself a cup of coffee and sat opposite Rachel and Hannah. Rachel gave him a smile that she hoped showed her gratitude for his quick actions. After they'd sat there awhile, her rage solidified into fatigue that weighed her down.

"You don't need to stay," Hannah said.

"Of course I do," Rachel replied.

Mark stood. "I'll bring the horses back home and close up the house for the night."

He kissed Rachel's forehead, patted Hannah's shoulder, and left.

"He's a good man, Rachel," Hannah said. "If you had to marry, I'm glad it was him."

"I'm glad it was too."

Hannah had insisted on sleeping on the floor with Isaac, so when night fell, Mark led Rachel up the stairs to Hannah and Isaac's spare bedroom. They were both too tired to talk much, but Mark needed the comfort of his wife after the day they'd had. Under the quilts, he pulled her into his arms, and she came willingly. Rachel had been strong all day, doing what needed to be done. But Mark knew first-hand how that strength would cost her.

As Mark held her and sifted his fingers through her hair, Rachel's tears wet the front of his shirt. He let her cry, too wrung out to cry himself. After a time, Rachel went quiet and he thought she was asleep.

"That could have been you," she said softly against his chest.

Mark knew she needed comfort, but he couldn't lie to her. "Yes, it could have been."

He pulled her closer, and she wrapped her arms around his neck, burying her face in the spot where his neck met his shoulders. Mark couldn't offer her any comfort when he was battling despair himself. So he just held her like that, until they both drifted off into an uneasy sleep.

Rachel awoke warm in her husband's arms. She didn't want to get up and face whatever had happened to her sister, but she needed to. She needed to be brave.

Downstairs, Dr. Smith had returned, and was making a pot of coffee. There was a gentleness to him that made Rachel trust him implicitly, even without Mark's recommendation. Hannah still slept at Isaac's side, but Isaac was awake, sweat beading his brow.

"How is he?" Mark asked, buttoning his waistcoat.

"Awake," Edward said. "I gave him some laudanum, but he's still in a great deal of pain. There's nothing else I can do."

They on the sofa, drinking their coffee and trying not to worry. Hannah woke up eventually, and she sat up, looking down at her husband.

"Hannah," he croaked. "I was trying to – "

Hannah took Isaac's hand. "You don't need to speak of it if you don't wish to."

"I want to tell you," Isaac said. "I was trying to help – with the plan. I climbed a tree outside the British camp. Wanted to see what they were doing. They heard me – they are good with those rifles. Shot my leg."

"I know."

Isaac squeezed her hand. "Climbed down. Well, fell down more than climbed. You – you found me. You helped me."

Hannah, who had remained stoic for this entire ordeal, finally let the tears fall down her face. And Rachel's heart broke for her sister.

Was it all worth it? All of them, laying their lives on the line? Rachel didn't know at the moment.

Rachel stood quickly. She went straight through the kitchen and out to the yard to feed Hannah's chickens and horses. The fresh air would do her good.

Mark came out a few minutes later, bringing her a piece of bread with preserves on it.

"Thank you," Rachel said, taking a bite. When was the last time she'd eaten?

"Edward said that he doesn't have a fever yet," Mark said, eating his own piece of bread. "That's a good sign, Rachel."

"It is," she said halfheartedly. The worry that was pressing on her chest wouldn't let up, though.

They muddled through the day as best they could, taking turns watching over Isaac. Rachel persuaded Hannah to eat some dinner. Mark rode back and forth, looking after their house and checking on his men.

By the end of the day, Hannah seemed more like herself. Isaac wasn't out of the woods by any means, but Hannah seemed to have pulled herself together enough to order Rachel and Mark to return home and get some sleep. Rachel reluctantly agreed.

"You'll come and get us if anything changes," she said to her sister as she put on her cloak at Hannah's front door. "Mark can get Dr. Smith in a matter of minutes."

"I will," Hannah said, smiling bravely despite her pallor. Rachel hugged her sister, then took her husband's hand as the daylight faded.

"Let me take care of you," Mark said when they were in their bedroom. There was a tightness in his voice and in his movements that made Rachel want to let him do this. Perhaps he needed it too. She sat down on the bed and Mark gently pulled the pins from her hair, setting them in a dish on the nightstand.

Rachel let her thoughts drift as he brushed her hair. The hairbrush felt heavenly against her scalp, and she tried to let the tension melt from her body. She tried.

It could have been Rachel that was hurt, but it could also have been Mark. It still very well could be Mark. How would she feel, if the man she had come to – she had come to love – was at death's door? Mark braided her hair and tied it with one of the pieces of leather he used to tie his own hair back. Rachel ran the piece of leather between her fingertips, watching as Mark undressed and cleaned his teeth.

"I don't know how you do this," she said to Mark when she was in bed beside him, tucked into his arms. "Knowing this could happen to you or any of your friends, at any time."

"Sometimes I don't know how I do either. You've seen what this has done to me."

She had seen that. "At least you acknowledge it. And you want to get better."

"I do." Mark sighed heavily. "I still think our plan is the best we can do. I think it has a chance of working."

"Will your men still be willing to help, in light of what has happened?"

"They'll be more motivated now than ever," Mark said. "This has to work."

"Monday?"

Mark nodded against the top of her head. "Monday. Lieutenant Feldman has made that clear. It's that day or wait until the spring. And nobody in Freehold wants to wait for the spring, I'm sure."

"And you'll go back after the work is done?" Rachel hated to ask, but that was the question that had been weighing on her mind. She and Mark were close. She wanted a real marriage with him, but he was a soldier, and she'd never want to ask him to choose between her and the men he considered to be his family. How could she?

And yet, how could she not?

"I'm not sure," Mark said. "It will depend on what your father wants me to do. And the decision I come to about my – my mind. I already feel fractured. How much worse could it get if I continued to fight, and continued to place stress upon it?"

"I don't know."

"Neither do I. I don't want to leave you, Rachel. You know that, I hope."

"I do." Rachel wasn't sure what else to say, so she kissed her husband instead.

CHAPTER 21

The next day was Saturday, and Mark and Granny set off on horseback first thing in the morning. They gave the redcoat camp a wide berth and rode toward the east. Rachel had wanted to stay with Hannah and Isaac, but if they wanted Monday to work, they needed to prepare. That couldn't wait.

"How far away can you set an explosion that could be seen from the camp?" he asked as they rode.

"Perhaps another mile or so."

That would draw the redcoats two or three miles away from their camp to the east. Hopefully that would be enough.

"And we haven't the manpower to fight them," Mark said. "So it will be a matter of taking the camp and holding it."

"I'm sure you boys will do well," Granny said.

They were riding slowly enough so as not to attract notice, and so far things were quiet. Granny rode well, sitting atop her mount like a queen with her purple headscarf.

"You and Rachel seem to be getting along well," she said.

"We are."

"I'm happy for you. You both deserve each other."

A grin spread across his face. "Thank you Mrs. Greene."

"You may call me Granny."

Mark's heart lifted. "Thank you, Granny. How did you meet your husband?" He'd been wondering that, and this was as good a time as any to ask.

She tilted her chin up to look toward the horizon, then looked back at Mark. "We were slaves in the same household. But we escaped together."

Mark couldn't think of a thing to say to that, so he let her continue.

"That was thirty years ago." Granny didn't elaborate. He supposed he hadn't earned enough of her trust yet to hear the full story.

"And you've lived in Freehold ever since?"

"For the most part."

Mark blew out a breath. "That's incredible."

"We were lucky," Granny said sadly. "There were – and still are – many who aren't so lucky."

"And how did you learn about explosives?"

She answered that question with a grin. "My master had us dig out a well once. We learned a great deal from the experience, and I've been experimenting ever since."

"I'm grateful," Mark said. "This will help. This might make the difference between success and failure."

Mark stopped his horse. He carried Granny's canvas sack for her – or he started to, anyway.

"Let me carry that, honey. I don't want you jostling any of my explosives."

Mark handed it back to her, eager to have it out of his hands. "By all means."

They climbed the nearest hill on foot, and when they reached the top, they could see all the way to the sea, glittering on the horizon. It was lovely, with the snowy trees and the blue sky and the quietness of the morning. Mark took a deep breath of the cold air, standing next to Granny. She assessed the area, pacing the clearing, but she seemed satisfied with the place they'd chosen.

"Will this spot work?" Mark said.

Granny nodded. "It's on a hill and the spot can be seen for miles. It's perfect."

"Good," Mark said. "Will you set the explosives tomorrow?"

"Yes. Early that morning. If I ride fast, I can get here in twenty minutes."

Mark looked around for a place for Granny to hide once she'd set the explosives. There was a small cave lower on the hill that might work.

"Would this place be suitable for hiding?"

Granny shook her head. "No – that's just a cleft in a rock. We'd be far too cold. Come with me," she said.

In a secluded area of the forest down the hill, Granny led him to a shack.

"This barely looks like it's standing, let alone able to shelter you."

She grinned at him. "Haven't you learned by now not to underestimate us?"

Chastened, Mark blushed. "I'm sorry."

Granny opened the door to the shack and led him inside. In the dim light, he saw that the shack had been reinforced from the inside, and there was a trap door in the middle of the floor.

Granny heaved the trap door open and peered into the dimness below.

"Let me guess," Mark said. "That cellar is stocked with food and supplies, enough that you could be comfortable here for several days."

"I wouldn't be comfortable," Granny said. "I'd be cold. But I could stay here for several days."

Mark shook his head. "Whose idea were these cellars?"

"Rachel's mother, God rest her soul. She started all of this work. But her daughters have stepped into her shoes nicely."

"That they have," Mark said. "I wish I could've met her."

Granny looked at him shrewdly. "I'd like to be polite and tell you that she'd love you, but I'm not sure. The Colonel is a good man, but he wasn't the best husband to his wife. She might have mistrusted you on sight."

Mark didn't respond right away. "I suppose it's a miracle that Rachel has chosen to trust me, isn't it?"

"It is," Granny said. "And don't ever forget it."

When he and Granny were satisfied with the location they'd chosen for the explosion, they rode back to Freehold.

It was Sunday, the day before they were to enact their plan, and there were a few details that they needed to work out. Rachel's friends and Mark's men were gathered in Rachel's sitting room, going through all the details for the hundredth time. Rachel had to hand it to Mark: he was commanding, making sure that everyone in the room knew every detail of the plan.

"There's one thing we haven't worked out though," Will said, frowning. "How will we get into the camp once we've cleared out as many redcoats as we can?"

Mark crossed his arms. "We'll have to fight our way in. It might get messy, but I don't see another way."

Rachel felt the idea burning in her mind, and wanted to speak up, but she could practically hear Hannah's disapproving voice. Yet as she looked at Mark, she remembered how brave she had learned to be in the past few weeks. She liked being brave.

"I have an idea." Rachel's voice was barely above a whisper, so she cleared her throat and spoke again. "I have an idea."

Every head in the room turned to look at her, and heat rose to her cheeks. "It might be foolish, though."

"By all means," Mark said.

Rachel stood, clasping her hands in front of her. The eyes of a dozen trained soldiers were on her, and she straightened her shoulders. "Sergeant Neumann expects a delivery of clothing from me in the next few days. The wagon has a deep bed. What if some of you hid in the bed of the wagon, underneath the clothing? I could drive the wagon into the camp, wait for the right moment, and give some kind of signal."

"And we could climb out of the wagon and surprise them," Mark said. "A trojan horse of sorts."

"Exactly," Rachel said.

"And how would you get to safety?" Mark said, his face grave.

That was the part that Rachel was trying not to think about. "I could roll under the wagon."

"What if the horses were spooked?" Hannah said. She'd insisted on coming to this meeting, declaring that Isaac wanted it this way. "Rachel, this is foolishness. Surely you know that."

Rachel knew the words were coming, but she fought the urge to shrink under them. "I'll think that through. But it could work. And it could save lives."

"By putting your own at risk?" Granny said gently.

Mark's warm arm went around her shoulders. "I think it's brilliant."

"If she were a man, she'd be a major general in no time," Will said. Rachel smiled at the compliment, though her friends were looking at her as if she'd gone daft.

"You can't consider this, Rachel," Hannah said. "I can't lose both you and Isaac."

"Isaac will heal," Rachel said to Hannah with more confidence than she felt. Isaac was hanging onto his life, still laid out on his sitting room floor. He'd been much the same for the past two days, waking occasionally to drink some broth. There was no fever, though, and that was a great sign.

"Rachel might not wear the uniform, " Mark said. "But she is a soldier in this war, the same as every person in this room. And as such, only she can decide the risks she wants to take."

Tears sprang to Rachel's eyes. It wasn't terribly romantic, her husband defending her ability to risk her life. But he respected her like nobody else in her life. And that was why she loved Mark Johnson.

"We'll work it out," Granny said.

"We're running out of time," Jim said. "We have one more day."

"You're doing this all wrong," Jim said to Will, who lay crouched in the bed of the wagon that afternoon.

Will sat up and used his rifle to push himself to his feet. "Fine. You try."

Mark was sitting behind Rachel on the bench of the wagon, both of them facing the wagon itself, which was currently stuffed with four of his men and their weapons.

Jim climbed into the bed of the wagon, steadying himself on the wall of Rachel's barn, where the wagon was hidden.

"Climb out, all of you," Jim said.

Edward, Tom, and Will climbed out, grumbling about it.

"I still think I should stay with Isaac," Edward said, brushing dust off of his breeches.

"We need all of us if we are to stand a chance," Mark said. As it was, all of their best efforts might not be enough. He fought back the worry that threatened to cripple him. His men needed him to be fearless right now, and Rachel needed him to be strong. He had no room for weakness.

"What do you think, Jim?" Mark said.

The other man paced the bed of the wagon, testing its strength. "I think we should cut a hole in this wagon."

"I beg your pardon," Rachel said. "I just got that wagon back; I'd prefer you don't cut any holes in it."

"What we could do, Miss Rachel," Jim said. "Is cut a hole large enough to slip through; a trap door, if you will."

Mark was beginning to see Jim's idea in his mind, and a grin spread across his face. He watched with pride the moment the realization dawned on his wife as well.

"And some of you would slip out beneath the wagon?" Rachel said.

"It would be easier than trying to climb out the top." Jim rested his hands on his hips.

Mark pictured the sequence of events, thinking through everything that could go wrong. "I like it, Jim. That does seem less risky."

"I'll get an ax," Will said. "Where do you keep yours, Miss Rachel? Unless you'd like to do the honors?"

Rachel laughed. "I'll leave you to it."

It did Mark's heart good to hear his wife's laughter, despite all of the worries in his mind. An hour later, they'd built a crude trapdoor into the bottom of the wagon.

"Now we have to arrange ourselves again," Will said. "And our weapons."

Mark climbed into the back of the wagon. "I'll throw the hatch when Rachel gives us the signal. That means I have to be here."

He lay down on his side. It was uncomfortable, but it would work. And he could carry an ax, his knives, and a pistol.

"It feels strange not to have any rifles," Will said, climbing in beside Mark. "Mine will miss me so."

"Your rifle is safe under the seat," Rachel said from overhead.

"You know why." Jim climbed on Mark's other side, lying next to him. At least they wouldn't be cold. "Rifles are too slow and too large for what we need to do."

"There's one problem." Tom's face appeared over the top of the wagon. "I won't fit. Not unless I lay on top of all of you."

Will groaned. "Let's try again."

After they were in bed that night, Rachel watched Mark with open sadness in her expression. She didn't want to say goodbye to him yet,

and that was entirely possible, given what they had planned for the next day. Mark climbed into bed next to her and pulled her into his arms.

"It's killing me to see you looking so frightened."

"I'll try to stop," she said with a watery laugh.

"I love you, you know," Mark said against her hair. That startled her; he'd never told her that before.

"You do?"

Mark nodded, meeting her eyes. She saw nothing but sincerity in his face, and her heart ached. "I love you too."

Mark grinned. "This will all work out. You'll see."

Once Rachel fell asleep, Mark eased his way out from underneath her and lit a candle. He was too nervous to sleep, and he had to do something with all the energy coursing through him. He wanted to show Rachel how much she meant to him.

He tiptoed downstairs, walking into Colonel Staples' office. A stack of paper sat in an orderly pile on the desk. If he didn't make it through the next day, Mark wanted to give Rachel something to remember him by.

Mark opened the bottle of ink and got out a pen. Taking a deep breath, he began to write.

Rachel awoke to a warm bed with Mark sleeping softly beside her. She hadn't the heart to wake him yet, so she sat up. Beside her on the nightstand was a letter that hadn't been there the night before.

She opened the seal.

Dear Rachel,

Meeting you is the best thing that ever happened to me. If I don't come back home today, know that I wish I could've spent my entire life being your husband. I love you.

Mark

Her heart ached. He'd known how much this would mean to her, and he'd made the extra effort to make sure she felt loved. And she'd repay him by making him the best cup of coffee he'd ever had in his life.

"How are you so calm?" Mark asked when he finally pried himself out of bed.

Rachel whistled as she cooked them a simple breakfast. Mark could barely stomach his coffee.

"I'm excited," Rachel said. "And hopeful."

Mark wished he could be the same. Usually before an assignment like this, he would be nervous because his men's lives depended on him. But today there was the added pressure of Rachel's life being on the line as well. Mark's men came into the kitchen, all seriousness, as soon as it was light enough to see.

"Is everything ready?" Jim asked.

Mark nodded.

"Good. Tom, go." Mark gestured to Tom Jones, who took off running for the British camp. Tom would watch the action unfold and come back when the time was right.

They scarfed down their breakfast. Rachel fed the animals, then they went out to the barn and harnessed a horse to the wagon. They were all too nervous to do anything else, Mark especially, so they paced in the barn.

About two hours later, Tom came running back.

"It's time," he said, breathing hard. "The camp is as empty as it's going to get." He gasped for air. "Granny set an impressive explosion."

All right then. Mark and his men climbed into the wagon, fitting themselves into the wagon bed in a kind of puzzle. It was tricky with their weapons, but they'd finally found the best way the night before. Rachel covered them with layers of fabric, making sure they had enough room to breathe. Then she stacked empty wooden boxes on top of that. The aim was to disguise Mark and his men so Rachel could choose the right moment for them to appear.

"Heaven help us," Rachel said. The wagon rattled onto the road, and Mark tried to calm his racing heart.

This part of the plan was entirely in Rachel's hands. Their surprise depended on her steady nerves. Luckily Mark had complete faith in his wife.

CHAPTER 22

It was too late to turn back now. That thought echoed through Rachel's mind as she drove the wagon to the camp. Had it only been weeks ago that she'd driven to this camp for the first time? Mark's men were silent in the bed of the wagon, covered in layers of fabric and boxes.

The redcoats waved to her as she rode into the camp; the guards didn't even question her presence this time. The camp only contained about twenty soldiers that Rachel could see; their plan had worked. At least the part that had been executed so far. It would all be for naught, though, if Mark's men couldn't do their part. Sergeant Neumann appeared at the entrance to his tent and greeted Rachel with a wave.

"Good morning Mrs. Johnson. I've sent some of my officers to Ms. Marshall's house to take a look at her weapons. Thank you for setting that up. Have you brought us the clothes you promised?"

"I have," Rachel said. She pulled the wagon around so the horse was facing the entrance to the camp, and climbed down.

The harness rattled in her shaking hands as she undid the buckles.

"Problem with your harness?" the Sergeant said. He and his men moved the empty wooden boxes out of the bed of the wagon. Rachel had a moment or two to act.

"It's only loose, I suspect."

At the last word out of Rachel's mouth, Mark's men burst from the bed of the wagon, above and below, and sprung into action. Rachel climbed onto the horse's back and pressed her knees into his sides. She galloped toward the entrance of the camp. Rachel didn't look back. That was the agreement she'd made with Mark. Though there were shouts, screams, and gunfire behind her, Rachel rode like her life depended on it.

She'd scarcely made it past the entrance of the camp when there was a tug on her cloak, and she lost her grip on the horse. Toppling to the ground, she rolled away from the horse, who was still galloping down the road. Rachel lay there for a moment, breathing hard and making sure nothing was broken. She'd hit her shoulder when she fell, but other than that she was unharmed. She didn't move, though, not until she knew what was going on around her.

Sergeant Neumann stood over her, loading his pistol.

Mark had watched Rachel ride out of camp. He'd told himself to concentrate on the battle, but of course he hadn't been able to take his eyes off of his wife. Sergeant Neumann had seen her too, and was following her out of camp. She didn't make it very far. Mark ignored the chaos around him and sprinted after Rachel. He reached her side as Sergeant Neumann finished loading his rifle, standing above Rachel and breathing hard. Mark's heart was pounding and he didn't hear anything else but the clink of the bullets being loaded. Mark took Rachel's hand, tucking her behind him.

"I don't want to do this, you know," Neumann said. The British soldier loaded the bullets slowly, deliberately. Mark felt his whole body go cold. "But you gave me no choice."

Mark had time for one last prayer before Sergeant Neumann pulled the trigger.

CHAPTER 23

Rachel had seen the stars stamped into the bullets that Sergeant Neumann loaded into his pistol. She'd seen them, and she'd prayed that Granny's idea had worked.

The shot of the pistol was loud, so loud, and Rachel instinctively ducked, pulling Mark with her.

Sergeant Neumann's pistol hit the ground with a thud and he clutched his face, blood streaming from between his fingers. Rachel grabbed Mark's hand and they hauled themselves off the road and into the forest, running along the outside wall of the encampment.

"You," Mark said. "Are brilliant. Did you know that?"

"That was all Granny," Rachel said. "Be sure to thank her."

"I will."

Mark absolutely couldn't believe it. He pulled Rachel against a wall of the encampment, tucked against the stacked logs, and hid, shielding her with his body. The fighting was dying down, but Mark wouldn't be able to live with himself if Rachel was hurt because of him. Rachel tucked her hand into the collar of his shirt, resting her palm against his skin. That contact kept him breathing, kept him calm.

"It'll be alright," she said.

Mark was beginning to believe it would be.

Eventually the noise died down, and Mark stood from his crouched position, walking around to the entrance of the camp. Somehow, the Continentals had taken the camp. A weight lifted from Mark's shoulders at the sight of a dozen or so redcoats being loaded into a wagon. Jim was supervising. Every minute that passed brought more Continental soldiers, and Will stood by the entrance, greeting them as they came in. One soldier in particular Mark recognized, and he reached out to shake Lieutenant Feldman's hand.

"I thought you could use the help," the older man said. "But I can see you and your men have things well in hand."

"We could always use more help," Mark said. "We don't know when the rest of the redcoats will come back, but it will be soon."

Lieutenant Feldman shouldered his rifle. "When they do, we'll be ready for them."

He and his men went to work organizing the redcoats' ammunition and supplies. Rachel stood at Mark's side, her hand in his, watching it all with wide eyes. Her dress was muddy from falling in the road, and she looked tired, but she also looked as happy as Mark felt.

"I'm going to take Isaac and Hannah," Dr. Smith told Rachel, cleaning off his spectacles. "It'll be safer there, in case some redcoats are still running around near here."

Rachel nodded. "And I'll stay here with Mark."

Surprise shot through Mark at her words. "You will?"

"Of course." She smiled up at him, and peace came around Mark's shoulders like a blanket.

That night, when all was quiet, Mark and his men built a fire and shared some of the cider that they'd confiscated from the regulars. After a supper of some of the food stores, Mark had a full stomach, and a pleasant sense of contentment settled over him. Rachel sat next to him on a log, tucked against his side. Around the fire, Will, Jim, and Tom sat with tin cups of cider.

"So which of you has done the most outrageous thing in the name of an assignment?" Rachel asked.

His men came to life at that, arguing with each other.

"Will is the clear winner," Tom said. "After that assignment in Long Branch."

Will studied his boots, a grin spreading across his face and pink rising to his cheeks. Mark laughed at the memory. "You have to tell her."

"Yes, tell me," Rachel said.

Will took another sip of his cider and cleared his throat. "So this was a few months ago, at the end of the summer campaign. We were in Long Branch, watching for a supply delivery that we were due to intercept."

"We had a plan," Jim said. "You should have stuck to the plan."

"The plan was tedious," Will said.

"Anyway," Mark continued, looking at Rachel. "There were more redcoats than expected on the boat. We needed a way to distract them so we could take the boat they'd brought in."

"And redistribute the supplies," Tom added.

"The *plan* was to divide them up and pick them off in the forest," Jim said.

"But Will thought that plan was too slow," Mark said. "So he –"

"Let me tell my own tale of glory." Will raised a hand. "It was a warm day, you see, Mrs. Johnson. So I thought of a way to distract the redcoats that was *sure* to get their attention."

Rachel laughed. "What did you do?"

"I took off all my clothes, and ran into the forest, screaming. They didn't even shoot at me."

"They were too shocked to do anything except follow," Mark said. "All thirty of them."

"It *was* an efficient way to get them away from their boat," Jim said.

"See!" Will said. "It worked like a charm."

"As his Captain, I had to reprimand him," Mark said to Rachel. "He did risk his life."

Rachel was laughing so hard that tears ran down her cheeks. She wiped her eyes, gasping for air. "I think I would like to be a part of your regiment," she said. "It sounds like you all have quite the time."

Her words were spoken casually, but they hit Mark right in the stomach. If only she could work with them. But would he want to see her in danger? And could Mark go back? That was something he still had to work through. Not tonight, though. He wrapped his arm around Rachel and pulled her closer to his side. Tonight, he savored their victory.

Mark and his men spent the next several days cleaning out the camp. They returned animals to the people they'd been stolen from in Middletown and Freehold, and delivered the extra ammunition and weaponry to Continental camps. A few units of Continental soldiers stayed in the camp, holding it in case the regulars decided to attack. Things had been quiet – there had been no word of Sergeant Neumann or any of the other regulars that they'd driven out – and Mark was perfectly content with that.

"Captain," Will said, coming into Mark's tent. "It's time."

Mark took a deep breath and followed Will, Jim, and some of his other men to the back corner of the encampment. His heart beat faster as they walked, and he tried to calm himself. He wished Rachel was with him, but she was sitting with Isaac. This was something Mark needed to do alone.

"We've found a place outside the camp," Jim said.

The prisoners at the back of the camp were still tied to the trees; they'd been left out here in the snow and cold for weeks. Mark had never been able to find out who they were. But he hoped their souls were at rest now.

"Can I help?" Ezekiel Elliott came into the clearing behind Will, wearing a cloak and tricorn hat. He looked better than he had the last time Mark had seen him; perhaps he was recovering from his injury after all. With him was Reverend Alder and a few other men from Freehold.

Mark shook the other man's hand. "We'd love the help. Thank you."

It was exhausting, digging in the near-frozen ground, but Mark used the repetitive motions to say a prayer for each man and his soul.

"I can't believe you've done it," Ezekiel said. "Driven them away."

"We still have to *keep* them away," Mark said gently.

"And we couldn't have done it without Miss Rachel and her friends," Jim said.

Ezekiel didn't respond right away. He took to his work, bearing his shovel into the ground and tossing the dirt into a pile. If Mark hadn't seen his injury, he never would've believed it by looking at the man. But Abigail had told Rachel that Ezekiel still struggled with his memory.

"I'm grateful for your help," Mark told Ezekiel again.

The other man gave him a thin-lipped smile. "It's good to feel useful."

Once the prisoners were buried with simple wooden crosses above their graves, Reverend Alder said a simple blessing over them. How many more men would die like this before the war was over?

Rachel looked around their tent, hands on her hips. She'd brought over a few of her belongings from home, and Mark had constructed a pallet for them to sleep on. Hannah and Isaac were still at Rachel's home, farther away from possible danger. Rachel would stay with Mark in the camp for the next few nights. Then – then what? What would happen next?

Well, that depended on Mark.

Rachel undressed and dove under the blankets. It was tolerably warm, but it'd be better with her husband at her side. He came into the tent a short time later, a contented smile on his face.

"Everything all right?"

Mark took off his weapons and laid them next to the pallet so they'd be ready at a moment's notice.

"We finished burying the prisoners. Lieutenant Feldman has everything in hand for the night, and I'll take charge in the morning. I think he's excited to see some action."

"He did look rather thrilled, pacing in front of the entrance to the camp with his rifle over his shoulder."

Mark took off his outer clothes and climbed into bed next to her, pulling her into his arms. Rachel sighed. That was better.

"What happens next?"

"I imagine your father will arrive shortly to discuss that very matter."

"And what will you tell him?"

"I don't know." Mark laid on his back, his hands behind his head. "The Continentals will need to hold the camp so the British don't capture it again. I imagine my men and I will be a part of that, since we know the area so well."

That was good news. "So you could possibly stay here for a time? Before you are sent away?"

"I would like that, yes. I'd like to be close to you."

Rachel couldn't stop the smile spreading across her face. Some days she still couldn't believe that this man was hers. "What about after that?"

"I don't know. It's arrogant to assume my men *need* me. I would miss them to be sure, but I have faith that Will and Jim could command the unit in my stead. I believe in the Cause, but not at the cost of my own wellbeing."

Hope bloomed in Rachel's chest. "And you know there are ways to work for the Cause that don't involve combat."

"Yes there are. And I'd be honored to work at your side." Mark kissed her, and she wrapped her arms around his shoulders.

"Enough talking for tonight," Rachel said.

Mark ran his hand up her back, achingly slowly. "I agree. It can all wait."

Rachel smiled. Indeed it could wait. For now, she wanted to celebrate with her husband.

EPILOGUE

"Stop twitching. You're going to give us away." If Rachel wasn't nervous herself, she would laugh at Mark's antics.

He had barely slept the night before. And now he was looking around at the green forest around them, bouncing his leg on the floor of the wagon. She was sure he had been on plenty of deadly assignments before, much more dangerous than delivering some ammunition to Millstone.

A lone man on horseback passed them, and Rachel gave the man a casual nod – at least as casual as she could muster with Mark gripping her hand like that. Mark breathed easier after the man passed by.

"It's so much more pleasant traveling by wagon during the summer," Mark said.

"It is," Rachel said, trying to keep her voice gentle. "Especially not being concerned about frostbite."

The white tents of the army camp came into view. As supply runs went, it was one of Rachel's less interesting ones. But Mark was still nervous every time.

"The army is moving toward Freehold soon," Mark told her.

"And you won't be a part of it. Does that feel strange?"

"Not as strange as I'd thought it would be." Mark looked toward the horizon, his face shaded by his tricorne hat.

Father had been disappointed by Mark's leaving the Partisan Corps, but as Mark was a volunteer, he couldn't force Mark to continue. Of course Rachel was thrilled that Mark would be working at her side, and she hoped that Mark would eventually feel the same way.

"Do you still feel guilty?"

He shook his head. "Not any more. This is important work too. After all, we never know when one of these bullets could save a life."

"One of Granny's bullets saved *your* life after all."

Mark laughed. "I can't believe you knew the whole time that it was one of hers."

"I saw the star stamped into it when Sergeant Neumann loaded the rifle."

"Yes, and I was busy making my peace with the Almighty."

"It was quite noble of you to place yourself in front of me like that," Rachel said.

Mark wrapped his arm around her shoulder, and she shifted the reins to her other hand so she could embrace him back. "I had to. I couldn't imagine my life without you."

"I feel the same," Rachel said.

"And I'm honored to be working alongside you." Granny and Hannah loved Mark, of course, but they had been hesitant to let him work with them. The good thing was, though, that the way Mother had set up the network of Couriers, none of them had too much information about the whole group. They only knew their small section of it.

"You can keep working alongside me," Rachel said. "As long as you stop bouncing your leg."

Isaac had made a full recovery from his bullet wound and returned to the army at Hannah's insistence. Rachel still prayed for him every day, and thanked the Almighty that she got to keep Mark with her. As for Mark, he was slowly gaining more peace the more time he spent away from active combat. Mark's men came to visit when their assignments allowed, and while Mark missed them, Rachel could see the light inside her husband growing every day. And besides, he was still fighting in the war; just not with a rifle.

Ezekiel and Abigail were still recovering from the horrible night of the fires. Ezekiel seemed to be regaining his memory, but it was a slow process. He'd become a kinder, gentler man as he learned to rely on other people for help. He'd even grudgingly conceded that Rachel's work was just as important to the war effort as the Continentals'.

As for Rachel, she had learned to be brave. And she never looked back.

Thank you for reading *the Reluctant Courier.*If you enjoyed this book, there are a few things you can do to make my day!

Leave a review on Amazon.

Subscribe to my newsletter.

And if you enjoyed this book, the next one is coming soon! Preorder here.

AUTHOR'S NOTE

A note about Native American representation. As far as I can tell by my research, this area of New Jersey was originally home to the Lenape tribe. This tribe was forced out of New Jersey as a result of the Treaty of Easton in 1758; they moved west, eventually settling in modern-day Ohio. Any residents of Freehold that were Native American would have been forced to "blend in" to be accepted in Freehold. There's a whole lot I could say about this, and I would love to have more Native American characters in my future books, but for the most part, theirs is not my story to tell. For further reading, I would recommend *An Indigenous Peoples' History of the United States* by Roxanne Dunbar-Ortiz. In my research, I read *the Lenni Lenape Indians of New Jersey: Who They Were and Who They Are Now* by Alice M. Rainey. Thank you Ms. Rainey for your research.

Granny's story is in part based on accounts I read in *A Black Women's History of the United States* by Daina Ramey Berry and Kali Nicole Gross. Free Black women in the time of slavery had to carry papers proving they were free, and there were occasions that these papers were forged. I hope by telling Granny's story I am telling a story of power and agency in a time when these women had so few options.

The Partisan Corps was a real group of soldiers. I found an article about the Corps entitled "American Light Dragoons and Partisan Corps in the Revolutionary War" in the Revolutionary War Journal (www.revolutionarywarjournal.com). Part of their job was to: "not only provide valuable service during major battles, but to conduct reconnaissance and surveillance, engage enemy troop movements, disrupt delivery of supplies, raid and skirmish enemy positions, and organize expeditions behind enemy lines to gather intelligence." We'll be seeing more of the Partisan Corps in this series!

I did not read anything about a group of women like the Couriers; this was one of the parts of history where I have to ask, "Why couldn't it happen?" instead of "Did it happen?". Women were just as active in the conflict against Britain as men; their service to the Cause looked different.

ABOUT THE AUTHOR

Elsa Stanley spends most of her time doing things for other people. A pastor's wife, a mom of young kids, and a general people pleaser, writing is one of the only things she does for *her*. She loves escaping to another time and place, and often stays up way too late to finish a book. When she's not writing, she loves to organize, read a good romance, or crochet. She lives in Colorado with her family.

www.ingramcontent.com/pod-product-compliance
Lightning Source LLC
Chambersburg PA
CBHW020411110726
47899CB00006B/1944